THE NORTHREPPS GRANDCHILDREN

The Northrepps Grandchildren

by

Verily Anderson

Braiswick 2002

Braiswick
61 Gainsborough Road, Felixstowe,
Suffolk IP11 7HS

ISBN 1 898030 67 7

© Verily Anderson

First published 1968 by Hodder & Stoughton Ltd
Reprinted 1979 by Mallard Reprints
Reprinted 1983

British Library Cataloguing in Publication Data
available.

Produced in Milton Keynes
by Lightning Source

Braiswick is an imprint of Author Publishing Ltd

DEDICATED TO MY UNCLE CHRISTOPHER
OF NORTHREPPS

Acknowledgments

NOTHING but help, kindness and encouragement have been my lot from those who have lent letters, diaries and memoirs concerning the family history of Northrepps Hall. To them I owe my most grateful thanks. Also to Geoffrey Bles for allowing the publication of excerpts already published in *Family Sketchbook* of E. Ellen Buxton's diaries, arranged by Ellen R. C. Creighton, who has also most kindly lent their full text from which further extracts are included here. Also to Jane Vansittart for allowing extracts to be used from letters edited by her in *Katharine Fry's Book*, and to her publisher Hodder and Stoughton.

V. A.

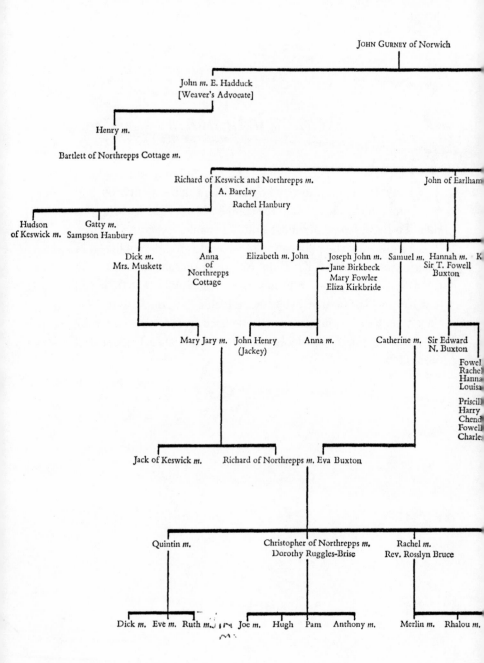

JOHN GURNEY of Norwich

John *m.* E. Hadduck
[Weaver's Advocate]

Henry *m.*

Bartlett of Northrepps Cottage *m.*

Richard of Keswick and Northrepps *m.*
A. Barclay
Rachel Hanbury

John of Earlham

Hudson
of Keswick *m.*

Gatty *m.*
Sampson Hanbury

Dick *m.*
Mrs. Muskett

Anna
of
Northrepps
Cottage

Elizabeth *m.* John

Joseph John *m.*
Jane Birkbeck
Mary Fowler
Eliza Kirkbride

Samuel *m.*

Hannah *m.* K.
Sir T. Fowell
Buxton

Mary Jary *m.*

John Henry
(Jackey)

Anna *m.*

Catherine *m.*

Sir Edward
N. Buxton

Fowell
Rachel
Hannah
Louisa

Priscilla
Harry
Chend
Fowell
Charles

Jack of Keswick *m.*

Richard of Northrepps *m.* Eva Buxton

Quintin *m.*

Christopher of Northrepps *m.*
Dorothy Ruggles-Brise

Rachel *m.*
Rev. Rosslyn Bruce

Dick *m.* Eve *m.* Ruth *m.*

Joe *m.* Hugh Pam Anthony *m.*

Merlin *m.* Rhalou *m.*

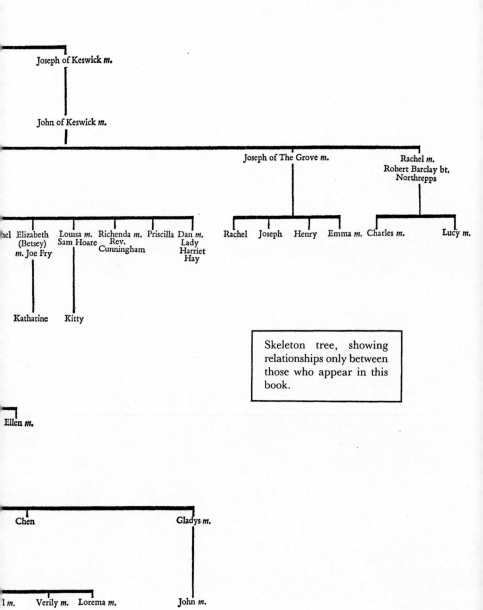

Joseph of Keswick *m.*

John of Keswick *m.*

Joseph of The Grove *m.*

Rachel *m.*
Robert Barclay bt.
Northrepps

hel Elizabeth (Betsey) *m.* Joe Fry   Louisa *m.* Sam Hoare   Richenda *m.* Rev. Cunningham   Priscilla   Dan *m.* Lady Harriet Hay   Rachel   Joseph   Henry   Emma *m.*   Charles *m.*   Lucy *m.*

Katharine   Kitty

Skeleton tree, showing relationships only between those who appear in this book.

Ellen *m.*

Chen   Gladys *m.*

l *m.*   Verily *m.*   Lorema *m.*   John *m.*

Contents

Index of Illustrations

Introduction

Several decades have passed since I came back to Northrepps to write this book. Everything still relates back to those earliest memories, either because it has changed or because it has not. Sounds and sights and smells remain. You can still find white violets near the Shrieking Pits and hear turtle doves purring on the way to church. Shucks Lane, where smugglers fought and killed a hundred years before our time, still winds up between the same banks under many, but not all, of the ancient oaks that have stood there for centuries. Wind has caused the most noticeable changes, felling, as Humphry Repton said they would, the outer ranks of beeches planted under his direction. But the child-sized hole in the hollow oak in the sunken lane can still be crept into by today's grandchild, as when I crept in, my mother crept in, her mother crept in, and hers before that.

The garden at Northrepps Hall is unchanged but for a real swimming-pool replacing the seashore of our imagination, in which, when it was too blowy to make the trek to Overstrand, we used the slowly moving shadow of the kitchen-garden as the rising tide. The church fête is still held in the garden with tea, as always, drunk from parish cups under the mulberry tree: the train still moves through the bottom of the park, though less like the leaping deer to which my grandfather joyfully likened it, when it first arrived.

Snowdrops, lent lilies and fluffy pheasant chicks still follow each other in the same delectable rotation in the woods. Up till a few years ago, Uncle Christopher spent his winter evenings, as he had done for forty years, charting up Scout and Guide camps in the fifteen places he chose for them in clearings and sheltered corners of the fields. He spent his summer evenings making sure there was enough firewood for new arrivals and then visiting camp fire sing-songs with a few of his own grandchildren in tow.

Then camping became caravanning. At first the conservationist in me was appalled to see the small Repton-inspired cornfield, set in the magical depths of the Cottage Woods and left unreaped to encourage the birds, enlarged for caravan camping, with the beloved gamekeeper's cottage turned into the headquarters of the site. But when I saw the first family arrive from Birmingham just as we had, and burst out of their car to scamper down into the Green Drive to see if the rhododendron tunnel was still there and then up again into the bracken to make sure that the sea below the cliffs was still there—my heart leapt up. Now there would be hundreds, no thousands of children to look lovingly back on so many of the same delights that we and all those others before us had known.

My mother lived just long enough to rejoice in my re-marriage (when I was already a grandmother myself) to the great great grandson of Louisa of Earlham. Louisa's eleven-year old journal records a visit to Northrepps in 1796, with romps whose merriment exceeded even some of our own. Although my husband, Paul Paget, is technically more of a Sidestrand grandchild than a Northrepps one, we must have both caught our first shrimps in almost the same sandy pool left at low tide at Overstrand, and been dried in the same bathing machines at Cromer. We never knowingly met. Now it is our turn to dandle the succession of visiting grandchildren in the North Sea.

Verily Anderson,
Northrepps, 1979.

CHAPTER ONE

Golden Days

C ERTAIN sounds and smells and tastes and tricks of light take me back more profoundly than any yellowing photographs to the wooded estate and flint-built house of my mother's Norfolk home.

The hoo-rooing of a wood-pigeon on a London roof bears me instantly back to the tree-fringed lawn sweeping down to the library windows. I can feel the spring of moss under my feet where the lawn merges into the long grass, hidden by snowdrops in February, wild daffodils in March and red-golden fallen leaves when the pheasant shooting has begun. I can breathe again the fresh keen air from the sea only a mile away and stretch my arms and legs as though I were still a child. A whiff of gunpowder from a spent cartridge takes me right into the woods themselves, and the smell of beeswax on mellowed timber takes me into the house. The rare taste of nectarines has never failed to produce in my nose the musty jungle smell of steam and moss of my grand-mother's greenhouses, just as the sight of purple clematis in a particular kind of morning sunlight takes me instantly to the summerhouse beside my grandmother's window.

Northrepps goes with me wherever I go. It is built in. It is part of me, colouring my whole view of life. It affects my behaviour, the way I speak and dress and work and run my home.

Even in 1840 Caroline Fox reports on her first visit to Northrepps Hall that it is 'a droll, irregular, unconventional place which must have had some share in shaping the character of its inmates.'

She was right. I am only one of a long procession of

grandchildren who have loved Northrepps in detail since before they could remember, but we have all, to some degree,
been made droll, irregular and unconventional by having
been inmates of Northrepps Hall, if only for intermittent
spells.

Twenty years after Caroline Fox, another grandchild was
expressing a sentiment shared later by us all. 'I think,' wrote
Ellen Buxton in her journal, 'that *everything* at Northrepps is
so *vastly* supperior to *any*thing at home because everything is so old
and old-fashioned.'

Other estates were acquired by the family earlier, but over the
years Northrepps has probably changed least. Peacocks still grace
the mellowed walls. Ducks still drift round the pond as they
did in the last century when a visitor staying there complained in
a letter to his small son: 'My room looks towards the duck pond
and the ducks were quacking quite into the middle of the night.'
Later the visitor, John Henry Gurney, became master of Northrepps himself. The avenue of elms still forms a tunnel half
a mile long up to the gates, where a pair of gentle-faced terracotta lions continue to stand rampant, if slightly battered by
weather and over-affection from grandchildren climbing up to
fondle them.

Indoors the Sunday tea-parties of relations of all ages and their
dogs go on as they always have round the circular table in the
hall. The same red leather armchairs—bought for the house in
1792—are pulled up and the same stools and drawing-room
chairs are fetched to make room for children and late-comers.
Tea is drunk from the same shallow rose and gilt-lined cups, and
sponge-cake is eaten from the same scalloped plates from the
same recipe, whose main ingredient I always believed as a child
to be fine blonde sand from the Cromer shore.

Once heard, the ringing tones of the family voice is recog-
nisable in any generation, and so are the grandchildren with their
flaxen or apricot coloured hair, clear pink and white skins and
blue, often short-sighted eyes. Slim legs and full busts have

usually distinguished the women, and heavy shoulders and well-worn clothes the men.

There has always been something of the holiday house about Northrepps Hall. With the sea within walking distance through the woods, pheasant and partridge shooting, and woods harbouring a greater variety of wild birds than in almost any part of England, this sporting, nature-loving, though philanthropic and prayerful family have continuously been drawn back to Northrepps for rest and recreation. For none can the holiday spirit have been stronger than for the endlessly recurring families of grandchildren who have stayed there, many of them regularly several times a year.

Just as the trees and gateways and furniture have lasted, so have the toys and playthings and secret hiding places in the nursery and garden. Tree-houses and huts built by one generation of children have been kept green by the next, to be revived and played in by the grandchildren of the first. Animals and birds have overlapped the generations and their places been taken by others so like the last that the changes have been almost unnoticeable. Family servants have outlasted one generation and carried on into the next, taking with them a ready-made affection for the next batch of grandchildren.

So much must have happened countless times over that many of the memories of one generation must have often become confused with the stories of the last. Some of mine I know to be direct memories from finding evidence years later. There are many more that may well have been reconstructed in my mind after hearing a story told and knowing its environment so intimately. It would have been easy enough, and pleasant too, to identify oneself with the little granddaughter who rolled out of the lowest branch of the mulberry tree while trying to climb up to get the dark, tart, juicy fruit, for every niche in the back of the branch and every undulation in the grass below were well loved and familiar; was it her, or me, or some other little girl in a light summer frock who, finding herself on the grass

B

under this tree with the deep purply black fruit under her and all around her and her frock already spoilt—completed the job by rolling again and again in the delicious, squelchy mess?

My own initial arrival at Northrepps seems more like my memory than my mother's, so clearly can I see the front door with its potted plants and pink conches just inside, and so used was I later to seeing long-clothed and bonneted babies being carried through it. But as I was only six weeks at the time I can hardly have remembered it. I was screaming loudly, after a newspaper boy had spilt scalding tea on me as he handed it into the train. In spite of the lusty sounds to the contrary, my mother was sure I was dying, so that this entrance made more of a stir than any I have made since.

The small lozenge-shaped scar on my right hand had always been the greatest comfort to me, as a portable, visible link with Northrepps.

My first real memory must have been of a year or two later. If I had not made a point of keeping it green I might have doubted whether it had really happened to me or whether I had confused it with the story of my great grandfather's earliest memory, which I read years later. His was in 1820 when (also aged about two), 'After being dressed in my best Nankin trousers, buttoned almost to the neck,' he wrote, 'I remember running into the garden and trying to climb on a giant gourd, which, being too ripe burst open and I fell into the huge caverty.'

Mine was of plunging into the nest-like centre of a clump of ornamental pampas grass. On the same lawn, my brother Erroll flung himself into another. The sight of his rounded legs kicking uppermost in his nest was one I used to cherish long after we had gone home. There was no background to this memory, except for the protective arms and skirts and aprons of those about us, leaning slightly towards us to hold us up and keep us safe. It was a kind of homogenous mass of the sweeter qualities of those who loved us —our mother, our nurse, our experienced elder sister, our father and perhaps a make-weight of maids and aunts and uncles all showing their interest. Through it all came the voice of my grandmother, using words I could not yet under-stand to reassure us that we were enjoying the moment to its utmost.

Every time we went back to Northrepps I would return to the pampas grass to refresh my first ethereal memory and strengthen it with details that had since become more familiar. Now I could see my grandmother clearly, peering through her blue elliptical gold-rimmed spectacles. There she was, tall and long-skirted with a huge hat that dipped in front like the petals of the purple clematis blooming on the canopy outside her drawing-room window. Indeed the whole canopy itself seemed to have been built on the same lines as her hat, so that to see one instantly conjured up the other.

Near the pampas clumps was the slatted door in the garden wall and beside it was a wheeled tap for a fire hose which only needed a little exertion on Erroll's part to produce a magnificent spray, reaching almost to the cedar tree whose lower branches spread themselves flatly out to be lain on. Here Erroll, or it might have been any of the cousins of the same era, and I swung, feeling the faint prickling of the pine needles through our jerseys.

The cedar tree was on the garden side of the lawn that divided the house from the wood. On the other side a gigantic fir rose high above the woods and house. It was called the Rescue Tree because the family had used its upper branches to experiment with a new kind of life line that could be thrown out to sea to drowning sailors. We supposed it was the current aunts and uncles who were responsible for this attractive adventure. It was just the kind of afternoon entertainment they in-dulged in. But no, it was the aunts and uncles of a hundred years before.

So much still remains from their day. The path behind the

fir tree still winds round to a low hooped iron gate, wide enough to admit a pony chaise. Here we would often stand, entwining our fingers with the pattern and sometimes, when I shut my eyes just before sleep, I can see it in exact detail, each hoop interlacing with the next—the gateway to the most magical of my grandmother's gardens, the kitchen garden itself. Here red and white currants clustered under fisherman's nets on the roseate walls. Gooseberries, whiskered and red and sweet, hung from the lace-curtain-covered bushes, homely protections against the birds.

Sticky raspberries, as we called the wineberries clustering behind their finger-pointed leaves, grew at the corner of two crossing paths. And beside a taller hooped gate leading into the meadow, the cherry-plum tree rained delicious little mirabelles on to the path for us to pick up and crush in our mouths—'Mind the stone! Spit out the stone!' still means for me sweet juice running down the chin and a taste of all fruits at once eaten under a ceiling of leafy branches revealing glimpses of blue sky and fluttery cloud. It was always a garden of the greatest promise. Although we already knew down to the last pebble, a few marked spots—such as the tunnel of ripening pears and apples through which we shunted as trains, feet together and hands up for buffers, and the rustic summerhouse with the built-in seat—if we had been allowed to wander far, we should have been lost. It was the same in the Home Wood, where one or two clearings belonged essentially to the nursery. To these we would be wheeled in the mail-cart, without certain knowledge which paths led to these darling places. Here we were set down to creep in and out of the nearby undergrowth.

The mail-cart was an airy conveyance, built on the basic lines of much of the Northrepps furniture, with wooden handles and legs like a wheelbarrow's. Even the pram in which I took my nap was estate carpentered. In the cart we sat back to back on its highest platform with our feet on wooden slats and our arms resting on railings each side of us. Though known as the mail-cart, it is doubtful whether any postman ever pushed it, even if it had ever possessed the necessary wicker superstructure to enclose the parcels. So high were we perched that when we returned from the woods we put our heads on our knees as we passed under the doorway into the backyard, hooped as most of garden gates are at Northrepps, to avoid what we believed might be decapitation. Once inside this sheltered square, we would descend and shunt up and down the asphalt paths that criss-crossed the cobbles, pretending they were railway lines. This could last for as long as it pleased our Annie to stay and gossip with Mrs. Royal the washerwoman, old Loynes who milked the white cows or any other backyard personalities who lurked half in and half out of the dozen or so doors below the pantiled roofs rising from many levels. The kitchen, scullery, servants' hall, game larder, wood shed, oil store, Sunday-school room and carpenter's shop all had access to this courtyard, whose pear trees skirted their southern walls.

From the plucking shed came a wheedling old man's voice merging with the squawk of a fowl. Once we peeped in and glimpsed for a moment a feathered neck held in gnarled hands. 'Come on, my pretty,' we heard, 'I'm not agoin' to hurt you.' We saw the promise broken and ran for our lives.

Into the back door we clattered, along the flagged corridor with its exclusively ancient scrubbed smell, past the log-bin and up the dark back stairs rising steeply between wooden walls. As we passed the dangling bell rope we gave it a push, knowing that one real pull would ring the bell under its wooden shelter on the top of the house and bring old Riseboro out of the potting shed, two would bring Carter from the coachhouse and three George from the pump house up in the wood. A continuous ringing meant that Northrepps Hall was on fire. Then under gardeners, garden boys, farm workers, gamekeeper and estate carpenter would all, we supposed, come flying in to take the scarlet leather buckets of sand down from their pegs all along the back corridor. 'Don't touch it,' I warned Erroll as he raised

one hand to the bell rope. Terrified by the thought, we panted
up to the gate at the top of the stairs to emerge into the safety
of our own dear nursery passage with its sunshine and fresh sweet
air. Bare, but for the thick cork overlay, this lovely broad alley
stretches from the back of the house to the front with two shallow
steps mid-way to jump down, bump a truck down or even drive
the pedal-propelled horse and cart down. Other passages leading
off our alley to bedrooms and the bathroom meant nothing to us
then. We were still bathed in a round shallow tub before a coal
fire and rubbed dry on warm towels on the knees of our admiring
betters, in whose presence we were balanced on elaborately
scalloped and gilded chamber pots to sit beside the fire, with our
night attire airing on the fire-guard.

Of course we knew every inch, every millimetre of the
nurseries themselves. If I were led blind-folded into the day
nursery now, my first finger could find its way instantly to the
brass ring, set into the window-sill, for raising it in two hinged
parts, to reveal the hiding place of the long disused shutters.
Both my forefingers would know exactly how to hook themselves
round the rings. My ear could still pick out the particular rumble
of the sliding cupboard doors from any collection of like sounds.
We knew which corners of the floor sloped too much to stand
soldiers on. We knew each join in the wallpaper where the story
of John Gilpin started again and we pressed our fingers to the
places where his wig flew off, so that every wig within four foot
of the floor was smudged.

From the sofa below the window we had an intimate view of
the front door and forecourt, with all arrivals and departures.
Some visitors came in big open cars with hoods, guyed in wet
weather with leather straps to the headlamps. Others used
traps or riding horses or bicycles with an intricate network of
strings to keep their skirts out of the wheels, if they were ladies.
The doctor came in a jaunty basket-work gig with yellow wheels
and a tall whip standing in its own tubular basket.

The night nurseries looked the other way over the backyard,

with sounds that reached up into our dreams and became part
of them—the clatter and clank of cans and bins, the mournful
sighing of the knife-cleaning machine with old Carter's husky
voice coming up through the floorboards, hissing as he mumbled
on to the maids below, as though he were still grooming the
horses that were once in his sole charge. In the walls was the
shuffling of mice—outside was the bellowing of cattle from the
farm-yard beyond the pond, where the ducks still quacked all
night. There was the bray of the donkey and then, just as all was
quiet, the sudden passionate scream of a peacock sounding, when
half in a dream, like a long drawn-out cry of 'Help'.

Our elder brother and sister, Merlin and Rhalou, being at
that time more than twice our ages, slept and ate in a different
wing of the house, guarded over by a governess. Our most constant
companions were the other tottering, toddling, scrambling grandchildren and their nannies and nursery maids. There were half a
dozen of us of an age, within a year or two, sharing the nurseries,
though not all stayed at Northrepps if they lived near enough
to come for the day.

Even before I understood the actual words: 'Eve's a good girl!'
'Joe's eating up all his porridge!' 'Dick never spits his out!' I got
the message that in our own nurse's eyes our cousins' behaviour
was always exemplary and our own severely wanting.

It is with complete clarity that the untampered memory
remains of the eldest of our group—fairer, curlier, pinker and
whiter and more dimpled than any of us—as she sat at the nursery
table on a cushion with an embroidered bib over a white lace-
edged frock, licking the white sugar butterfly off her brown
Playmate biscuit. Round and round went Eve's pink tongue and
Oh, the triumph and relief of watching her wickedness which
surely for once was greater than my own!

And so it must have been, ever since the mahogany and wicker-
work highchair that could be turned by the twist of a single
brass screw into a low nursery chair and table, was first brought
into the day nursery with the assortment of semi-highchairs.

Baby grandchildren must have been settled round this table by their nurses who, no doubt, always built up the behaviour of the other children in the hopes of nipping in the bud their own charges' waywardness. Little girl and boy cousins' faces must have been sponged and their flaxen hair combed ready to be taken down to the drawing-room after tea, some hand in hand, some clinging to their nurse's skirts and some still in their arms.

Enchanted memories of the drawing-room after tea remain. Among the toys brought out for us to play with on the floor was one that delighted me so much that even now if I pass a market place on a sunny day I can almost feel the soft comfort of the carpet under me as I gazed at the little gaily painted greengrocer's stall that my grandmother set before me. Tiny, glossy oranges could be picked up between finger and thumb and rolled into a miniature barrel. Minute bunches of carrots and crates of cauliflowers could be moved about the stall without ever detracting from its charm.

The big wooden letters, hewn by the estate carpenter, were interesting too but in a different way. My grandmother would arrange them on the floor in biblical texts which we learned to recognise in their entirety long before we could read. GOD IS LOVE, KNOCK AND IT SHALL BE OPENED UNTO YOU, SEEK AND YE SHALL FIND were all as familiar patterns as the Noah's Ark and Gardens of Eden she built for us with the wooden bricks, wedges and blocks brought from the timber yard, polished by two centuries of handling and each one eventually known individually by every grandchild.

On Sundays we came down to tea itself round the hall table, sitting on piles of cushions between the many loudly chatting, shouting (since deafness abounded) and, when young enough, yelling relations. It would have been easy enough to tell when it was Sunday even without this, for, though bricks were allowed after tea on account of the texts, certain other toys were not. The market stall was banned—no shopping on Sunday—and so were the sewing cards. The papier mâché horse on a wheeled stand was taboo—horses must not work on Sundays and so, strangely enough, was a stone idol, brought back from Africa by an ancestral missionary and very pleasant to dress and undress and put to bed in the wicker doll's pram. A stuffed alligator, out of which sawdust continually poured, was only allowed on condition we did not, as on week-days, ride on it.

CHAPTER TWO

Family Prayers

GRADUALLY our environments began to expand and Annie's vigilance to relax a little. We were now bathed in the bathroom itself, a large square room lit by a skylight. This skylight must have been added when the bathroom was converted from a bedroom with a three foot thick outside wall, beyond which other rooms had since been added. A fully glazed window remained in this wall, as we discovered when left alone for a moment wrapped in bath-towels, and we unlatched its shutters. It was quite in keeping with family construction merely to hook up the shutters and draw the curtains over them rather than take the original window away and brick up the hole.

At Earlham, the Northrepps-like home of our great-great-grandparents, had been found, we were told, long after it ceased to be used, the earliest bath to be installed by any of the family. It was described rather alarmingly to us as a great black leaden tank under a heavy wooden lid, with the ceiling perforated above it for a servant on the next floor to pour pitchers full of water down through the holes on to his master in the tank in a cupboard below. When alone in the bathroom at Northrepps we would tease ourselves with thoughts of the same thing happening to us, till I was afraid to look up at the ceiling in case holes appeared through which an arm stretched with a pitcher of water.

When we were not alone, the bathroom at Northrepps was a cheerful place, smelling attractively of seaweed and adhesive plaster. The seaweed we brought in ourselves and the adhesive plaster lived in the cupboard built into the thick outer wall.

The plaster we always associated with Aunt Chen, the one unmarried daughter left at home. Aunt Chen had been to the front as a Red Cross nurse, and so obviously was the person with whom to connect plaster. In fact the whole bathroom we associated with 'our front aunt' as we boastfully referred to her, though others besides herself must have used it since it was the only one in a house with eighteen bedrooms. Probably the real secret of her ownership lay in the communicating door between the bathroom and her bedroom, which we did not discover till we were left alone again. Then silently, cautiously, nakedly we crept through it and gazed reverently up at her hats, balanced saucily on stands along a shelf. We passed on to examine the other doors. Two led into passages and one into our grandmother's dressing-room. The fifth led to a dress cupboard in which there remained, characteristically, from another generation, part of a staircase.

Erroll pushed in between the dresses. I followed, feeling them silky, rough and woolly against my bare skin. Erroll gave a door beyond them a shove, releasing dust and plaster as the door burst open. Through it we could see another world—a landing and stairs and passages that seemed higher, grander and very much pinker than the Northrepps we knew. We shut the door quickly, and scuttled back to the bathroom, only a few days before we were officially introduced to that grand high other pinker world.

We had heard talk of the Water Closet Wing, that had been built on by our Victorian grandfather, with its spacious pair of lavatories, and to these we were now taken, not without pride, for one of the more worldly of the cousins of our group had boasted on our last visit that he had been inside both, and one had a door that closed very slowly as though by magic. It was not so much a wish to see this wonder that gave us such pleasure, on setting out on the longish journey for the first time, but from the eradication of shame from failing to be allowed to keep up with our four-year-old cousin.

The Water Closets, as they were always referred to in full, were reached from the passage we had seen from the dress cupboard, which formed as imposing an entrance as any long front drive.

A high glass dome of stuffed birds stood to one side of the twin brass-edged doorsteps, like a baytree beside a pair of town front doors.

Erroll and I chose a lavatory each and we stuck to them always, with Annie waiting outside by the stuffed birds. Mine was the one with the brake on the door that caused it to close very slowly with a soft whirring sound mingling exquisitely with the cooing of the wood pigeons that wafted in from the woods through the barred window. And how wonderful was the feeling of being really alone! How I loved the Water Closet of my choice, with its broad step up to the splendid, shiny, mahogany seat, stretching from wall to wall, on which I could stand to look out of the window on to the great lawn sloping up to the tall trees bordering the lawn. Consciously I reviewed my good fortune in being there. 'Here I am, at Northrepps, and I go to one of the big lavs, called a water closet, and stay here all by myself.' But soon the door would groan and Annie would come in to hurry me away.

One day I tried to prolong the delicious seclusion by sliding the polished brass bolt across the door. Annie tried to persuade me to unbolt the door which I stubbornly refused to do. Annie hammered on the door but I made it clear that I did not wish to be disturbed. She fetched others. There they all were, gazing at me through a pair of glass panels high in the door that I had not even noticed before. I could hear them dragging up chairs on which to stand till both windows were filled with gesticulating faces. At last it seemed that they had begun to go away, but no, Merlin had been sent out on to a flat roof to peer through the burglar-proof bars behind me. With him he had a fishing-rod which he passed through the bars in an attempt to push back the lock. But the wavery tip of the rod fell short and now messages were being signalled to him through the glass panel on how he could extend it. How unsecluded after all was my lovely place!

Only when, through the crack beneath the door, Rhalou offered me a chocolate did I begin to relent, for though my

pleasure was already spoilt, I had felt till then bound to hold
out longer than was necessary. Slowly I came down the step and
crossed to the door and pulled back the bolt, even though I knew
well enough that she had no chocolates to give.

The pleasure after that was barely perceptible. The door still
cooed with the wood pigeons. I was still allowed to retain my
status, but now Annie always came in with me and conscious
thought was no longer possible.

It can hardly have been cause and effect but at about this
time I began to be considered fit for Family Prayers before
breakfast. Family Prayers were not, of course, before breakfast
for us, who had already eaten well round the nursery table, had
our bibs removed, our faces wiped, hands unstickied and our
hair flicked up with the brush. But it was before breakfast for
everybody else. For now we were daily led even further along the
new passage and up a short flight of steps along a dark, arched
passage and out into the softly carpeted landing leading to the
front stairs. Beyond it, through an open door we could just see
a vast roofed and curtained bed as big, almost, as one of the
trams in our home town.

Down the front stairs we went, leaning heavily on the light
polished handrail against the wall to see what it felt like to be
lame. They had put this extra rail there for a lame girl to drag
herself up by. I liked hearing about this little girl who lived here
till she grew up and then moved to a house in the woods on the
way to the sea with her rabbits and puppies. At the bottom of
the stairs stood her wheel-chair. It had a padded red leather back
and arms and to the wooden spokes of its two heavily built
wheels, other wheels were joined within so that the girl could
propel herself about with her own hands. We had tried it out
ourselves and found it a most satisfactory way to move about.

Down in the hall the grandfather clock ticked on unhurriedly.
A snake skin as long as a man hung beside it. The logs stacked
under the stairs gave off a mossy, pithy smell as though the
woods had come into the house. Beside them baskets were kept

for every conceivable purpose—long flower baskets, round black berrying baskets, oblong shopping baskets, square picnic baskets and a long tubular basket that I had last seen strapped to the Bath-chair to hold my grandmother's parasol.

Mixed with the smell of logs was the smell of linseed oil from the study, where our uncles kept their guns, and now the smell of fried bacon and toast and coffee was added. I did not like bacon or coffee and had already had all the toast I needed in the nursery but these smells were so closely connected with the occasion that to me they were like incense, without which our prayers could not have been carried upwards. Already they had come some way. It was a long jaunt from the kitchen with many twists and turns and a trip upstairs to the pantry and another one down again at the other end of it, all of which the parlour maids would soon be making too with their heavy deep-sided trays.

Through the arched doorway we could see my grandmother sitting at the round table in the hall with the Bible open in front of her. She kissed us in turn as we came in, and I would have liked to scramble up on to her silky lap and put my head against the lace on what we called her 'body', but I was quickly drawn away towards the red-cushioned window-seat on to which the other grandchildren were climbing and turning round and sitting down to swing their legs, in a flutter of frilly drawers and twill knickerbockers.

It was at Family Prayers, with so much time to look about, that people began to separate out into individuals. Except for Aunt Chen, the aunts and uncles and grown-up guests were ever changing, and so not easy to sort out. But the single file of maids filtering in through the swing door from the kitchen passage never varied in their processional places. Most of the faces I could identify but one or two I never saw anywhere else except in the two rows as they seated themselves with a starchy rustle. In the mornings they all wore big, enveloping linen aprons with stiff bibs that stood out well away from their bosoms as our Annie's

did. She, too, wore a striped dress in the mornings and a plain
white mob cap which she exchanged in the afternoons for a hat,
indoors and out. Harriet, our grandmother's tiny frizzy-haired
lady's maid, I could recognise, for she was always bustling about
the nursery corridor and in and out of her housemaid's cupboard
near the top of the back stairs, clanking her hot water jugs. And
tall, quiet Knights was easily distinguished too, with her dark
hair and sallow skin and low serious voice. Knights never sent us
away if we strayed into the kitchen where the walls were embossed
with copper jelly moulds and silver plated meat covers. There
were sizes to fit anything from a cutlet to a brace of peacocks.
There were cooking pots too for all occasions. One set we particularly admired rose up, one pan above another into a tower, taller
even than Knights when she put it on the range. A kind of
chimney went up the side, collecting the steam from each compartment. This way, Knights said, she could do the different
dinners for the dining room, the nursery, the schoolroom and the
servants' hall, all at once. Yet she still had time to lift down from
a high shelf a box full of pink and white sugar mice, that were
really kept for decorating birthday cakes, and she would let us
choose the ones with the longest string tails.

The maids I thought I had not seen before must always have
been lurking behind the copper in the back kitchen or else made
themselves unrecognisable by changing in the afternoon into
black frocks with lacy aprons and goffered caps with streaming
black velvet ribbons.

Family Prayers began with a shuffle that led on to a rousing
unaccompanied hymn. I stood up on the window seat with Erroll
below me in his blue smocked overall, holding a hymn-book to
look as though he were reading it. I did not bother with this
pretence yet, and unashamedly sang at will. Then down on our
knees we went on the floor. Tightly I squeezed my eyes shut for
just long enough to feel God's approval. Then my fingers began
to explore the door knobs and little round holes in the cupboard
under the window-seat. There can hardly be a wrinkle in the

paint or a strand in the great, knotted, fringed cable holding back the curtains that I and countless other grandchildren before and after me did not trace with forefingers during Family Prayers.

Up we all came at last, as in a game of Ring o' Roses, some bouncing up, some scrambling, some creaking and some heaving. Now we had to sit very still while my grandmother read from the Bible. Her voice rang out like a bell, musically pleasing though I understood not a word. Even when she read 'Verily, verily, I say unto you', I had no idea what she meant except that she referred to me. Erroll was not mentioned in the Bible, nor Merlin nor Rhalou, though from time to time Rachel, my mother, was. Among the cousins of our age, Joseph and Eve were sometimes mentioned and stories about their doings both in and out of the Bible were still confused in my mind. I had looked in vain for Joseph's coat of many colours in the nursery and when Eve was reported to have found a frog in the garden it seemed hardly worth mentioning, since she was known to talk to snakes. Her brother, Dick, I had always confused with Adam, believing that it was Dick and Eve who went naked in the Garden of Eden, even though their nannie always shielded them with such modesty when undressing them on Overstrand beach for a bathe. It seemed to me that it was more likely to have been the voice of their nanny that caused them to rush off and cover themselves with leaves.

Another lusty hymn and the maids filed out. Instantly talking and laughter broke out. It was as if God had withdrawn to the kitchen passage with the maids, and all the more so when, after a very short interval, a particularly masculine sound began to boom out from just beyond the swing door. But I knew the gong, for I had often seen it hanging there and had even given it a ping in passing.

Sometimes on sunny mornings my grandmother would take us into the drawing-room with her before she had breakfast. How fresh and sweet the roses smelt, arranged in their bowls on the many little tables! How light-limbed and free this golden room made us feel with its white marble mantelpiece on which stood a clock under a glass dome with all its works revealed. Beside it flower encrusted candle-sticks branched out with china babies clambering about them.

Our grandmother would throw open the french windows so that we could run out into the dewy morning. Just in front of them the geometrical pattern of little paths, edged with low clipped box hedges, surrounded a mosaic of brightly filled flower-beds. Along these paths we chuffed and shunted with even greater joy than in the backyard and kitchen gardens. The box hedges swished against us as we moved between them and the smell of wallflowers and the feeling of our grandmother's approval added further delicious qualities to our journeys. These paths and hedges and flower-beds are still there and even now when I see them an overwhelming desire comes over me to shuffle along them, palms turned out with the feeling of dewy box leaves brushing my legs.

The aviary beside them is still there too, leaning against the high fuchsia-covered wall which, three generations before, had fallen down in a heavy fall of snow, burying one of the peacocks, which three days later was dug out none the worse. Through the hooped garden doors in the wall, grandchildren are still attracted to 'The World' in the front courtyard. There was a 'World' at Earlham too, in much the same position, described by a grandchild as 'a medley of flower-beds cut in loops and rounds and triangles, planted with geraniums, marigolds, begonias, dahlias and calceolarias with little box-edged paths between them.'

The real trains that passed the bottom of the park must have had some influence on our passion for shunting and shuffling round the paths. To us, who could not yet tell the time, the coming of these trains was always unpredictable and added a tremendous excitement to whatever game we might be playing. Specially we loved the goods trains. 'Oh, God let it be a goods train,' we were guilty of praying when the first sight of smoke over the distant woods made us drop what we were doing and

c

stand gazing over the railing. When we heard the slow rumble, with the hollow change of tone at the bridge, we knew our prayers had been granted. And, oh, how satisfying it was to see the low work-a-day trucks filled with coal and up-ended timber and drawn by a short, friendly little engine. The wheels turned so slowly that moving patterns of light showed enchantingly between the spokes. Sometimes we stood hoping for a train, and the wind in the trees, or old Riseboro's wheelbarrow crunching on the gravel or a far-off threshing machine or even just a rumble in our own heads that stopped as soon as we started to examine it, would set our hearts beating faster as we eagerly scanned the trees for a trail of smoke. But no train came, only the rooks flew over, cawing teasingly. We did not want rooks then, we wanted a train. And then suddenly, almost as soon as we had turned away to make do with some other occupation, the Liverpool Street Express itself would be upon us, rumbling and roaring and thundering over the bridge and then snorting to a standstill, as it always did, just beyond the park where the high embankment dissolved into a cutting. This was so that half of the train could go on into Cromer and the other half could be collected by a smaller, lesser engine to be taken off through the Felbrigg woods on its way to Sheringham.

Once we watched the end of this procedure on a pram walk, from the bridge beyond the avenue, and how almost unbearably touching it was to see this Sheringham train sliding away, a wreath of its own smoke rising into those fairy-tale woods! It produced a sensation that I was reminded of years later when first witnessing a cremation.

But the trains only remained mysterious when we were outside them. When we were in them, pounding along this same line on the last lap of our journey to Northrepps, all was familiar right down to the round metal basin, clinging like a limpet to the tiny washing compartment wall till it was lowered for a final prink up, which action produced a steamy trickle of water from its inner rim. Since we believed this to come direct from the engine's boiler, we were reluctant to waste a drop in case the engine lost pressure and our speed was reduced.

After the prinking, noses were pressed with renewed vigour to the windows searching for something—some tall elm or grey flint cottage or leafy lane—that would have set in motion the metamorphosis from being ordinary twentieth-century city children to country grandchildren belonging to an almost pre-Victorian age. And suddenly—it was all there—the whole well-loved scene, easing itself into place like a magic lantern slide: the hedges, the cornfields, the little box-bordered gardens round the grey flint cottages. The train clattered over the bridge whose every echo we knew from underneath, and there, rising among the trees, was our dear grandmother's house itself. At least it was there to see if we managed to keep awake till the end, which was not always the case. Sometimes the first we knew of the journey drawing to a close was the sight of old George's long grey moustaches under his peaked cap as he carried us in turns in his arms, still apparently asleep, from the train to the waiting Vauxhall.

CHAPTER THREE

The Coachhouse

IT was a long journey from Birmingham, where our vicarage was, with a change and several hours' wait at Leicester. Not that this deterred my mother in the least, even though my father rarely came with us to help to convey the party, for his parish kept him too busy to go away every time my mother decided it was time to 'go home', as she still referred to Northrepps.

At Leicester she would leave the towering pile of great shining black round-topped trunks and strapped rush-baskets on the station platform, with Annie and the two maids who came to visit their mothers too in Northrepps village. She would then set off with us to look for what must have been a mythical toy-shop, for we never found it. The scramble to get back in time to catch the connection and push us and the luggage and the maids all into it only seemed to increase my mother's natural elation.

There was another shorter wait in Norwich, and during one of these journeys, as dusk was gathering, the station-master came to the door of our carriage and poked his face in with news that put the whole family into a state of alarm.

'Zeppelin' was all I heard, but that was enough for me. It was so terrible a word—even when shortened to 'Zep'—but to my mother it was merely a signal for more fun. She set about pulling down the blinds and moving us about with as much organising excitement as though we were still rushing for the train at Leicester station. Not that she intended to lie down under the impending air attack. Somehow she managed to sidle out of the door with the maids holding coats round her to prevent any light going with her. She had gone to advise the guard to start the train at once. Presumably he must have explained that the risk of hitting the Up train was considerably greater than that of being hit by anything the Zeppelin might drop. Anyway we did not stir and soon she re-entered, as though from the sea into a bathing machine, with coats once again held up.

Next she set about making the carriage bomb-proof by piling cases up against the windows. Erroll remained aloof, though he knew as well as I did that Zeps were full of darkness and sudden death. We must have been about four and three.

Soon the suspense was more than I could bear. I can still remember the rough feeling of the upholstery against the bare patch between my 'drawers' and the tops of my leather gaiters as I edged towards the window and whipped the suit-cases aside and gave the blind a sharp tug. Up shot the blind to reveal the end of a glorious sunset such as can only be seen streaking the vastness of an East Anglian sky. Bunches of pink-tinged cloud clung together like clusters of apple blossom from which single petals detached themselves to float for a little alone. Golden arms stretched out behind it and then faded softly into the yellowy blue. I saw it and sighed deeply. It seemed to me a Zeppelin was a glimpse of heaven.

Of course they crowded instantly to my end of the carriage and whisked the blind down again with a scolding that even I knew was made fiercer with their own fear. But it had been worth it. I had seen a Zeppelin even if, at the time, I might also have allowed a Zeppelin to see me. For a long time after that, the sight of any beautiful sunset with floating clouds of pink and gold gave me a thrill of mixed exhilaration and terror, which inevitably sent me hurrying for shelter.

According to the Visitors' Book, we went to Northrepps for two longish stretches the year after peace was signed. If there were any changes now that the war was over, we did not notice them. Perhaps there were more uncles at the Sunday teas and garden boys in the kitchen garden and possibly we took more notice of the pill-boxes and barbed-wire entanglements that still remained on the nearby Overstrand cliffs, just because they were now obsolete.

'They used to have them in the war,' we said with the superiority of those who had lived on from another era. There was still something grim about the word, but all the same it was very pleasant to run in and out of the little round house with a sandy floor just beyond the Green Drive.

There was some talk among the nannies, hopeful, no doubt, that the butler and footman, whose places had been taken by one parlourmaid, would be replaced. But they never again were. And anyway, I learnt much later, it had not been the war that had taken them away, but an overpreponderance of pregnancies stemming from the pantry.

The old brigade had long been considered safe enough in this respect on their brief visits to the pantry, and now, with the war over, they continued to prop each other up, with a certain amount of overlapping of each other's job to allow for bronchitis and rheumatism. All, however, were ready to run, or anyway hobble, towards the Hall should the fire bell be rung.

George's job was somewhere between chauffeur, lamp-trimmer and nursery-footman. He was always there at hand with his bushy moustaches and dead-pan banter, and, if we happened to be by the sea, his trousers rolled up all ready to rescue us. For a long time I confused him with the uncles home from the war. He wore the same long coat as they did, and carried us over the stones if our shoes had been packed under the sandwiches. He drove my grandmother's Vauxhall as they did and pulled the thorns out of our thumbs when we went blackberrying on Toll's Hill, swathed in the long khaki putties that had bandaged our uncles' legs in the war. If we behaved badly George was never cross but gently chided us with apt texts.

'For Verily, when we were with you, we told you before that we should suffer tribulation,' he would quote as I kicked and screamed on the floor for the second time in one afternoon.

Carter, still known as *the coachman*, was more inclined to

shrink away from us when we gave trouble, muttering 'Whoa up' and other restraining horse commands. Old Riseboro occasionally chased us out of the peach houses and Reynolds growled at us in the woods if we went within a hundred yards of his pheasant coops, reminding us that there were still man-traps lurking in the undergrowth. He was right. There still were, with gruesome jagged claws, put there incongruously by our reform-loving ancestors, to break the legs of passing poachers, which barbarous practice was not prohibited by statute till 1861, leaving few enough years by Northrepps standards to catch up with the times and spring the traps.

Loynes only had to hold up a half-strangled hen to create respect. Billy Silver, the estate carpenter, won his by sheer age and ability.

Almost everything at Northrepps that could conceivably be made of wood and bent iron, and bearing the same stamp of 'bold, basic and built to last', stemmed from Billy Silver's, hammer and saw. Gates, farm implements and furniture—sledges, prams and ironing-boards—doll's beds, Noah's Arks and cricket bats. Even the North Wing itself was said to be Silver-made from timbers sawn from wreckage pulled out of the sea after a storm. There was always something of the longshoreman about Silver, with tales of rum-running and smuggler's hide-outs under the Silver floor-boards. But could it have been our Billy Silver who drove a cart three nights running to Norwich, using the back lanes and avoiding the turnpike, and being paid for his trouble not in money but in brandy? The same boy first came to Northrepps Hall to weed the paths at the age of nine for a shilling a week (which was the usual pay in the eighteen-thirties). He then rose to be estate carpenter. It must have been our Billy Silver's father, but it made no difference, their works, like the Chippendales, were indistinguishable.

The product that must have given the greatest pleasure for the most years—whichever Billy Silver built it—must surely be the boat. Shaped like a hump-backed bridge when turned upside down (and indeed often used as one) its curves exactly matched the Northrepps pram and all the hoops over the gates, suggesting that the same jig was used to shape them all. The boat was not designed to be put to sea and would certainly have sunk if it had been, but as a rocking boat none could have rocked higher nor contained more children at once without tipping up. There are two tiers of seats at each end and room in the middle for more. A fretwork design provides appropriate hand-holes for lifting, and holding on.

According to the sketch-books the boat was kept in the hall in the eighteen-sixties but in our day it was always being moved about the garden, as though drifting on a wayward tide. As soon as we found it we would run to get the best seats, the boys for bloodthirsty pirate games and the girls to play at willow patterns, chasing the lovers across the lake as in the story on the plates. Equally agreeable was merely to rock gently backwards and forwards with a congenial child to balance the other end, to the sound of the mowing machine not far off being pulled by the donkey wearing leather boots over its hoofs. Presently the mowing party would come in sight with old Riseboro at the donkey's head and young Willy, his grandson, behind the mower. A whiff of new-mown grass would reach us on the breeze, and as the donkey turned, we could hear the bees. Presently the Riseboros approached to move the boat again.

Sometimes the donkey pulled the watercart round the garden with the tank on its pivot clanging as the water lapped its sides, and sometimes, if our grandmother needed a turn round the woods and kitchen garden without exposing herself to the rain, the donkey would be harnessed to the Bath-chair with its great black leather hood shaped like a poke bonnet. On fine days she preferred the wicker pony chaise, drawn by Hippolyta, the skewbald pony, and so did we, for there was room for two beside her and at least two more at her feet.

Hippolyta, so called from being bought out of a herd of unbroken ponies on Midsummer's Day, was often in the garden, saddled for the older grandchildren to ride at will. We, however, had to be held on and led. Once I found her all ready to ride and fetched an inlaid mother-of-pearl table from the drawing-room and put it beside her in the hopes of climbing on alone. But Hippolyta must have known it was forbidden, for every time the table legs were well dug into the grass she took a few steps forward and then waited for me to move it again. I followed her with the table across the lawn till Rhalou, deeply shocked, found us and sent me in to our grandmother to say I was sorry.

Our grandmother, ever-forgiving, promptly ordered the goat carriage to be brought round specially for my benefit. It was not unlike the mail-cart and obviously of a Billy Silver pattern. It was drawn by a stubborn old nanny-goat who pleased herself about which paths she took, for all the shaking of the reins from the box. It was some consolation, but not a lot, for I could see Rhalou cantering in the park, in complete control of Hippolyta.

She took Hippolyta very seriously, spending hours in the stables with Carter, building up the simple care of the fat elderly grass-fed pony into the elaborate grooming, feeding and watering of a stable full of carriage and riding horses. Carter still regarded the harness room as the heart of the estate and lit a fire there daily in the range on which bran mashes for the horses and breakfast for the grooms, who used to sleep in the loft above, had always been cooked. Where once great bran mashes were boiled up on this range, now only Carter's tea mulled slowly in its pot. Shining harnesses hung from every peg, polished assidu-ously by Carter, though now only dulled by the sweat of Hippolyta, the donkey and the goat. Very occasionally the angry mule, left over from the war, was brought into the cobbled stable-yard for an unsuccessful attempt to harness it.

All this Erroll and I witnessed when taken to the stables for Annie to gossip with Mrs. Carter. The coachman's cottage adjoined the loose-boxes and might have been built entirely of grey eggs, so perfectly matched were its cobbles. Our pleasure here, since we were discouraged from helping Carter and Rhalou, was in the coachhouse which sheltered vehicular traffic of all ages.

There was no hard line drawn yet between shaft and sparking plug. The Vauxhall rubbed shoulders with the little governess cart known as 'The Tub'. A dog cart towered above Aunt Chen's neat little two-seater Wolseley with its dicky at the back with a railing round it. Erroll climbed at once on to the fire engine whose solid wooden wheels and pumping poles led us into lasting arguments about its age. Erroll was sure it was the stock family fire engine that could be bought any day from the Army and Navy Stores in London. I believed it had been made by Noah, or anyway by Billy Silver. Though its leather hoses were too heavy for us to lift, they inspired games of daring rescues, sousings and burnings to the ground. My grandfather's sleigh, slightly kicked by the mule which had been the last to draw it through the snow, also produced games of great daring with some throwing to the wolves. But our favourite was the brougham with its dove grey upholstery, fringed blinds and windows that disappeared into the doors as in a railway carriage. The matching footwarmer and rug had been borrowed, supposedly at first only temporarily, for the Vauxhall.

Each of these we drove in turn, sometimes playing together, sometimes in little herds with the other cousins and sometimes in lonely grandeur. It was as though a box of wheeled toys had been turned out on the nursery floor and we had been made miraculously small enough to be able to get inside them all.

But it was only to us that they were toys. Carter still did the day-to-day shopping in Cromer in the governess cart, donning his livery with his long frock-coat and the cockade in his half-high hat and bringing his spanking little turn-out to the back door for orders. Once a week he took soup to the alms-houses. The pony would be tied up to a ring in the ivy-covered wall, while Carter made several slow journeys across the backyard. Even though he only carried two soup cans at a time, with their lids wedged into place with greaseproof paper, the soup always slopped out as he went. It was made specially nourishing for old people, we were told, out of meaty bones and vegetables. It sounded horrible to us, but with each can went half-a-crown and the latest gossip from Carter.

Up till only a few years before, the carriage had been brought to the front door at a quarter to eleven every weekday morning for more than a hundred years.

'The Ark is at the door, Mrs. Noah,' our great-great-grandfather would announce. The mistress of the house could then drive down to Cromer to visit the many relations who, whatever the century, were assembled there.

Once, when our grandmother was young, her little son, our Uncle Christopher, then aged about three, appeared clean and neat at the carriage door and his mother, supposing him to have been presented thus by his nurse, took him into the carriage and drove off with him at her side to Cromer.

In fact he had started off for a nursery walk with the pram and then found an intriguing hole in the hedge and crawled through it. His nurse did not see him go and by the time she and the nurserymaid had discovered the hole there were no signs of him anywhere. As the ditch the other side of the hedge drained into the lower pond they could only think that he had mysteriously drained there with it. They set off back to the house. Nobody had seen him there and now consternation broke out. The fire bell was rung and the pond was about to be dragged when the carriage returned with the missing boy smiling contentedly beside his mama.

Since then there was always an elaborate exchange of whereabouts of all children before the mistress of the house departed. This practice continued, though now it was the Vauxhall that came daily to the door at a quarter to eleven, with George in his maroon livery at the wheel.

CHAPTER FOUR

Farther Afield

WHEN we went to the village with the mail-cart, we always slowed down to view the famous hole in the hedge just before the lower pond where Uncle Christopher had disappeared. When we came to the railway bridge we climbed out for the pleasure of running along the raised footwalk that hugged the wall of the bridge, shouting to hear the echo, while Annie splashed through the puddles where the lane dived under the bridge.

At the post office and general store we alighted again to mount the two steps and run along the garden path between bachelor's buttons, stocks and pansies. Even we children had to stoop under the honeysuckle that tumbled over the porch. The door handle had hardly to be touched before the bell above it sprang into action. Inside, the smells almost overpowered us with their richness—candles and raisins and corn-plasters and brandy balls and bacon rinds and sacking and bootlaces made variously of leather and string and liquorice. We only bought a stamp or a twist of peardrops, but Annie's talk was long and often behind the hand. With post office gob-stoppers in our cheeks and more in the jars for the hinting, we were in no hurry to leave. When we did the bell was still ringing itself out long after we had climbed back on to the mail-cart.

Next there were calls to be made on our own maids from home who were visiting their mothers in the village. Ada's mother was plump with a tiny head that seemed to go back into her body on a stalk like a Cox's orange pippin. She kept nut toffee in a tin with the King's picture on all four sides. The cottage smelt agreeably of boiled washing any day of the week.

Rosa's mother was frayed and wrinkled as a dish-cloth. Rosa wore the latest fashions when she stayed with her mother, with a belted blouse that almost reached to her knees.

In the afternoons Annie pushed us down to Overstrand for a paddle. It was coming back that made the impression. Would we ever get to the top of the gangway dragging our spades and buckets and wet seaweed, with our yellow oilskin paddlers pinching our thighs where the sand had lodged in its folds? It was all right trundling in the mail-cart along the footpath to Overstrand church. But when we turned into the lane that curves up through the Cottage Woods our combined weight was too much for Annie and we were put out to walk. Soon our weights were too much for us too. What a relief it was to come to Northrepps Cottage itself and there be regaled with cakes and milk by whichever family of cousins were 'there' for the summer. This was the house in the woods where lame Anna eventually lived with her rabbits and dogs, looking after the sailors cast up after wrecks on the shore.

It was—and still is—a cottage in shape only, with the twisty chimneys, overhanging eaves and small decorated windows of a gingerbread house, yet large enough to hold a huge house party.

Here came the overflow from Northrepps Hall who could not be fitted in when we were all there. Three hundred yards higher up the hill, a house of about the same size accommodated a further overflow. One year we went to Hill House ourselves for part of the summer. Both houses were then more extensions of the Hall than houses in their own right. Furniture, crockery, linen and usually one or two maids were lent from the Hall for the visit.

In Cromer there were other family houses—fifteen of them at one time—filled with cousins with strong Northrepps associations who turned up for Sunday tea or at any other time when their children wanted a change from the shore.

There was one curious thing that George used to tell us about Cromer pier. Not far from the end of it, deep under the water, lay the original harbour town of Shipden. One night a great storm had come and swept the whole town into the sea. The old pier and harbour were washed away and the church had toppled over the cliff with all the houses and shops behind it.

'At certain times,' said George, 'You can still hear the church bells ringing under the water. Hark!' and we harked—surely it was church bells we heard and not just the waves and the seagulls or the ringing voices of the relations greeting each other?

Naturally we supposed George was talking about something which happened in his childhood, as he often did, particularly as he said he knew a fisherman who had caught his oar in a pile of rocks that had once been the church tower. It was a long time later that we learnt that Shipden church fell into the sea in 1350.

George told us that if we went down to a little covert just beyond the Long Wood, known as Graveholes, we should also hear, on certain nights, wailing coming from the shrieking pits.

'The what?'

'The shrieking pits, Master Erroll. Where the old sea kings buried their heroes, with the view of the sea they'd asked for.'

But we did not go down to Graveholes. Again we supposed that it was in George's lifetime that the Vikings had buried their dead there and not a thousand years before. Then there was Shuck's Lane, twisting up through a tree-tunnelled cutting behind Northrepps Cottage. George assured us this was haunted. Shuck was a two-headed dog, had eyes like saucers, sometimes turned into a ball of wool and caused any man who saw it to drop down dead within the twelvemonth. Women were excused.

Shuck's Lane, and Shuck himself, were both notorious tools of the local smugglers till a round-up was made in this sunken lane by preventive officers, with fatal consequences.

Long before that, something no less nasty, if slightly more honourable, had occurred. 'In 1250 a duel was fought here on behalf of Agnes de Reymes, daughter of the Manor of Over-strand, and one Roger of Northrepps, concerning a lease of eighty marks of silver', reports the Hundred's Roll of that time.

But it was on trips in the Vauxhall off our usual beat that George really excelled himself as a narrator.

Slowing down at a hump-backed bridge he said with a reflective smile: 'This was where the family diamonds was lost, Miss Verily.'

'Where?' 'In the river?' 'From a highwayman?' We all wanted to know.

'In your great-aunt's head, Master Erroll. The horses bolted and she, wearing the family tiara, was bounced up to the carriage roof coming over the bridge.'

'But where did the diamonds go?'

'They were drove down into her, Master Joseph.'

Once I was to go on a long drive alone with my grandmother. Normally the Vauxhall was crammed to capacity but today, due to an unusually low tide causing a keen shrimping expedition, only I was prepared by Annie in white socks and shoes, tussore coat, white cotton gloves and a flower-wreathed hat with fresh and unchewed elastic under the chin. I was taken out to the waiting Vauxhall where George had soon so terrified me with wayside anecdotes of the road we were to take, that when my grandmother came out I was already under the rug.

Usually, if we could not get the seat beside George in front, we children were packed in on footstools on the floor among the folds of canvas falling from the extendable windscreen which was drawn round my grandmother after the rug had been spread over her knees. On this occasion, however, I travelled behind the windscreen, with my white shoes on an embroidered footstool. I was quite glad, for once, not to sit beside George with his bloodthirsty anecdotes, knowing my grandmother would only point out the churches and ancient houses in which our ancestors had lived—all good people—or anyway nearly all. There was just one great-grandfather who was brushed rather obviously over.

'Look, that's where the eleven Gurneys of Earlham lived—all such good people—and three of them your great-great-grand-parents—two of them twice over. Their lives covered a hundred years and their combined ages, when they died, were six hundred and seventy. Just think! Six hundred and seventy years of Christian goodness! Though,' my grandmother's voice tailed off as though she spoke now more to herself, 'their friends did display great anxiety as to what would become of them when they were young—', she dropped her voice even lower, 'and perhaps a little wild.'

Keswick Hall, where we were going to tea, impressed itself deeply on me in a strange ethereal way. Its huge rooms and large-patterned Chinese wallpaper made Northrepps and even my tall grandmother seem small and homey. There were only good people here, it was clear—a great-aunt and great-uncle of singular decorum.

Unexpectedly, I was not sent away to any nursery for tea but was allowed to perch on a knobbly carved chair and nibble a rolled asparagus sandwich like the rest of them. The rain pelted against the vast windows and the thunder and lightning that would at any other time have sent me scuttling to the nearest knee, seemed here entirely in keeping. After tea the rain stopped as suddenly as it had begun, and I was sent into the garden to look at the stork. It stood disdainfully on one leg on the edge of a sheet of water—a lake or river or pond. A weird, yellowy light shone out of the dark, lowering sky and lit a willow tumbling its branches towards the water, so that the leaves seemed like a dazzling silvery green fountain. Soon it was raining again in sharp spikes that hit the water at an angle. I left, still not sure whether the stork was alive or of bronze.

On the way home my grandmother pointed across the fields towards a tumble-down farm and said, 'That's the *real* Keswick Hall.' I understood. What she meant, as I learnt years later, was that the mansion we had just left had been built by ancestors who had become too rich to want to live in so modest a hall as the original one. But I nodded in complete agreement. Certainly the Keswick Hall we had just visited had seemed anything but real to me.

The next time we went to Northrepps there was a big change, not in Northrepps but in ourselves. I was now no longer the baby. We had a new one, five years younger than myself. Moreover Lorema was one of the new kind of babies who dispensed with a nanny. Annie had irrevocably damaged her leg.

Now, instead of occupying the nursery wing, we abandoned it to the still nannied cousins from London, who had also brought a new baby, Pam, with them. The North wing, which we now occupied—Silver-built seventy years before—was made for our great-great-Uncle Charles to fill with his children for the summer months. Along one side of it stretched a narrow passage with all the rooms off it looking on to the woods, and in some places almost touching them. The schoolroom, formerly used for the purpose by Merlin and Rhalou, now became our nursery. From its windows we could see right into the heart of the woods.

Still all the families continued to trail to the only bathroom, which also contained the only upstairs taps, apart from those in the housemaid's cupboard where Harriet filled copper cans almost as big as herself and distributed them at least twice daily throughout the bedrooms.

Harriet did not at all approve of our nurse-less state. It was not only that we were more likely to stamp mud into the house and rub sticky fingers over her polished door knobs but—well—it was just not in the way of things.

Without Annie to prevent us, we now roamed at will all over the house and garden and into the woods. We went down the steps of the pond and tottered out to the end of a fallen tree that formed a pier. We went into the kitchen garden and, while old Riseboro's back was turned, helped ourselves gooseberries and redcurrants. We barged into the kitchen till Knights gave up handing out sugar mice. Except during Family Prayers and at meal-times, which we still had in the nursery with the other cousins and their nannies, we could not often be easily found.

Another change had come over me. Now I could read. The names painted below the row of bells, hanging high on coils in the kitchen passage, now revealed themselves as belonging to my grandmother, and my mother and her brothers and sisters.

We followed the wires upstairs and along the passages and in and out of cupboards to find out which rooms they had all had before they left home. We followed them up into the attic crawling after them under the rafters, testing as we went the triangular springs on which the wires changed direction, so that bells in the kitchen passage set up a continual jangle. One, marked 'The Anteroom', hardly surprisingly, turned out to be Aunt Chen's room with the five doors.

Out in the stables I was at last able to spell out horses' names written up over the stalls: Jumbo, Sambo, Frisco and Nellie. In the coachhouse I read the directions, protected by a sheet of horn inside a miniature door, for looking after the fire engine, which turned out to have been built in 1734 by Richard Newsham of London, whose 'new water engine for quenching and extinguishing fires' he patented in 1721. Well, he was nearly Noah.

Learning to read certainly opened up the past as nothing else had. That Northrepps was an actual place on the map, independent of the family, came as a shock. When I first read NORTHREPPS 2½ on the signpost, I felt an intense resentment that it was necessary to point it out. Surely, anyone needing Northrepps would know where to find it without written directions? As for the thought of Northrepps and the surrounding country existing without the family, it had never occurred to us. We took it for granted that it all began and ended with us, till someone let fall the unpalatable truth that others before the immediate family had been returning to our haunts for half a million years.

Old axes made out of stone by prehistoric men 5,000 years ago were still, apparently, being found near Cromer.

'Then were there ape-men here till *we* came?' we asked, aghast.

'Oh, no. There were all sorts of other people in between.'

'Well, who were these people?'

'Oh, Urn Folk and Danes and Weavers—Walloons, don't you know,' we were told with some ambiguity. And it was easy enough to see them in one's mind's eye, swinging on the low branches of the trees as we did, picnicking in the green ride and drifting about the garden—the Urn Folk replicas of the Mothers' Union who after their meetings drank tea made in a tall metal urn with a tap at the bottom, the Great Danes barking at the ducks on the pond, and the Walloons—big woven balloons floating silently about the woods.

Next we learnt to our further dismay that the woods themselves had not existed till the family planted them. Every towering elm and smooth barked beech, every multi-trunked ilex and out-stretched oak had been deliberately heeled in as a sapling by one or other of our many-greated-grandfathers. Even the wild daffodils that followed the snowdrops in the spring had been brought by them from Devonshire. The woods had not, as we supposed, always been there exactly as we found them every time we returned. Each winding path and broad green ride had been carefully cut. Each mossy glade had been deliberately left open for the sun to reach it.

All our ancestors found when they came was an open, heather-and gorse-covered heath with an occasional ancient windswept oak and strand of pine trees that were said to be directly descended from the forests that had once covered Europe.

Northrepps Hall itself was little more than a crow-stepped and rectangular farmhouse of cut flint and cobble, sheltering beneath a cluster of tall trees that narrowed into the avenue. Even the sea had not always been here but had crept up over the marshes between us and Germany.

And the railway! Perhaps it was hardest of all to imagine Northrepps without the railway. It was even more part of it than the sea and yet, it turned out, not 6,000 years but only sixty years before there had been no railway lines at the bottom of the park, no railway bridge on the way to the village and no express train pounding over it. When the grandchildren came to stay they had to drive from Norwich by coach, or ride the rest of the way on their ponies, for that was as far as the trains from London came.

We now mostly came the whole way by car for my father had become Rector of Herstmonceux in Sussex. As a parting present his Birmingham parishioners had given him a Model-T Ford. Into this our mother stuffed us to drive to Norfolk via the Gravesend ferry whose list of fares always delighted us by showing the difference in price of carrying a coffin with or without a corpse.

CHAPTER FIVE

Children's Garden Party
—with Walloons

FROM our next visit onwards my grandmother's frail health had begun to make what was called in the family 'a great invalid' of her. She stayed in her room till late in the morning, when all blinds and curtains were drawn on the stairs, in the hall and in the drawing-room for her coming down; for she believed that if her already partially blind eyes were subjected to light she would choke, and if she choked she would die. A nurse in a black dress, but no white apron, waited on her night and day, backed frequently by Harriet who ran ahead to clear the way for the coming downstairs. But I refused to be cleared. This was my grandmother and I knew she would not be distracted from the business of getting downstairs by my being there.

It did not seem to me such a sad or awe-inspiring sight, my once tall grandmother bent forward between her nurse and Harriet as she moved slowly along. It was just the way Granny liked things done, just as, when we went to see her in her bedroom, she liked us to put on dark pinafores over our lightly coloured frocks or shirts; and if we ran in forgetting about this, she would have a purple velvet cushion put over our knees.

Otherwise life went on as usual. Her children and grand-children came to stay and those who lived near enough continued to come for the day. Missionary meetings and huge children's parties went on as usual even though our grandmother could not eventually attend them even in her hooded and darkened Bath-chair.

For her last summer party, she had herself taken into the Bow

Room so that she could look through her blue spectacles on to the lawn and woods where the children's tea was laid out. It was a good tea, with grapes from the greenhouses that very much impressed the visiting nannies. We sat on benches at trestle tables heavily draped in white damask.

Round the woods we went in the donkey cart, the pony chaise and the goat carriage; and our grandmother, who had invented the party, was alone upstairs. I decided to call on her and give her a few details of the delights. I ran up the front stairs and turned the painted china door knob of the darkened Bow Room without knocking, and ran in, forgetting to cover my party frock with a cushion. There was my grandmother with neither nurse, Aunt Chen nor Harriet. With her head bowed almost on to her purple Shetland shawl, she was rocking quietly, though whether in pain or prayer it was hard to tell. Once I had attracted her attention I knew that my coming was right. She wanted to know exactly who was there, focusing her mind on each name as though each child stood in turn before her.

'And Dick,' she repeated after me. 'And Eve.'

'Yes. And Ruth.'

'And Ruth.'

'And Tommy,' I said. 'I think it's still Tommy. Only he's grown awfully if it is.'

She looked puzzled, and then smiled.

'Ah, Tommy,' she said.

'And Peter and Polly and Guy—'

'I'd like to see them all,' my grandmother said, and to my surprise groped for her ivory-handled stick.

'Stand quite near me.' I moved near her and braced my back as she laid her thin hand on my shoulder and rose shakily to her feet.

Together we made slow progress through the shadows to the window. I pulled back the curtain, forgetting, as my grandmother must have done, the blaze of sunshine that would pour in. She leant forward into it, seeming to gaze out. A dozen or more bunches of balloons had been let loose and, like soap bubbles from a clay pipe, they blew about over the flower-beds with the children leaping, chasing and running after them. This is what I had once thought Walloons would be like.

'All these grandchildren!' my grandmother murmured. They were not all grandchildren. There were great-nephews and great-nieces and first, second and third cousins, who were once, twice and three times removed. There were even a few children who were not related at all. But to her they evidently all felt like descendants, even the balloons.

Presently the slight weight on my shoulder was renewed and we turned and she moved very slowly back to her chair. We had just reached it when Harriet appeared.

'Oh Miss Verily, what are you doing disturbing your poor grandmama!' she scolded me. 'She doesn't want you chattering round her while she's trying to rest.' She shooed me out and I turned to see the old lady, just as I had found her, nodding away in her chair as though quite unconscious of her party going on in the garden below.

Supposing she died, I thought, as I hopped down the front stairs, pretending to be lame through force of habit. A terrible feeling of anguish seized me with the realisation of the possibility. Then I would want to die too, for my mother would never be able to bear life without her mother, just as I should never be able to bear it without mine. I prayed, therefore, as I reached the baskets by the garden door, that God would kill us all three at the same moment. A solution having been found, I was then able to join the game of Hide and Seek without further anxiety.

Next time we came to Northrepps we had turned into 'others' and all the baby brothers and sisters of all the families into 'little ones'.

While the nursery party paddled and made sand castles at Overstrand, we others were now permitted the more sophisticated attractions of Cromer beach. No longer were we stripped in the open by our nannies in nothing but the shelter of a breakwater.

We were now paid for and led up the steps of a bathing machine, not one each of course but one large one divided down the middle for the boys and the girls. It was a little disappointing, on my first inauguration, to find that the machine was really nothing more than a beach hut on wagon wheels. I had hoped that, once we were undressed, a horse would be harnessed to the shafts and we should be pulled down into the surf. But the horses on the beach were all busy pulling up the crab boats, and rarely now took the bathing machines right down into the water, except for the most eccentric or old-fashioned customers. I had expected too to find some sort of machinery inside, as in a mill, though for what purpose I had not thought.

Aunt Chen, renowned in the family as a great swimmer, often bathed with us, supporting us in turns under the chin as we floundered under our water-wings. She wore, as we girls did, a pale red thick rubber bathing cap set into a wide band, and the new skirtless bathing costume with a scooped-out neck, sleeves to the elbow and trousers to the knee, edged with white, which was worn by boys and girls alike. When Merlin appeared on the bathing machine steps in the knee-length trunks that were regulation at his prep school, there was a little gasp.

Picnics now were farther afield and became increasingly noisy. On Sundays we new 'others' now came down to lunch in the lofty Victorian dining-room that had been my grandfather's most solid contribution to the house. Some of us were just beginning to be able to see what was on the sideboards but the multi-storied mantelpiece was still high above all our heads. We were all, however, able to see all that was visible of our two great-great-grandfathers whose busts, larger than life and carved in alabaster by the same sculptor, still dominate the dining-room on their marble pillars. They, like so many of us sitting beneath them, shared the same grandparents. Joseph John was, we knew, as good as he was handsome and a worthy Quaker preacher. His bust was insured for a hundred pounds. But Richard Hanbury of Keswick —well, for certain reasons not yet divulged to us, our grandmother could not bring herself to insure his bust for more than thirty bob.

Sometimes twenty or more of us sat round the carved mahogany table, which still had extra leaves in the pantry for more. While the maids in their Sunday goffered caps and aprons staggered round under silver-plated dishes, we heaved the weighty crested spoons and forks off the Crown Derby and up into our temporarily silenced mouths. We swallowed as best we could, with throats constricted by starched table napkins, stuffed by a passing parlour maid, as we sat down, into the tops of our frocks or shirts.

My grandmother hardly came downstairs at all. Her life was becoming darker and more and more detached. She was so closely watched by her bodyguard that it was impossible to slip in to see her unnoticed. On Sundays the most we saw of her was a tray with a few of the best grapes from the greenhouse or a peach going into her room, or the same tray with the grapes almost untouched, and possibly a peach stone coming out.

When the news came that our grandmother had died, I did not, after all, want God to kill my mother too and myself. Far away, at home, her death seemed natural and proper, if solemn. Only Merlin, among her grandchildren, went to the funeral in his new uniform as a Dartmouth cadet. We stayed at home with black ribbon, instead of grey, round our Sunday felt hats.

And that, so it seemed, would be the end of Northrepps. Aunt Chen could not go on living there by herself, and her brothers, married to two sisters, had houses of their own.

But with our grandmother dead, what did it matter? We would never want to go there again. In fact there was almost no need. For Northrepps was already part of us. We could not love it more than we did already. Nobody could take away what was stored inside us.

There was talk of distant relations taking it, but it barely held our interest till we heard that Uncle Christopher had suddenly decided to throw up his job and his house in London and take his family, Joe, Hugh, Pamela and Anthony, to live at Northrepps.

Grand children living at Northrepps sounded incongruous at first. Northrepps was a place for grandchildren to go to, not to live in. But, my mother pointed out, she and her brothers and sisters had been grandchildren of Northrepps and yet brought up there, indeed most of them were also born there. How much more of a pull, I then realised, must it be for Aunt Chen, who had never known any other home, to have this drastic upheaval.

And yet when we went to stay with Aunt Chen that first summer, in the lodge next to George's, where she was staying till she settled on a house of her own, she was her own cheerful self, as busy as ever with good works and nephews and nieces. And there was Northrepps—darling, mellowed, gentle, humorous Northrepps, the same down to the last half-buried cobble bordering the path to the stables. And there was the new mistress of the house, Aunt Dorothy, already part of it, welcoming us at any time of day and in complete sympathy with all the grand-children's love of every detail of the place.

And so it must have been with each death and replacement at Northrepps. The new master and mistress took up the reins and moved quietly on without disturbing the rhythm.

We ex-grandchildren—some now children of the house and some now nephews and nieces—went on where we had left off, repairing our tree-houses, remaking the raft on the pond and taking messages through the woods to other cousins at Northrepps Cottage and Hill House. Presently, Erroll and I were back in the same beds in the North Wing we had slept in when our grand-mother was there. We were climbing up the same narrow back stairs and giving the same bell-rope a push as we passed. We were sitting on the same cane chairs round the nursery breakfast table, presided over by Nanny Pink, and drinking out of the same gold-rimmed nursery cups we had known since before we could remember.

Of course certain changes had to be made in a house where a

modern young family were to live permanently, but there was no feeling of sacrilege about these. We viewed each one with interest.

The bathroom was being partitioned into two and the old shuttered window was turned into a door into the passage. Now you could take your choice and bath in the old bath with celluloid boats to play with or in the new one, beside which a decorative jar of bath salts now stood. 'Boats or bathsalts?' you were asked, and so were the bathrooms named.

Uncle Christopher made his own electricity. Its engine snorted erratically into a silencer that only helped to amplify the sounds in the back yard. When a thunderstorm, or any other cause for a breakdown, caused the lamps and candles to be brought out of the pantry cupboard it was good for a short time to see the rooms and passages bathed in the soft light and to smell again the gentle paraffin fumes. But when the clear, bright light came on it was nevertheless greeted with a congratulatory cry.

Family Prayers went on but with certain modifications. Uncle Christopher read the prayers and each of us read a verse from the Bible, sometimes in a different tongue, for there have always been enough Bibles at Northrepps to cover any of the languages we were learning, dead or alive. We took it in turns to accompany the hymns on the harmonium; if they were too difficult for one, they were played as duets.

Freed of her ties, Aunt Chen was now able to go abroad and on long visits. In her absence her dog was returned to Northrepps. It was on one of these occasions that Kelpi, by now a good seventeen, passed on and was buried without ceremony in the dogs' graveyard in the wood.

It was not so much the lack of a ceremony as the lack of a coffin that worried us. After what we hoped was a suitable lapse of time—at least two holidays—we decided to inter Kelpi's bones and give him a decent funeral. Other family dogs had tombstones with such noncommittal epitaphs as 'Little Melly who lived happily among her rabbits'. It was not difficult to identify the unmarked mound. We went out at dusk and started to dig silently.

We had already prepared a shoe box suitably lined with flowers.

'Here's a bone,' said one of the boys. 'Not sure if it's a bit of Kelpi or just his favourite buried with him.'

But a matching one showed that it was Kelpi and now I felt we were going too far. I had not expected to find anything under this leaf-mound beyond ordinary earth. This was a shock, bringing home the reality of death in a sickening way.

'Cover it up, Joe,' I begged. 'Let's not go on. He's quite all right as he is.'

'Here's another.' I was relentlessly ignored. 'Pelvis, I think.' They bent down to pick over the excavations.

I dug half-heartedly on, but I did not like it. When they decided they had all of Kelpi, they scooped up the bones into my skirt.

'Aren't they going in the coffin?' I asked.

'We'd better take them back to the light and pick them over to make sure they're all there,' I was told, and we went back to the house. They were laid out on the garden door step in the thin shaft of light that shone from the library window. I could hardly bear to look at the pattern the bones made, but, to hurry things on, I tried to sound keen.

'A very nice skeleton,' I approved hopefully. 'It's all there now.'

'Except for one leg. Just nip up to the wood and see if you can find the missing one, will you, Verily?' urged Hugh.

But I could not, and all night, as I lay in the darkness in the Red Room along the North Passage, I thought of Kelpi's three-legged skeleton and soon even began to think I heard him limping about on three legs below.

To the delight of the boys next morning at breakfast, Nanny Pink described how I had come hurtling down the nursery corridor at three o'clock in the morning and had burst into the night nursery and flung myself frantically under the eiderdown at the end of Pam's bed.

Nanny Pink was even inclined to suggest that it was I who

had led the boys on in the re-interment of Kelpi. But this was an old accusation, dating back to their bouncing at the other end of the pram that deliberately caused it to upset my end.

Once Nanny Pink came into the nursery in answer to my yells to find me beating my heels on the floor. The three pirates in the game knelt in a beaming row beside me, having successfully lashed me to the yardarm with my own hair.

'Don't lead the boys on,' was, as usual, all the sympathy I got. But nobody could have lavished more when we were in trouble not of our own making. Falls from bicycles, ladders, and roofs counted in Nanny's eyes as acts of God and were rewarded with the highest standards of nursing and treatment for shock. To lie on the nursery sofa under the window with a wad of witch-hazel on the forehead smelling watery and fresh, with a triangle of Nanny's home-made toffee wedged into one side of one's mouth and Pam's dolls' pram cover over one's knees, Anthony's fat hand stroking one's face and Nanny reading the *Pip, Squeak and Wilfred Annual* out loud to soothe, was almost worth the fall.

All the same, I could not agree with Nanny on all points. It had never been my idea, for instance, to put pins and pennies on the railway line, yet somehow it came under the old heading. The boys had offered to make me a pair of doll's scissors in exchange for two pins which I readily gave them. They said they could even make a penny for every halfpenny I gave them, and these I gave them willingly too. We went to the end of the park and climbed over the forbidden railing and out on to the top of the railway embankment. The two pins were laid crossed on the line with the halfpennies beside them. Joe looked at his watch.

'She'll be along presently. It's nearly twelve twenty-five,' he said, and our danger suddenly dawned on me. I scuttled down the bank and the boys came at a more leisurely pace. Now the train that we had loved so much when we were small had a new note in its distant rumble as it came nearer and nearer. It clattered over the bridge and stopped in the siding. I froze, sure that for once this was not its usual stop and that the driver and guard already knew who had caused it. But presently the Sheringham engine came. The train moved off as usual in two halves, and as soon as both were out of sight the boys scrambled up the bank and I followed more timorously. There were my doll's scissors— flat and joined in the middle, if not exactly a working model. I picked them gently off the shining metal line and held them in the palm of my hand. There too were my newly-made pennies, which the boys picked up for me, a little thin perhaps but penny-sized and though not quite legal tender, worth twice their former value to me. The engine, indeed the whole train had been right over them, only just missing, as Joe pointed out, doing the same to us.

Most of our games had an element of danger in them. When we were not shooting at the bell on the top of the house with the air-gun whose pellets ricochetted off the lead with considerable force in any direction, we were hurtling round the paths in the wood in Aunt Dorothy's Baby Austin, teaching each other to drive. We swam at Overstrand only if the red 'No Bathing' flag was flying, taking our bicycles into the water with us and competing in swimming out the furthest. We climbed about the roof with the abandon of those believing themselves to be safely surrounded by railings. And we experimented with cooking and eating berries and fungi that should have put each one of us into an instant coma.

CHAPTER SIX

The Ancient de Gournays, and the New
of Norwich

M ORE and more we took part in the activities of the
other cousins, joining them to sing songs round the
piano at Northrepps Cottage, to get up a concert at
Northrepps Hall, a circus in the stable-yard at Hill House or
a gramophone dance at Colne Cottage in Cromer, only stopping
to dash to the end of the pier together to watch the lifeboat go
out.

There was nothing new about it. The family had been sharing
holidays on these lines since long before 1803, when Rachel
Gurney wrote to her sister from Cromer:

'Our time here is spent in a way that exactly suits the place
and the party. All are left in perfect liberty to do as they like all
day, or to form any engagement. Yet the party is so connected
that hardly a day passes but some plan is fixed for us all to meet.

'I will tell thee how we generally pass the day. The weather
since we came has on the whole been fine, so imagine us before
breakfast, without troutbecks on'—hats—'and coloured cotton
gowns, running in all directions on the sands, jetty, etc. After
breakfast we receive callers from the other houses, and fix with
them the plans for the day; after this we now and then get an
hour's quiet for reading and writing though my mind has been
so taken up with other things, that I have found it almost impossible to apply to anything seriously. At eleven we go down in
numbers to bathe and enjoy the sands, which about that time
look beautiful; most of our party and the rest of Cromer company
come down and bring a number of different carriages, which

has a very pretty effect. After bathing, we either ride on horse-back, or take some pleasant excursion or other. I never remember enjoying the sea so much, and never liked Cromer a quarter so well. Some of us continually dine out, whilst the others receive company at home. We always dine in the kitchen; Nurse is our cook, and makes a very good one. We have short afternoons, and in the evening all the party meet on the jetty and we divide and mix as is agreeable and spend the evening with music, something of that sort.

'The day before yesterday we spent at Sheringham wandering about the woods, and sketching all the morning. Everyone met at a beautiful spot for dinner with three knives and forks and two or three plates between twenty-six people. All manner of games took place after dinner. We completed our day by a delightful musical evening.'

She goes on to speculate about a dance they are going to and ends up by 'in such a party as this, strong health and spirits are really necessary.'

There seemed to be no lack of either in Rachel's time or ours. From hearsay we had collected a hotchpotch of descriptions like this and anecdotes about our ancestors, that might have happened to any of us. But only gradually did we begin to wonder which was which and where they had all come from.

One rainy afternoon at Northrepps I put this question to a cousin who was older and wiser, if only by a year or two. To get a better view of a green woodpecker, Tommy was known to have propped his pillows up in bed with a *Landed Gentry, Debrett* and *Burke's Peerage*. The bird had flown off, leaving him with his props. The result was that he was now, in our generation, the recognised expert on anybody's ancestors.

'Come into the library and I'll show you,' he said, and I expected him to make straight for the props. But Tommy spurned them.

'If you want some really bloodthirsty ancestors,' he said, 'you'd better flip through Dan.'

'Dan?'

'The Apocryphal book of Daniel.'

'The Bible?'

'No, Great-Great-Great-Uncle Dan.' He scanned the shelves in a business-like way and then with a practised hand slid down an enormous clasped and leather-bound tome and opened it at page 1096.

'All of it?' I asked.

'Well, you asked when it all started. Great-Great-Great-Uncle Dan can't get us farther back than Eudes—Eu, for short, in later generations called Hugh—a Viking prince who settled at a place called Gournay—meaning muddy swamp—in Normandy in 896—hence the name de Gournay.

'There were six Hue de Gournay's one after another who defended Gournay. Two of them fought at the Battle of Hastings and got some land in East Anglia. You can read all about it here. Dan gives them each an enormous chapter with all their armorial bearings, wives, children, Crusades—the whole catastrophe. One of the de Gournays (not Hue) murdered Edward II in a particularly repulsive manner. Dan spares you nothing, though I see our great-grandmother has written in the margin in pencil against the regicide "Not our branch". In fact this splendidly annotated edition should give you a lot of insight into the family.'

'But I only want to know about the Northrepps ones,' I said.

'According to Uncle Dan's reasoning, the son of one of these Hues must have been the first one to come to Northrepps. He says the third Hue de Gournay's son, Gerard, married William the Conqueror's granddaughter, Editha, whose father, Earl de Warren, owned all this land here. Thus, Gerard de Gournay would probably have come hunting here with his father-in-law. What could be more natural?'

'When Northrepps was being put into the Domesday Book?'

'Just about that time.'

'I'd rather know about the ancestors we know for certain were here.'

E

'You're right,' agreed Tommy. 'Not everybody's entirely swayed by Uncle Dan. His detractors like to remind us that he was a bit of a desperate man, born at a time when Norman ancestry was as necessary as silver-plate candelabra. He married the daughter of an earl and seems to have been torn between showing his own family what an ancient earldom his wife's was, and showing her family that the Gurneys were all right really, if you went back far enough.'

'So none of this is true?' I tried to lift the mammoth book but failed.

'Oh yes, Dan's research on the ancient de Gournays is absolutely sound. The trouble is he never managed to prove the missing link between the old baronial de Gournays who'd been living in the same house in Norfolk for twelve generations— West Barsham Hall—getting broker and broker, and the new Gournays who, at about the same time as the old ones appeared to die out, started to get richer and richer in the city of Norwich.'

'Hasn't anybody proved it since?'

'They've got a bit nearer. Some papers turned up showing that one of the last of the old Gournays or Gurneys—they still spelt it any old way—Francis, owed some money on a dud lot of pipe clay and was so worried he jumped, or fell, into his own well. He had a son John, born in 1655. Well, a youth of the same name and age turned up as a cobbler's apprentice in Norwich at about this time and made a fortune. Dan, who knew nothing about the suicide, always said this was Francis Gurney's son.'

'Was the suicide all on paper?'

'Rather! Samuel Pepys, *the* Samuel Pepys, was among the people who wrote trying to save Francis Gurney's property for his wife and children. They used to confiscate the goods and chattels of suicides in those days. Look, here it is, copied out on a piece of black-edged paper and stuck in by a Dan-supporter some years after his death. How Dan would have revelled in it!'

'"August 21st 1677. That noe Grant passe of the estate of Francis Gurney, of Malden, who drowned himself in his owne well on Sunday night the 12th of this instant August. At the desire of Samuell Pepys Esqr."'

'What about the young apprentice who made his fortune. Is there anything on paper about him?'

'Oh yes, plenty. It was recorded, among other things, that John Gurney of Norwich went to prison for his faith as a Quaker, married a girl who was good behind a till, and ended up a silk merchant with the freedom of the city and a son who was offered a seat in parliament after making a speech in the House of Lords that had their Lordships first in stitches, then in tears.

'The trouble was, the local weavers really were near to starvation due to undercutting by foreign and north country markets with cheap calico. Norfolk, having no natural coal or water power, could only press on with finer and more expensive weaves. A tax on imported cheap calico merely encouraged smuggling which was already rife all along this coast. Listen to this,' Tommy quoted from our ancestor's speech. ' "It is the common practice for the drapers to go in their coaches on Sundays and load them up with run calicoes sufficient to maintain both coach and horses." That's what made their Lordships laugh. It sounds as though this Gurney knew this part of the world pretty well,' Tommy suggested. 'As a Quaker he wouldn't have taken part in any of the smugglers' skirmishes, but he may well have watched unobserved from the cliffs. Anyway, a law was passed with a fine of five pounds for anyone wearing calico, and Gurney became a public hero. They called him The Weaver's Advocate and sold engravings of him in the streets. As his brothers were all Master Weavers they were among the first to benefit from the law. One bought Keswick Hall on the proceeds. The next generation got richer still. There was no law against importing home-made yarn from Ireland.'

'Was that quite fair?' I asked.

Tommy flipped through the pages of yet another volume.

'Other business men thought so. As Quakers, it says here, the Gurneys were respected for their quiet ways and honest dealings and men trusted them with their secrets and their money.'

'And these were the ones who came to Northrepps?'

'Their children were the first to buy land in Northrepps, though they all used to come here to shoot long before that, and put up in very uncomfortable lodgings in Cromer. The beds were too short.'

'Surely Quakers don't shoot?'

'These ones did. They all had a passion for sport. Some of the more pious ones eventually gave up bloodsport, but they still invited their friends and relations to shoot on their land. By 1790 there were five of them coming regularly to Cromer and, with roads and beds improving, bringing their families for the sea-bathing.

'There was the Weaver's Advocate's only grandson and heir, Bartlett Gurney, who also inherited some land in this direction through his grandmother who rejoiced in the splendid name of Hadduck, which she liked so well she gave it to one of her sons as a Christian name.

'Then there were the three Keswick brothers and one sister who spent so much time in each other's company that they were known as the Devoted Four. These were Richard, twice-married and a keen shot who had already bought land a few miles from Northrepps; John of Earlham, whose hair was so red as a boy that Norwich urchins had run beside him calling out: "Hi mister! You've got a bonfire on your head"; and Joseph of Lakenham Grove, who preferred hunting to shooting. The fourth was Rachel, sweet, gentle and pretty. In fact they were all remarkably good-looking. Three of them married Barclay cousins, whose great-grandfather, Barclay the Apologist, like the Gurney's great-grandfather, had gone to prison for his Quaker faith. Their great-great-grandfather was Gordon of Gordonstoun.' Tommy deviated to enlarge upon the current proposal to found a new kind of boys' school in our Scottish ancestral home. I steered him back to the Devoted Four.

'They were all nephews or nieces of ten Barclay daughters who, though singularly lovely of face, all had some slight defect of figure. You'll find them referred to in the records, with the usual all-embracing hyperbole of our family, as the ten, or anything up to thirteen, Hump-Backed Beauties of Urie. Urie was the Barclay stronghold in Scotland, which was said to be one of the last to be entered only by ladder.' Tommy said this not without pride, for he was a Barclay himself, though with strong Gurney descent on both sides.

He told now of the meagre spoonsful of chippings that were all that the workmen could disturb of the seven foot thick walls of Urie when at last it was decided to make a ground-level front door. And how, Barclay-like, the wall had withstood everything but gunpowder.

We returned to the eighteenth century and to the Devoted Four.

'Three of them had seven daughters apiece and between them they reared thirty-six children all of whom spent as much of their holidays here as we do. But that was not all. There were Hoare cousins who came too. The Gurneys and the Hoares had already started inter-marrying. The Hoares were also bankers.'

'Where did you find out about them all?'

'In their game books, in their sermons, in their journals and their letters and their graveyards. In Dan. The place is stiff with their story if you look into it. I've thought of picking out the ones who were often here and writing them up sometime.'

'It would take a lifetime.'

Tommy died before he had written more than a handful of poems on the subject. By then the habit of combing through old documents was established in me too, though it was a long time before I followed up Tommy's introduction to the sporting Norwich Quakers who helped to turn Cromer into a holiday meeting place for us all.

The first to buy land near Cromer was Robert Barclay, husband of Rachel of the Devoted Four. They had a large family—fifteen, of whom eleven survived—and as they lived in London, they

needed a country house near the others for the holidays. They
bought Northrepps Hall in 1790 from Richard Ellis for something over £5,000 and an annual annuity of £52. The Ellis
family had owned and lived in Northrepps Hall since 1602 when
the first Richard Ellis rebuilt it on his marriage to Miss Playford
whose family had, for two centuries, been Lords of the Manor
of Northrepps and much buried in the churchyard. Northrepps
Hall was mentioned as such in 1545. Judging by the thickness
of some of its cellar walls today it must then have been more of a
fortified farm-house than a mansion, probably dating back to
long before John of Gaunt's recorded ownership of the farmland.

The outside walls of the 1602 rebuilding still stand, though
now many are inside walls, showing clearly that the Ellis
manor was a simple rectangular house only one room thick, with
the usual dairy below ground. A later Ellis planted a straight
avenue of half a mile of oaks and elms. This was the third Richard
Ellis, who was a man of some importance in the neighbourhood.
As a popular attorney and steward of the adjoining large estate of
Felbrigg he no doubt felt entitled to an imposing front drive
reaching almost to Cromer. He was also responsible for collecting
dues to build and maintain a new pier at Cromer, a recurring
task, for Cromer piers had never lasted long. As distributor of
licences to set lobster coys off it, the first licence he allowed was to
himself.

By the time yet another Richard Ellis had sold Northrepps
Hall to Robert Barclay, the pier had been washed away again
but the dues went on, although all cargo, even coal, had to be
landed on the shore and then hauled up the gangway by teams of
five or more horses. The avenue has still survived, though for
years it has been used as a public road.

The Hall and farm buildings round it all tended to snuggle
down together out of the wind under the sparsely wooded slopes
rising gently towards the Overstrand cliffs. Under Robert and
Rachel Barclay's orders, soon the walls were heightened, the
mullioned windows were replaced by 'the new high sash windows'

to let in more light, ceilings were raised and the chimneys rose up to a final flourish of twisting brickwork. Inside, the old carved panelling in the hall was removed. Part of it was found years later up in the attic.

An extension to the drawing-room was added with a dining-room and study behind it, reached by an additional hall with arched double doors and a graceful mahogany-railed staircase. Upstairs, the master bedroom was enlarged and the Bow Room was built, a great bedroom with three bow windows and the sunny powder closet into which I had led my grandmother to view her children's party. Opposite it, the Pink Room was added with a sash window filling almost all of one wall.

On a smaller scale, the nursery wing was enlarged over new kitchen premises producing in its corridor the two beloved shallow steps without which many of our games would have lost their lustre. The corridor was extended to link the extra night nurseries that would be needed for the Barclay children and their Gurney cousins who were waiting eagerly to use them.

Only one bedroom appears to have been left untouched during these renovations. That was the ante-room—Aunt Chen's room—in which so many of the family were subsequently born or gathered to their forefathers, despite, or possibly because of, the five doors that gradually accrued with every fresh alteration to the rest of the house.

A porch supported by fluted pillars was erected over the front door and the house was then fashionably white-washed to give something of the effect of the classical villa then much in vogue.

Here, when the alterations were finished, Robert and Rachel Barclay came, with their large nursery party. Here also came the most frequent of all their many visitors, Rachel's brother, John, and his wife Catherine, whose eleven children exactly matched their first cousins, the Robert Barclays of Northrepps. Each claimed to have a fellow in the other family. Rachel Barclay and her brother John had been married the same year and the two families had multiplied at much the same pace, resulting in four sons and seven daughters apiece. Each family had a block of four girls, all born, with the help of twins in the Barclay family, in the four years between the autumns of 1782 and 1785.

Four years before Robert bought Northrepps, John Gurney had taken a leasehold of Earlham Hall, just outside Norwich, so that his children with their 'fellows' whenever they were in Norfolk, could enjoy the summer bathing in the river that wound through the park. Now, with Northrepps within walking distance of Cromer, the Gurneys of Earlham stayed with their 'fellows' and swam with them in the sea too.

CHAPTER SEVEN

Rich Man's Cottage in a Hundred-pound Wood

URING the Barclays' second summer at Northrepps a family tragedy occurred that was to affect them all. John of Earlham's wife died, leaving their eleven children between the ages of eighteen months and seventeen years, motherless. Kitty, the eldest, took on the full responsibility of mother to the others, caring for them and teaching them when their governesses gave them up in despair as they often did. Now, more than ever, they were sent off to their aunt at Northrepps for sea air and special treatment after colds, not that the keen east winds and perishing corridors at Northrepps always improved them.

'I have had rather a dis day, but a very happy ending,' wrote the small motherless Louisa of Earlham. 'How amazingly dull being here is, to be sure! I was most uncomfortable all the morning, I was so hurried and my cough so bad. Great was my joy to see Kitty. Hannah and my father arrived in the evening. Three days later we all left Northrepps.'

The youngest of the eleven Gurneys of Earlham became Great-Great-Great-Uncle Dan who traced the family back into the Dark Ages. Three others, Samuel, Joseph and Hannah became our great-great-grandparents whose children and grandchildren were all closely associated with Northrepps. Hannah, as mistress of Northrepps, spent more than half her life there, so that her memories were the most plentiful and far-reaching. Her earliest was of Lucy, one of the Barclay twins, being whipped in the seventeen-nineties for not drinking her breakfast beer in the new

Northrepps dining-room—now the library—and then being taken into the study and locked in till she drank it.

Joseph John as a small boy was also imprisoned at Northrepps when Hannah was trying to teach him geography and spelling and had to call Kitty to help her to manage him. Joseph John was shut up in the night nursery. Poor Joseph John! He was also whipped by mistake by his father for moving a lark's nest that turned out to have been placed on the lawn by an artist friend who wanted to draw it. His mother, on her death-bed, had described her gentle four-year-old as 'my bright morning star' and he remained the most saintly figure.

No amount of punishment had any effect on our other great-great-grandfather, Samuel, who, when sent to bed, said cheerfully that there was nothing he liked better. Samuel's independent character and resistance to schoolroom learning caused him to be sent to boarding school when he was only seven. His sisters went with him in the coach on the first stage and put him into the London coach all alone. But it was they who wept, not he, and all of them wrote frequently and sent him cake of their own making.

At Northrepps, Samuel liked to help on the home farm and, with his older cousin Charles Barclay, would lead the cart horses down to the horse pond to drink. Joseph John preferred to follow the bunch of small girls round, helping them to garden and pick flowers. They were a lively band, laughing and squabbling and generally brightening up the scene in the scarlet cloaks they always wore in the garden instead of the more usual bonnets and mantles of the time.

'I was in a very playing day mood today,' wrote Richenda, the eldest of the Earlham quartet of little girls—Richenda, Hannah, Louisa and Priscilla. 'And thoroughly enjoyed being foolish. I tried to be as rude to everybody as I could. We went on the highroad with the purpose of being rude to the folks that passed. I do think being rude is most pleasant sometimes.'

In a less playing mood she writes: 'I cannot help just mentioning my dinner, which was particularly delightful to me: I really felt true pleasure while I was eating excellent apple-pudding and partridge: how I did enjoy it.'

The Gurneys of Earlham were avid diary-writers, and much of the childhood life both at Earlham and Northrepps can still be seen through their eyes.

'We romped most of the morning. In the afternoon we read a novel. In the evening a blind fiddler came and we had a most merry dance and ended in a violent romp,' wrote Louisa, and: 'We lighted a fire in the field this afternoon and roasted potatoes in the ashes. There was company in the evening and my father would have Chenda and me dance a Scotch minuet—most dis.' Like most big families, they had a vocabulary of their own. There was 'dis' meaning disgusting, 'mumping' meant being down-hearted, 'a valley' meant a worry or disappointment, 'journal-wise' meant being retrospective, as, in the same diary: 'I have done nothing today to please anybody, not the least good. I am really a most disagreeable, common character, and the reason why people love me can only be from habit.'

'Goats' was their nickname for the Quaker Meeting House in Goat's Lane, Norwich, where they were taken, from which was derived 'goatified' for bored or subdued, as in: 'We eight went to Goats in the afternoon . . . I was very sorry to see that place again after a separation from it of a whole fortnight. We all came home rather goatified and cross.'

How they all loved Kitty! 'When I had a sore throat and was poorly on Friday,' writes Louisa, 'Kitty nursed me most kindly. I never saw so kind and sweet a nurse.' And how they hated their governesses! 'Governess, disliked by most of the family, sits in the drawing-room almost all day.' And again: 'Governess is going away: I am most glad she is, I dislike her so very much: I think it must do harm to the heart to feel such dislike as I do.' Eventually even kind and sweet Kitty, seeing the four commit their hates and adorations with such fierce glee to their penny note-books put a temporary brake on it.

'Kitty has forbidden us now to write more than six lines in our journals. I entirely see that it is now her plan to treat us as babies,' writes Louisa haughtily. 'I am very, very sorry.'

Among the many visitors to Northrepps Hall during the Barclays' first years there was Bartlett Gurney, when he came to shoot on his nearby property at Little Barningham that he had been left by his grandmother Hadduck.

Bartlett was so taken with Northrepps that when more land became available he bought it with the old farm, Hill House Farm, intending to build a fashionable country house in the middle of this beautiful unspoilt country where important guests and the children of his many sisters could be invited to stay. He had no children of his own, and, at thirty-seven, was very rich indeed. He was not only the senior member of the Gurney family, with a vast Gurney inheritance to add to his grandmother Hadduck's, but he had also made a tremendous success of banking, considerably increasing the transactions of Gurney's bank and establishing its principal branches. It was said that his father and uncle started the bank to give Bartlett some employment 'on account of his great dislike to the manufactures'. In fact at that time he had a dislike of any occupation except hunting and shooting.

'Hunting at Dereham today,' he writes in a note to a banking colleague. 'Send this from thence: if the fox makes for Rainham I will do myself the pleasure of seeing you; but it is on uncertain and precarious tenure.'

Bartlett decided that he wanted a house 'of a mixed kind, partaking of a villa, sporting seat and constant residence'. He chose a site on the crest of the open hill between Northrepps Hall and the sea at Overstrand. The views in all directions were magnificent but there was absolutely no shelter. Bartlett commissioned plans from the architect, William Wilkins, who was reaping the harvest of the Industrial Revolution with a spate of stately homes for Norwich merchants—the finest of them landscaped by Humphry Repton.

Bartlett already knew Humphry Repton, who had lived for some time near his Hadduck estate. Now Repton drew up one of his famous Red Books with designs and advice on laying out the land round the proposed new house at Northrepps. As usual he wrote it in the vein of a personal letter.

This slim book with embossed leather binding, now faded to pale brown, is still at Northrepps with a map showing Northrepps Hall, Hill House and a pair of cottages near it which are still standing. Repton has sketched in the many plantations that he suggested should be placed round the house. Bound into it are half a dozen of his delightful water-colours, each with a flap which lifts up to reveal underneath the suggested alteration. The flap could then be tucked into slots again to reveal the original scene. These 'slides', as Repton called them, saved having to paint the whole landscape twice, or more, for sometimes there were several slides to a scene. The last sketch in the Northrepps Red Book is of a bare hilltop with only two or three hedgerow trees, distorted by the north winds. Under the flap lies a splendid park flanked by our own Northrepps woods and dotted with sheep and clumps of trees. A neat front drive winds up to a large white classical villa which, however, was never built.

Although Bartlett was the first of the family to leave the Society of Friends, he must have decided that the mansion was too ostentatious for one brought up as a Quaker.

No Red Book survives of the house that was built instead in a fold in the valley at the foot of the same hill, and stands today as Northrepps Cottage Country Club. Tradition has it, however, that Repton had a hand in this too. If he had not, then Bartlett and Robert Barclay must have skimmed the cream of the landscaping advice given by Repton in his authoritative and lively manner in the Northrepps Red Book and adapted it to Northrepps Hall itself and the new house as well.

Certainly the new house is typical of Repton's other extreme from the Italianate villa, his *cottage ornée* crouched down in a dell with a background of trees against which a plume of smoke could be seen rising through a light mist. He had little time for the sea or large skies, and the glimpse of the sea beyond the then ruin of Overstrand church was planned to be so framed as to be like only one small gem in an eye-catching setting.

Repton introduced the idea of placing a kitchen garden out of sight in the heart of a wood—(he cannot have experienced the inevitable piracy of fruit by the waiting birds)—'yet situated near enough that dung may be brought from the stables' and this is where the kitchen garden lies in Bartlett's new house. Another typical Repton feature is the cutting into the hill to give a pleasant curve to the entrance and to give 'access to the poor', which was a favourite cry of Repton's, who condemned all fences and appearance of boundaries. No house could be more over-looked by the lane than The Hermitage, as it was at first called. This name was soon dropped by the family in favour of 'The Cottage', which, with its coachhouse and stabling for half a dozen horses, it has never been in anything but name.

The building of The Hermitage caused quite a stir in the neighbourhood for it was considered most 'novel to build a new house to look deliberately old-fashioned'. Visitors to Cromer—the newly-established watering-place—made a point of walking along the cliffs and turning inland to wonder at it.

A young doctor describes The Hermitage in the first guide to Cromer, 'considered as a watering place,' published in 1800, as: 'Flinted and thatched, with a Gothic porch, also thatched, and fitted up with the greatest neatness and simplicity; and stained glass which occupies the upper parts of the arches of the windows throws a very pleasing light into the apartments.'

Two of these panes of birds were copied from Bartlett Gurney's copy of Edwards' History of Birds. 'The parlour, which com-mands an elegant view of the sea, is decorated with coloured prints, extremely appropriate to the situation, such as the "Sailor Boy's Return", the shipwrecked sailor-boy telling his tale at the cottage door, and on the chimney-piece are shells and pieces of Derbyshire marble. Could it have been these prints that later inspired Anna Gurney, who from babyhood became a constant visitor, to take up her renowned work among shipwrecked sailors from this very house? Might the shells and Derbyshire marble have touched off her own scientific collection of minerals?

'Planting has been done with a liberal hand, and the healthy appearance of the young trees, when the situation so near the sea is considered, promises hereafter amply to reward the owner for his perseverance,' writes Dr. Bartell, junior.

For this purpose a hundred pounds worth of young trees were used, including some of the newly imported copper beeches which for all the irregularity of their gale-twisted trunks have grown to be some of the loveliest trees of them all.

In his Red Book Repton writes of the risks of exposing young trees in so bleak a situation to the powerful winds of the north coast. But he thought that if the trees were collected into great masses they would protect and shelter each other, 'though the outside ranks might shrink from the blast'.

This advice was taken by the whole family who diligently planted trees on the cliffs and hillsides where hitherto only an occasional storm-bent oak had fought for a lonely existence. These, Repton had said, should be left, however misshapen, to protect the younger trees.

Joseph Gurney, the youngest of the Devoted Four, planted his trees on the cliffs two or three years before enlarging yet another holiday house for his by then nine lively and remarkably good-looking children. Like his brother and sister, he too had seven daughters. Their home near Norwich was called The Grove, and indeed so was the whole family. 'The Grove are coming over to dinner', writes Kitty of Earlham. Earlham was only three miles from The Grove and Keswick only two, so long before the Devoted Four's children shared their holidays together they were 'like one huge family'.

The new house at Cromer was called The Grove too. The Cromer Grove still stands among Joseph's trees behind a cobbled

stable and coachhouse, its clear-cut but comfortable lines reflect-
ing Joseph's practical homely wife, from Darlington, who still
spoke 'the quick clipped tongue of the North'.

Joseph was a stricter Quaker than his sporting brother Richard,
though he had a ready sense of humour that made him well-
loved by everyone. By the time he built The Grove at Cromer,
he had given up hunting on principle, though he was always fond
of horses and continued to be an excellent rider.

He was stricter too than his more indulgent widower brother
John of Earlham, who became increasingly liberal in his feelings
towards other persuasions and who, though he wore Quaker costume
to a certain extent, never made a point of sticking to a suit of one
colour as his brother Joseph did, if drab could be called a colour.

The Grove children were mostly younger than their cousins, the
Gurneys of Earlham who, their father suggested, had a worldly
influence on them. He sometimes even admonished his nieces
themselves. They wore such brilliant coloured clothes and their
pranks were so unpredictable. One day they all joined hands
across the highway and held up the Norwich coach.

The other cousins who were warned against them were the
Samuel Hoares, who also came frequently to Cromer, though it
was young Sam Hoare, aged twelve, who caused Louisa, a year
younger, to write in her diary: 'Young Sam Hoare was most
disgusting; we were on most good terms for the first part of the
evening but at last he went so far as to give me a kiss; it was
most disgusting.' Still, possibly Louisa had led him on for she
had already decided in her diary; 'I am afraid I shall be a flirt
when I row up. I really do think I shall. To be sure I am not
a flirt yet, but I think I shall be.'

Meanwhile Sam's sister wrote that her father was making an
effort to prevent their being too closely associated with their
relations, the Gurneys of Earlham, 'who enjoyed more liberty
than he approved for us, and spoke on subjects connected with
religion in a manner he so greatly disapproved that he desired
that they might be excluded from our conversations'.

Certainly eleven-year-old Louisa had an uninhibited approach to religion—though hardly a dangerous one. She wrote: 'Two things raise my soul to feel diversion—nature and music. As I went down the dance yesterday, I gave up my soul to the enchanting Malbrook. I thought of Heaven and of God. I really tasted Heaven for a minute, and my whole heart thanked God for the blessings he enjoyed. These moments were delicious.'

For some years these cousins, the Samuel Hoares, had neither house nor land in or near Cromer, relying on the still far from inadequate lodgings and the days his landowning cousins took off from shooting to attend to their banks, when he would ride about their lands with his gun, getting off his horse to shoot indiscriminately whenever he saw a covey of partridges.

'My father was delighted with Cromer,' writes his daughter. 'As a sportsman he found an abundance of amusement and though having no land, there was some jealousy between him and those who had, the pleasure far outbalanced the pain.'

When, on the Cromer doctor's death, his house, Cliff House was put up for sale, Samuel Hoare bought it. Built, like so many of its neighbours, of flints taken from the beach, it still stands almost on the edge of the cliff with nothing but the North Sea between it and the North Pole. A long flight of steps, known as Doctor's Steps, lead straight down to the shore. It was a great relief to his family when Samuel Hoare bought and enlarged Cliff House and more relief still when he added some land on the cliffs for shooting, which put an end to 'feelings' with the cousins around.

John Gurney of Earlham never bought a house on the coast, possibly because his family already spent so much time at Northrepps Hall. However he usually rented a house at Cromer in the summer and autumn.

Meanwhile, just as the Devoted Four had settled their holiday homes and Bartlett had completed his, Rachel Barclay died and once more eleven children were left motherless. Robert immediately took them to Earlham to stay with their 'fellows'. They

F

remained there for several weeks in an atmosphere that could not have been more sympathetic, barely three years after an almost identical bereavement.

After that, Robert had no heart to go back to Northrepps, though his children always loved it, particularly Charles, the eldest. In 1795 Robert sold the whole estate to his brother-in-law, Richard of Keswick, with everything in the house left exactly as Rachel had arranged it for the huge holiday parties— the red leather armchairs in the hall, the tall grandfather clock at the foot of the stairs and the great four-poster bed in the Bow Room.

CHAPTER EIGHT

Sweet Danger

THE Richard Gurneys moved into Northrepps in the October of 1795. Richard, the eldest of the Devoted Four, was a bluff, amiable man, already getting rather stout in spite of all the exercise he took, much of it on a large grey horse. Although his nieces complained of his 'sarcasm', by which they meant teasing, he was particularly popular with the boys of the family whom he always tipped before they went back to school with a golden guinea, 'in an arch manner with a sort of nasal snort—"Here, boy, here. Here's a guinea for thee."'

His first wife had died when his daughter, Gatty, was born and she and her brother Hudson had been almost entirely brought up by their Barclay grandparents who were very much stricter than Richard. When he married again, they spent more time again with him. His second wife, Rachel Hanbury, was a 'sweet, tall Quakeress who inspired no "respect through fear". She was kind and benevolent without the force of character which her children had. Her influence over them was not great and her generosity and self-denial almost amounted to a fault.'

Her children, when she came to Northrepps, were Dick, a hot-headed, freckle faced boy of twelve who spent most of his time in the stables and Elizabeth, aged eleven, who was as gentle as her mother and adored by all her cousins, but especially by Louisa, who was the same age.

'Elizabeth and I had a sweet evening. I do love her so much.'
'Dearest Elizabeth was quite charming. I do love her so with my whole heart. It flutters me to think that such a charming person should make me her friend.'

The family had been there a month when Gatty was married

to her step-mother's brother, Sampson Hanbury. Sampson, aptly named, for he weighed seventeen stone, was a brewer, famous in three counties as Master of the Puckeridge Fox Hounds and, according to Surtees, the best judge of hounds in the county. All this appealed to his sporting father-in-law, who was also his brother-in-law, but not at all to Gatty's little cousins.

'I wonder that such a charming person as Gatty should marry Sampson Hanbury,' writes Louisa in her diary.

Hudson, Gatty's brother, now a handsome youth who yearned 'for the romance of being a poet', came home from his tutor's for the wedding. 'All my aspiring was to be author of one good poem', he writes of this time. 'All my worldly aspirations, should luck favour, London and Parliament.'

The family stayed at Northrepps for the autumn and returned to Keswick for Christmas. On New Year's Eve, Anna, the youngest child, was born, after a gap of eleven years. She was a strong vigorous baby but at ten months became crippled, it was said by a fall from her nurse's arms, though later reports suggest that she was more likely to have been a victim of poliomyelitis. Her mother took her to a celebrated surgeon in Leicestershire who put her too soon into irons, which were afterwards said to have done more damage than the actual disability. Her tremendous force of character coupled with her physical energy and intelligence made her a difficult baby to keep amused. From a small child onwards she refused to accept that she was handicapped and insisted on trying to do all that other children could.

The Gurneys of Earlham continued to come and stay at Northrepps, sleeping in the same beds as they had slept in when their other Aunt Rachel had presided and returning to their old haunts in the garden and on the shore. Sometimes one child went alone.

Louisa wrote in 1796: 'After breakfast, set off with Uncle Gurney for Northrepps and had a most dis drive but most glad to see Elizabeth next day. We walked about the roads then we went to the church. It was very cold. I felt everything very interesting in the church. We then rode down to Cromer. It was quite odd to me to see the sea.'

That year Bartlett of Northrepps Cottage stood for Parliament. His name had been put forward while he was away in the north, and so Hudson, who had just come of age, stood in for him at the election. His opponent was William Windham from Northrepps' adjoining estate of Felbrigg. Louisa's political enthusiasm knew no bounds. 'This morning I thought of nothing but the election; I was so interested in it. At ten we all set off for the Market Place, and there we looked out of a window all the morning. Norwich was in the greatest bustle. We had blue cockades and I bawled out of the window at a fine rate "Gurney for ever!" Hudson was tossed in the chair. He looked most handsome, I never saw him so handsome or so well. In the afternoon I was in the most dissipated mind. In the evening, as Eliza and I were walking, Scarnell' (the butler), 'came home and told us that Windham had got the election. I cannot say what I felt, I was so vexed. Eliza and I cried. I hated all the aristocrats; I felt it right to hate them. I was fit to kill them.'

Louisa's political views were certainly strong at this time, though like her religious views hardly, as old Samuel Hoare inferred, bordering on the seditious. She dealt shortly with democracy:

'I was very angry with Rachel for treating Chenda differently, just because she is a little older than me; there is nothing on earth I detest so much as this. I think children ought to be treated according to their merits, not their age. I love democracy, whenever and in whatever form it appears.' To prove it, she got up early and made a pincushion for nurse's sister. 'I think it is quite right,' she wrote, 'to pay these sort of attentions to servants, and if we do it out of kindness it is more a virtue to give a present to a person who has been rather ungrateful to you.'

As the family moved round from house to house rather often, Kitty found herself, between governesses, teaching others besides her own younger brothers and sisters. It was always a pleasure to include in the lessons, Elizabeth of Northrepps, who was said by an admirer of the Gurneys of Earlham, to be 'like one of them'.

Kitty used as a guide to teaching them all, a syllabus drawn up by her remarkably well-educated mother, on the lines of which she had started to teach her children before she died.

'. . . To be useful it is necessary and very agreeable to be well-informed of our own language,' she wrote, 'of Latin also, being the most permanent, and of French, as most in general request. The simple beauties of Mathematics appear to be so expert an exercise for the understanding that they ought on no account to be omitted, though perhaps scarcely less essential than a competent knowledge of Ancient and Modern History, Geography, Chronology. To these may be added a knowledge of the most approved branches of Natural History, and a capacity for drawing from Nature in order to promote that knowledge, and facilitate the pursuit of it. As a great portion of a woman's life ought to be passed in at least regulating the subordinate affairs of a family, she should work plain work neatly herself.

'Also, she should not be ignorant of the common properties of table, or deficient in the economy of any of the mass of minute affairs of a family. It should be here observed that gentleness of manner is indispensably necessary in women, to say nothing of that polished behaviour which adds a charm to every qualification; and to both of these it appears certain that children may be led without vanity or affectation by amiable and judicious instruction.'

Kitty, who was by then still barely twenty-one and whose own education had been cut short, felt herself sadly inadequate as she tried to follow the instructions her mother had set herself. She sighed over the Latin, French and Mathematics and groaned over the Ancient and Modern history, the Geography and Chronology, and gave up over the polished behaviour. It was difficult enough to teach the children simple spelling and arithmetic. It was not that they were stupid, but merely hard to

keep indoors. In the summer she solved this problem by teaching
them, whenever possible, in the garden.

'I do so like my liberty,' Louisa reminded her diary. 'In the
afternoon we walked about. I think it most silly to bring children
up always at work. I am sure I should be better and happier if I
did not learn much; it does try my temper so much.'

But it was not only the little ones who worried Kitty. Their
elder sister Betsey's concentration was appalling, unless it were
on the purple laces with which she had gaily fastened her purple
boots, and her spelling was most unreliable. 'This morning I
whent' [sic] 'to meeting although I had a very bad pain in my
stomach.'

The others were all rather sorry for her. She was so awkward
in her ways, so moody and given to fits of 'mumping'. And yet
when there was dancing and charades, it was Betsey who was the
gayest and most bright. By the time she was fifteen she was
engaged to James Lloyd of Bingley Hall, Birmingham, then a
charming park-enclosed country house. James, however, rode
away and Betsey turned her attentions elsewhere. This was the
girl who was to become the first 'Plain' Quaker in the family, and
eventually the prison reformer and friend of kings, queens and
princes all over Europe—Elizabeth Fry.

Rachel, two years older, was never any problem. Kitty described her later as a 'lovely girl, full of native charm and attrac-
tion, very sweet in her person, fair and rosy, with beautiful dark
blue eyes and curling flaxen hair'. She was very fond of dressing
up, and acting and singing to amuse the others, on whose teasing
she thrived.

John and Samuel were safely at school. The four younger girls
were now described as 'a joyous and happy quartet full of life
and enthusiasm, very industrious with their drawing'. John
Crome—'Old Crome' of the Norwich school as he later became
known to distinguish him from his son—was their drawing
master and often went with them to Northrepps to take them
out on sketching expeditions. Richenda, the daughter most

attracted to drawing and music and drama, who eventually became an artist of some talent, wrote:

'We had a good drawing morning but in the course of it I gave way to passion with Crome and Betsey; Crome because he would attend to Betsey and not to me, and Betsey because she was so provoking.' His 'attention' was to draw at least half of the sketch himself. Hundreds of these pencil drawings survive, for he taught the Gurneys of Earlham for years, as well as their cousin Elizabeth of Northrepps. Parts of them are small masterpieces and parts are the easily distinguishable efforts of these lively teenagers, one of whom, Richenda, became an artist of some little renown. However, because Crome, when he taught her, had contributed to her drawings and had a strong influence on her style, it has been the custom in the family to deny her kudos for many delightful drawings and water-colours executed long after Crome had ceased to teach any of them.

Many of the Northrepps sketches show the progress of the young trees planted by Bartlett and Robert Barclay. One of them shows a little round hut built like a hayrick, surrounded by straight young trees. This must have been the reed hut, first mentioned by Mr. Pitchford, a young friend of the Gurneys of Earlham who was staying at Northrepps Cottage in 1798 'enjoying the woods. After dinner we took a walk and drank tea in the reed hut, a summer house cut from the bracken for a surprise for Mrs. Bartlett Gurney.'

Later it was rebuilt of stone with a conical thatched roof and a romantic staircase curving round the outside to an upper floor from which the sea could be seen. Part of it still remains.

It was on that first visit that Mr. Pitchford noticed Elizabeth's charms.

'Elizabeth Gurney of Northrepps was, at fourteen, a most sweet girl, her manners uncommonly elegant, her beautiful hair between flaxen and auburn, her lovely blue eyes beaming with intelligence and full of inexpressible sweetness, her complexion exquisitely fair and her whole countenance full of the glow of youth,' he wrote, adding that if she were two years older he believed he would fall in love with her. Even as it was he did not know that he was quite safe.

John Pitchford was one of the many young people of different denominations whom John Gurney welcomed to Earlham. Another was the daughter of the doctor, Dr. Alderson. Amelia's lively writings had attracted the Gurneys' mother when she was alive. Amelia, also motherless, was about to marry John Opie, the Cornish painter who had already made a name for himself and divorced his first wife in London. Led by Amelia they all eagerly discussed religions, politics, literature and art, sitting on the lawns or wandering by the river. Naturally the young Gurneys listened eagerly and no doubt it was quotations from these animated conversations that caused old Samuel Hoare to ban them from his own dinner table. Indeed the elder girls admitted they were often 'carried off-centre' in their interest in the French Revolution. Their father, John Gurney of Earlham 'feeling at a loss how to treat the case' tactfully asked these 'charming young people, gifted by nature and much cultivated, highly pleasing in person and manners, with religion of sentiment but no knowledge of Scriptural truth', to restrain their visits. But it was too late for Rachel, who had already fallen in love with one of them—a Unitarian, and he with her. Her father insisted on a separation with a promise that if they were both in the same mind in two years' time they should be allowed to meet again.

Rachel bore the two years patiently and when Henry Enfield failed to reappear her father wrote inviting him to return. The meeting left Rachel no happier and when there was another long silence her father sent his coachman, 'an old and confidential servant', to make enquiries. The coachman came back with the news that Rachel's suitor was about to marry another. Not only Rachel, but the whole family, felt jilted.

'Rachel's grief was most bitter,' writes her sister Kitty unhappily, 'and she was for long in a great state of depression but by degrees her fine vigorous nature prevailed and her mind and affections turned to other subjects.'

The family picked themselves up and later Harriet Martineau, 'that dyspeptic Radical battle-axe' who was said to be the ugliest woman in the world, was tolerant enough to describe them as 'a set of dashing young people, dressing in gay riding habits and scarlet boots, and riding about the country to Balls and gaieties of all sorts. Accomplished and charming young ladies they were, and we children used to hear whispered gossip about the effects of their charms on heart stricken young men.'

But for all the gaiety of their dress, they still refer to 'our coalscuttles and plain silks', which old-fashioned bonnets and Quaker shawls they donned for more sober occasions.

In the summer of 1800, the Gurneys of Earlham took Northrepps Hall from Richard Gurney for five weeks, before Betsey's marriage to Joe Fry, son of the Quaker cocoa and coffee importers. It had been a stormy courtship after Betsey had, at seventeen, shocked the family by casting off all dancing and frivolous amusement along with her gay clothes, and taking to the sombre dress of a Plain Quaker. Joe Fry's family were Plain Quakers, much plainer than Betsey could have imagined possible, as it turned out. It was not Joe who inspired the change, but an American preacher with whom the sisters assured Betsey she was obviously in love. Betsey said no, it was entirely spiritual. Believing that marriage would divert Betsey, her father encouraged Joe Fry's attentions and even took the whole family to stay with their Barclay 'fellows' in London to be nearer to the Frys. At last, after they had returned home, urged on by her sisters who hid in the bushes to witness Joe's final proposal, Betsey accepted him.

Now the Earlham family were all together at Northrepps before the inevitable bustle of their first wedding. Here, on her walks on the cliffs and down by the shore, Betsey thought about her decision. In one of her letters to Joe in July 1800 she writes:

'Do not be alarmed at my numberous letters. Yesterday I

wrote one on love, and now I am going to write one on business.

'I wish to know what are the wages that have generally been given to the housemaid, and also the number of rooms she has to attend to. I have heard of a footman of very good character.' She goes on to ask practical questions about the house in London in which they would live. 'I begin to wish for the time of our again being together. If we be so blessed as to be a loving couple at Hempstead this time a month, having got through all the awful ceremony, how happy and how good we ought to be! I do not much approve of looking forward to dwelling too much on the future, but my nature is so set on that time where we may be out of the way of the world, and quietly enjoy in each other the beginning of our honeymoon at Hempstead. Farewell, thine own (that is mostly likely to be) affectionate and sincere friend, Elizabeth Gurney.'

The 'awful ceremony' was accomplished at 'Goat's' with Amelia Opie and John Crome among the 112 guests who all signed the marriage certificate.

Next morning, accompanied by Rachel on what she called only a 'treaclemoon', the bride and bridegroom set off for their honeymoon at Hempstead, an old mill house overlooking three romantic ponds near Barningham. Richard of Northrepps had bought this land next to Bartlett's Hadduck property so that they could shoot over the two properties together.

The following summer a nephew of Mrs. Richard Gurney, Thomas Fowell Buxton, who was always known by his grandmother's maiden name of Fowell, came to stay at Northrepps for the first time. He was enchanted with everything about it. 'Northrepps is perfectly delightful,' writes Fowell. 'I did little else but read books of entertainment except now and then a few hours Latin and Greek, ride and play chess.'

His headmaster had recently told his mother that her son was 'the greatest reader of books in his school—all of them trash.' He was known at school as the Elephant from his enormous size. One school friend remembered years later how he received

complete protection from the school's worst bullies in exchange
for doing the Elephant's Latin translations.

The fact was that Fowell's heart was not in school. He cared
only for shooting and hunting and games, perhaps because his
earliest influence after his father's death when he was six was
his 'guide, philosopher and friend', their gamekeeper. Abraham
Plastow had been huntsman of his Uncle Sampson's hunt, the
Puckeridge, and had taught the young Buxtons to shoot, ride,
swim and behave. When Fowell swore at his pony out hunting,
Abraham took him straight home.

Now, at sixteen Fowell was six foot four, and, having persuaded his mother to let him leave school two years before at
fourteen, devoted his life to nothing but sport. Now she was
trying to coax him to start studying again but with the expectation
of an inheritance from Ireland he did not consider education
necessary.

Fowell had lately made friends with the gentle Joseph John
of Earlham, and had taken him to stay with his grandmother in
her beautiful house, Bellfield, near Weymouth, where she had
more than once entertained George III. An incongruous friend-
ship had sprung up at once between these two boys of entirely
different dispositions. Fowell was physically active, exuberant
and bursting with affection for everyone whereas Joseph John was
shy, retiring and academic. Joseph John was the only one of his
family—boys or girls—who had declined to learn to swim either
in the river at Earlham or the sea at Cromer. Now, under the
tough tuition of Abraham and the Buxton brothers, who threw
him into deep water and then pulled him out again, Joseph John
learnt eagerly.

The Buxtons were not Quakers, though Fowell's great-great-
grandfather narrowly escaped prison as a Nonconformist at the
time that the Gurney and Barclay great-great-grandfathers were
in prison for their Quaker faith. When the Gurney's were trading
in silk and wool in Norwich, the Buxtons were trading in clothing
at Coggeshall where they lived in a beautiful richly-carved

fifteenth-century house, Paycocks, which still stands today. Later they made a fortune as 'Russian oylmen' in the City, meaning that they traded in oil with Russia.

After Fowell's first visit to Northrepps he went on to Earlham and was there when Betsey Fry returned to her beloved home with her first baby. All the family gathered on the front steps to greet them and Fowell saw a tall excited girl spring out of the carriage with the baby in her arms. This was Hannah. Fowell always said he decided the moment he saw her that she was the one he wanted to marry.

Soon he was joining in with all the romping, dancing, acting and singing. The piano rattled ceaselessly. 'This instrument is hardly ever silent,' writes Richenda. There was a new—and the family thought very apt—dance called 'A trip to Cromer'. Richenda sang 'Sally in our Alley' and the others sang the chorus, taught by Amelia Opie.

Soon, too, Fowell was joining in with the animated talk under the trees, and taking part in religious and political discussions, that were now more safely backed by some 'knowledge of Scriptural truth'.

Fowell found himself even joining the reading groups that began in the garden before breakfast to study the subjects under discussion. He returned home having decided to do as his mother wished and go to university. His mind, he said later, never lost the impulse received during that first stay. 'They were eager for improvements—I caught the infection,' he wrote. 'In the college of Dublin, at a distance from all my friends and all control, their influence, and the desire to please them kept me hard at my books and sweetened the toil they gave.'

CHAPTER NINE

The Three Dear Pairs

EARLY in the spring of 1803, Bartlett Gurney died. Somewhat to the disgust of his six already immensely rich sisters, he left Northrepps Cottage, with Hill House Farm and the Hadduck property, to his cousin Richard Gurney of Northrepps Hall and Keswick, so that the adjoining estates could continue to be shot over as one.

Richard's son Hudson, through Bartlett's decease, was to take a step up in Gurney's bank, so came hurrying home from France only just in time to avoid being interned by Napoleon. He had had a lot of trouble with his carriage, which he 'woefully repented bringing instead of a new one. There is always something breaking, the roads being intolerable.' A few more delays of this sort and he might well have had to spend many uncomfortable years in France, with the several thousand English who were arrested and detained within the next few weeks. In France, he said, he had met nothing but troops. 'Thousands of poor young peasants, marching over the mountains with the little wallet containing their few clothes slung over their shoulders, together with the black loaf their liberators allowed them, escorted by French Gens d'armes on horseback to the regiments they were forced from their homes to form.

'That there will be war is the general opinion at Paris,' he wrote to his father and within a month war was declared.

With the daily expectation of the descent by Napoleon on the Norfolk coast, preparations at Northrepps were made as anxiously as anywhere. A great bonfire of furze and pitch was made on Toll's Hill above Overstrand, ready to be lighted as part of a chain of warning fires all along the Cromer ridge, if the enemy landed. Northrepps farmers had their wagons ready to convey the women and children inland, if the need arose. In Cromer Doctor's Steps below Cliff House—the Samuel Hoares' house—were removed and wreckage piled up at the bottom of them above the gangway. Volunteers trained assiduously. Later, even the younger sisters at Earlham were making a few tentative plans. Priscilla writes: 'I think we shall be in a very unprotected state if the French should land whilst my father is away, without a single man or even boy to take care of us. We had quite a serious conference about it yesterday morning; thee would have been entertained to have heard the various plans that were proposed. It is, however, now finally decided that as soon as ever we hear the news of their arrival we six sisters, Danny, and if we can manage it, Molly and Ellen' (two of the maids), 'are immediately to set off in the coach-and-four, for Ely where we are to take up our abode, as my father thinks it a very safe place, being so completely surrounded by marshes. I hope, as soon as ever you hear of the French being landed in Norfolk that you will imagine us setting off post haste for Ely. Mrs. Freeman is to stay to take care of the house, as it will be necessary for somebody to be here.' So much for the Gurneys of Earlham's democracy when put to the test! 'My father intends to write down directions for every individual of the family, so that there may be no confusion or bustle whenever the moment of danger arrives, if it ever does arrive.'

It was just as well the moment of danger did not, for the military plan was to flood the marshes between Norfolk and Ely and the party would certainly have been drowned.

Troops were mustering in all the towns and young John of Earlham, now twenty-two, joined the Volunteers, for which he was promptly disowned by the Society of Friends.

It was a blow. Just when at last he was seeming to be proving his manhood he was awarded this disgrace. John was 'singularly handsome and more of a man of fashion than most of his family. He had very fine silky auburn hair which he wore long.' When at Cambridge with a tutor (for he could not, as a Quaker, enter the university proper), he was termed an 'elegant scholar'. But he was easily depressed, perhaps due to his being sandwiched between three elder sisters and four younger ones and so cut off from his three anyway much younger brothers. John now found it hard to reconcile himself to the rebuff, which might have been easier if the enemy had actually come. But he could not bring himself to drop the Volunteers and seek a re-entry into the Society of Friends as his father hoped he would do.

It ought to have been some comfort to him that Hudson, older than himself and more of a man of the world, was also disowned for subscribing to a military fund. Hudson had just seen the miserable condition of the countries occupied by Napoleon's army and gave willingly towards raising corps to defend his own country. His Barclay grandfather wrote to him, much hurt, signing himself 'Thine afflicted grandfather.'

Even the benign John Gurney of Earlham was 'far from being in a comfortable state of mind' over his son's religious indiscretion. However, neither the war nor its consequences deterred the family from gathering as usual after the annual Quaker meeting, for shooting and romping by the sea at Cromer, where barricades and the absence of Doctor's Steps went unnoticed.

London-bound Betsey received details, right down to how drawer-space was shared out, from her sisters in the lodgings in which they were grouped about Cromer. Richenda, Hannah, Lucy Barclay (who was whipped for not drinking her beer when she lived at Northrepps) were in a lodging house to themselves with one of the maids. 'Father, John, Kitty and Louisa in another, throwing a damp over us all by coming in uncommonly dull minds, Louisa so poorly that she was quite overcome by seeing us.' John and his father's damps were due to the religious disagreement, Kitty's to her favourite brother, Joseph John, leaving home to go to a tutor in Oxford, and Louisa's to love.

Fowell Buxton and his little sister, Sarah, were there and 'The Grove'. The Hoares were at Cliff House, and at Northrepps Hall

Bartlett's nieces, who had hitherto stayed at Northrepps Cottage, stayed with the Richard Gurneys. Elizabeth and Dick of Northrepps Hall joined the party every day and their eight-year-old lame sister, Anna, insisted on being carried down to the sea to learn to swim with the rest of the smaller cousins of her own age. Elizabeth was more attractive than ever and Dick was now a keen connoisseur of the girls, though hefty, ruddy of complexion and conspicuously lacking in the polished manners that his half-brother Hudson displayed.

In place of the holiday snaps of a later age, scenes were vividly reproduced for Betsey, both in letters and sketches.

'All of us were in white gowns, blue sashes and nothing on the head; after dinner we all stood on a wall, eighteen of us, and it really was one of the prettiest of sights—such a number of young women, and so many, if not pretty, very nice-looking.' Hannah describes the bathing, riding on the sands, the picnics and the dances.

'This afternoon was delightful and the sociables, the horses and walkers on the sands formed quite a beautiful scene. On the sea there were supposed to be 400 vessels on sight and the sea was such a colour!

'John continues with us and seems to enjoy the party though he is in a flat state about his affairs. He stays overnight to be at a dance which some very agreeable people who are in Cromer, Mr. and Mrs. Wyndham, are going to give and which I think will be pleasant.' This was at Cromer Hall where Hannah was to live twenty years later.

Love was now rife in this generation and Richenda reports what was all too noticeable in Cromer that summer.

'Sam Hoare completely neglects Louisa, though he was so attentive a little time ago, as you yourself saw in London. He appears to be in love with Elizabeth, and is completely taken up and absorbed by her. Louisa has behaved with great spirit and propriety, though this neglect has taken off a good deal of her pleasure in the party. I think Sam is so uncertain, that I should

G

never be surprised if he never married Elizabeth at all, but went
off to some other unknown fair one. I really do not know what to
say to him, or how to treat him when he comes up to me.

'Rachel is on the whole in good spirits. I have not seen her so
since her unhappy affair. She has felt Sam's neglect of Louisa
more than any of us, having been through the same herself.

'I have not mentioned Charles Barclay and Anna Kett which is
one thing that is now very much on the carpet. She is much less
shy and really seems to take pleasure in his society, which is a
most favourable symptom. I would not have a doubt of her
accepting him, were Mrs. Kett not in the way. She is such an
obstacle that I doubt if he can accomplish his end at all!'

Charles was still faithful to the neighbourhood he had loved
so much as a child, and here he presently accomplished his end
and won his cousin Anna Kett. The mother of the Devoted Four
was an earlier Miss Kett, descended, according to her grandson
Dan, from Kett the Rebel who supported the cause of the people
and was hanged in chains for it from Norwich Castle.

Dick of Northrepps now singled out pretty, feminine little
Priscilla who was the most fastidious of all the Earlham sisters,
and a forthcoming engagement was hinted at. But Dick's follow-
up of his somewhat brash approach was probably what caused
the affair to peter out.

With no mother to engineer suitable occasions for proposals,
nor to prove an obstacle to be overcome, the Gurneys of Earlham
fanned love's flame for each other. When Fowell and Hannah
were suffering agonies of indecision, Kitty and Rachel shut them
up in a room together till Fowell had proposed and Hannah had
accepted him. 'They both looked miserable,' wrote Rachel, 'but
we stayed with them a minute or two and laughed at the difficulty
they both seemed to feel in speaking and then we shut the door
on them. When an hour and a half had elapsed and no effort
was made by either to disengage themselves, we were almost
surprised as well as comforted to see them walk off into the garden
arm in arm and on into the meadows beyond the pond. They at

length joined the others and sunshine prevailed on every countenance when they came in. Fowell looked like a person who
had been condemned to be hanged and had gained a reprieve.
Hannah quite easy and cheerful as if her mind had cast off all its
burdens.

'When Fowell had gone we all sat down on Chenda's sofa to
hear Hannah's story.'

It was necessarily a long engagement, for Fowell was still only
nineteen and had two more years at university. It was not only
an engagement to Hannah but, in a way, to all the six remaining
sisters, who loved Fowell as a brother long before he was even a
brother-in-law.

In the summer of 1806 Fowell went with the family on a tour
of Scotland and the north of England. Elizabeth of Northrepps,
Sam Hoare and Mr. Crome with the sketching equipment were
also of the party. They travelled on horses, in three chariots, and
the whisky—a high light trap for two—which was sometimes
attached to the back of the carriage and sometimes driven.
They changed places whenever they stopped, and picked John up
as they went through Cambridge.

The roads were 'good, bad, and almost impassable'. The
country was still in a state of armed defence, with press gangs a
terror on the seaboard. On open heaths travellers were warned of
danger by the corpses of criminals swinging from the gallows.
John Gurney's party put up at wayside inns into which not all
of them could always fit. At Ambleside, Fowell, Samuel of
Earlham and Mr. Crome had to lodge separately from the rest
of the party, which gave them an admirable chance to dress up as
widows and go and beg for alms from the others. This kind of
practical joke was a favourite diversion in the family, producing
acute embarrassment when genuine beggars, parsons, highwaymen
or whoever they happened to be portraying, were shooed away
with gales of laughter.

John was again 'mumping' after a love affair contracted during
a former family holiday at Brighton, then only a small fishing

village known as Brighthelmstone. The object of his affections
had been persuaded to refuse him on the grounds of unequal
wealth. John poured out his sorrows to gentle Elizabeth of
Northrepps during her turn with him driving behind the others
in the whisky. Elizabeth, who was exceedingly well endowed
herself, sympathetically agreed that it was not necessary for a
couple's incomes to be identical. From then on, the vicissitudes
of the tour threw them constantly together, and they came home
engaged.

At first the marriage was absolutely prohibited by Elizabeth's
father, Richard, not on the grounds of unequal richness, but
because marriages between first cousins were strictly forbidden
by the Society of Friends. The fact that John had been already
disowned only made the marriage less desirable.

But gradually Richard began to weaken. Rachel wrote to
Fowell in December: 'Tomorrow Hannah and I go to Northrepps
for a few days, to see our new sister-elect. John's last visit to her
seems to have been a very happy one, and our uncle a little more
favourable towards the close of it. Elizabeth writes as if she
became more and more dependent on him.'

Perhaps it was Elizabeth's engagement to John that brought
Sam Hoare to his senses. Since he first kissed Louisa when she
was eleven he had always returned to her between conquests, if
only to receive a rebuff for temporary neglect. Though they too
had travelled alone in the whisky on the 'Scotch Tour' they had
not been able to bring their affairs to a satisfactory conclusion.
Now Sam took his whole family—parents, brothers and sisters—
to stay at Earlham. 'How foolish it is to discolour absent people
in your own mind!' Louisa wrote to Fowell while they were there.
'This has often been our case with regard to the Hoares, but
they have much heart and are so very agreeable as companions.'
Old Samuel had evidently forgiven the liberty he had objected to
at Earlham, or else was enjoying indulging in it himself. Louisa
went on to say what a success the house party was. 'On Thursday
they dined out but Friday was a rout from morning till night.

We had a large party at breakfast; a larger at dinner, and largest in the evening, so that at supper the table extended from the top of the bow to the sideboard in the Great Parlour. Dancing succeeded till nearly twelve, when we supped, after which, for a wonder, the whole party migrated to the anteroom, and the farewell boulanger was not over, I suppose till past one. The clock has struck nine and the tray has just rattled through the hall. So think it is time to put an end to this letter.'

After which Sam and Louisa were soon announcing that they were to be married at the Quaker Meeting House on Christmas Eve, and would spend their honeymoon at Cromer.

John and Elizabeth were married a fortnight later, at North-repps church, but none of the parents attended. In fact Richard was compelled to show himself ostentatiously walking in the opposite direction with his other son-in-law, Gatty's husband, Sampson, so as 'to avoid any chance of being said to witness or even countenance it'.

Hannah, who had been the first of the young Earlham lovers to get engaged, was still waiting for Fowell to get through his finals. In March that year the long awaited news arrived.

'My dear Hannah, the examinations are over but alas I cannot describe the disasters that have befallen me. Think how dis-agreeable a circumstance it must be to me, to have all my hopes disappointed, lose the certificate, to have my gold medal stopped, and what is worse, to know that my Earlham visit, as it was the cause of my idleness, was the cause of my disgrace.

'Think of this, and fetch a very, very deep sigh and look very grave, and then think how happy I must be, to have to tell you, that my utmost hopes are realized and that I have the certificate, and *valde in omnibus*, and what is better, that I can ascribe my success to nothing but my Earlham visits.'

Fowell and Hannah's Quaker wedding took place six weeks later. 'The house was overrun with bridesmaids in muslin cloaks and chip hats,' Rachel writes in her minute to minute account of that 'mild and summerlike day' in May. 'At dinner were my

father's fifteen children and children in law and four grandchildren. Afterwards the whole party dispersed in different parts
of the house. Hannah sat with Elizabeth in her room.'

A fortnight after their marriage Rachel writes: 'I accompany
my father to Northrepps to visit our three dear pairs. The sight
of them, all so happily married—John and Elizabeth, Sam and
Louisa, Fowell and Hannah—was delightful, particularly to see
the sweet and happy looks on my dearest Fowell and Hannah.'

Kitty, whose life work was to bring up her brothers and sisters,
leaving her no time to marry herself, continued her work after
their marriage. 'I strongly recommend, dearest Hannah, thee
keeping thy mind at rest about the future.' This letter ends:
'Now I must give thee a lecture. As thee are likely to have
children to educate, I really think it is of consequence for thee
to take more pains with writing and spelling. Two words are
spelt wrong in thy last letter, and thy style is most inelegant, and
even incorrect. Pray profit by these hints.'

And Hannah earnestly tried to do so, though she had some
cause to worry about the future. While Louisa and Elizabeth
were comfortably established in Hampstead and Lynn, where
both their husbands had solid positions in their family banks,
Hannah and Fowell were waiting in a cottage on his grandmother's estate near Bellfield for the Irish inheritance that never
materialised. It was a time of 'great damp', ending in Gatty's
M.F.H. husband, Sampson, whom Hannah had always disliked
so much as a child, turning out to be as good a judge of men as of
hounds. He now offered his nephew, Fowell, a small place at a
salary of £300 a year in his brewery with a chance of partnership
later, if workable suggestions could be made to save rising expense
in the firm. Fowell and Hannah moved to London and Fowell
made a brilliant success of his job, putting up the profits by such
unexpected expedients as hiring a schoolmaster to teach the
employees to read, and telling them 'This day six weeks every
man who cannot read and write will be discharged.' Not a man
needed to be dismissed.

'Do it with thy might' was Fowell's family motto which he carried out to its extreme. 'I can brew one hour; do mathematics the next; and shoot the next and each with my whole soul.' He beamed through the oval spectacles that he now always wore.

The family met whenever possible. Betsey and Joe Fry were also in the City with young Samuel of Earlham living with them to work in Fry's counting house, where he turned out to be much better at business than he had ever been at his school books. In fact he was already showing signs of the financial genius he became later. Now those who had found his childhood wearing looked forward to his cheerful and inventive company. Louisa and Sam Hoare were not far off at Hampstead, whose then completely rural heath they were later able to save from being built over by giving land, money and time in fighting speculators. The sisters came to stay with them all in turns and in the autumn they all went off as usual to their Norfolk shooting and seaside activities.

CHAPTER TEN

Distant Rumble of a Social Conscience

THE Three Dear Pairs, were all expecting their first babies. Louisa's 'lively Sammy' was born first, and then in the spring Hannah's 'bonny Prissy' was born at Earlham. Elizabeth and John looked forward to their baby in the summer. But before the summer came, the baby was born prematurely and died, and Elizabeth's health slowly began to ebb away. John refused to leave her side night or day and insisted on carrying her downstairs every morning and up again at night, even after the effort had damaged his back, making him complain of every movement.

During the night of May 12th, 1808, lovely Elizabeth of Northrepps died, leaving John in a state of depression bordering on dementia which he seemed to make no effort to throw off. He walked permanently with a limp due, he repeatedly said, to the damage done to his back carrying Elizabeth.

Elizabeth's early death was a terrible blow to the little circle in which she had been so intimately brought up. Many of her cousins had just married, or were about to be, and it seemed 'suddenly to arrest the stream of prosperity and earthly happiness in a family whose unity was such that if one of its members suffered, the others all suffered too'.

A year later they were all gathered together again for another of the long drawn out Quaker funerals, which Dan wrote afterwards were 'particularly painful and devoid of religious comfort—the multitudes attending—the exhibition of the family—the preaching of the men and women.'

Kindly, indulgent John of Earlham had died after an operation. As the whole family knelt before their father's open grave,

Betsey threw herself forward in an attitude of prayer and made her first public offering in the ministry, to Dan's intense embarrassment.

From then on she began to speak at meetings and to work towards the reform of any social inadequacy with which she came in contact. Regardless of contagious diseases, she carried her own young babies into prisons and doss-houses to speak to the inmates in a voice that was magical in the effect it had on them. She taught them to read and to study the Bible and, above all, to love and take pride in their appallingly neglected children.

The other sisters raised eyebrows over Betsey's own children— of which there were the inevitable eleven—and helped where they could with the cheerful but obstreperous bunch referred to affectionately by their aunts as 'Betsey's brats'. Joe Fry was not an inspired business man and financial crises overtook the Fry family with varying degrees of seriousness. But though Betsey worried, she went on with her voluntary work outside the family, with her own children dotted about among her relations, during the crises which included a sad move to a smaller house that it was hoped would be less expensive to run. The married sisters included the brats with their own children and the unmarried took them home or trailed them round with them.

'Priscilla came here yesterday, bringing with her three of the little Frys', was not an unusual piece of news. But when there was sickness it was always Betsey they sent for and Betsey who was always first on the scene with soothing words, experienced hands and a variety of remedies. She had trained not only herself but other young ladies in the most up-to-date methods then known in nursing.

It was not only Betsey but also Fowell who was first shaken into a fervent desire to better conditions everywhere by the impact of an initial visit to Newgate Prison. Particularly moving to both was contact with young women and boys under sentence of death. The effect it had on Fowell was to cause him to write to Hannah: 'I must pray—you must pray for me—that I might at length stir myself up to devote myself, my influence, my time and above all my affection—to the honour of God—for the happiness of men.'

But he did not expect Hannah to abandon her nursery for practical work outside their home in Spitalfields. By this time Sam Hoare had become as interested as Fowell in the many social deficiencies, whose relief was still entirely in the hands of amateurs. Louisa, like Hannah, confined her contribution to prayers and hospitality for the field workers, while confirming the opinions she had always held on how children should be treated in a number of publications, two of which, 'Hints on Nursery Discipline' and 'Friendly Hints on the Management of Children', became widely read and followed. Thanks to these modest publications she was recognised by the literary society of Hampstead and, through William Blake, she and Sam befriended the young painter, George Richmond, who often stayed at a nearby farm. He and his companions called themselves 'The Ancients' and made long expeditions into the country by moonlight. Blake was their high priest living in rooms which they called The House of the Interpreter. Richmond used to kiss the doorhandle whenever he entered. Soon after Richmond returned from Gretna Green after a runaway marriage, Sam Hoare gave him one of his first commissions. It was to paint Louisa. Eventually he painted over fifty portraits of the family and became one of the most successful of the Victorian portrait painters, in much the same way as photographers became later. Richmond always did 'a certain something for his sitters' and usually painted three or four copies of the same portrait so that each member of the family could 'take Papa away and hang him over the mantlepiece'.

Through their wives and their spare-time interests, Sam Hoare and Fowell Buxton came to like each other more and more, and in the holidays they shared a shoot adjoining Richard Gurney's Northrepps estate. From then on till the end of their lives they kept a joint game book. When once they arrived in Norfolk early in September with their families, they scarcely ever missed a day's shooting from Monday to Saturday, and if they did, the reason appears in their game book—'No shooting— Missionary and Bible meetings'—or whatever the reason might be.

Besides the birds shot (or, if unusual, seen) are recorded such incidents as this from Fowell: at Earlham 'caught two poachers and lodged them and their guns, their snares and their dogs, in Norwich gaol'. Bad weather led on to 'there were more wrecks off Cromer than ever before'. And bad shooting to: 'out of twelve shots, Joe Fry killed nothing on September 28'. Joe Fry was always somewhat of a trial to his wife's family who found themselves more than once feeling bound to put their hands into their pockets on his behalf. But Fowell bore him no more grudge for bad shooting than for bad banking, twinkling at him through his gold-rimmed spectacles and calling him 'a good trier'. Though extremely short-sighted, Fowell was an exceptionally good shot. 'Had twenty-one shots and killed twenty,' he records excitedly. He was not above a little flutter on the bag. 'Laid a wager of 6d three times against S.H. to kill 15 out of his first 20 shots. Killed 200 head in the last two hours' and 'nearly caught in a man trap'. The only record of a poacher being caught in one of these nightmare contrivances which had so terrified us in the woods when we were children, reveals that when he recovered he became one of the young gamekeepers at Northrepps, who set the traps for other poachers.

While the husbands shot, the wives took the children on the shore where they were sure to find 'The Grove' who had come running down the path from their house on the cliffs. The Grove children, who were themselves all particularly attractive-looking, were enchanted by Hannah's babies. The youngest of The Grove, Emma, wrote to her sister: 'Little Fowell is very much pleased with picking up pebbles; he is certainly very handsome, I am afraid our darling nephew will not be quite so much so, but we still love him most. Henry found a nice piece of the right sort of seaweed. Has anyone told of his luck in finding a large piece of amber? I also found a piece of jet, but have lately lost it.'

'I have thoroughly enjoyed swimming this year and have brought the art to a much greater perfection than any of us have ever done,' writes, at the same time, her sister Rachel of The Grove (not to be confused with Rachel Gurney of Earlham who was seventeen years older; both were particularly vivacious and very much the 'clowns' of their families). 'You would be entertained to see me in the sea surrounded by my pupils, of which I have seldom less than six or eight. All the ladies are so envious that in imitating me they nearly drown themselves, so that yesterday the bathing man said he would not draw them in again without they promised to be sober.'

Hannah and Fowell not only took their own children. Hannah's young brother Dan, and Fowell's younger sister Sarah, who were the same age, were often with them too. When it was time to start lessons again, the families often did them together.

The year after Elizabeth of Northrepps died, Sarah stayed on to do lessons with Anna, and for a while Dan of Earlham did lessons with them too, after recovering from scarlet fever. Rachel of The Grove also joined them. Dan was fascinated with Anna's interest in the old sea kings from whom he later claimed they—and we—were all descended, and the children would all go down to the shore to see what kind of a landing the Vikings could have made when the cliffs still stretched out into the sea. Rachel of The Grove writes again of Hannah and her babies, who were once more staying at Northrepps:

'Hannah looks very nice. It is a real treat to see her. The baby is a nice child, not very handsome, and, of course not very interesting, as it is at present but a sleepy bit of clay. I wish you could see the other children; little Fowell is the brightest looking child I ever saw. Louisa's two are very sweet.

'I must now go and read with Dan, if I can make him, which is doubtful, for he is, to tell the truth, rather idle. P.S. Dan *would* tear this open.'

When Dan and Rachel had left Cromer, Sarah remained at Northrepps with Anna. Sarah was older than Anna, but, though

by no means backward, she had to work hard to catch up with the
determined questioning child with a mind that was 'independent
and almost masculine' in its approach.

Anna was struggling to become as valuable a person as her lovely
sister Elizabeth had been. She could never hope to be as beautiful,
but she could be interesting and she could study and do good
to others. She could never run, nor ride, nor dance gracefully as
Elizabeth had done, for she could only walk a few steps at a time,
and those only awkwardly on two sticks or, with the aid of the
extra rail, pulling herself up the stairs. But she could be active
in her own way; she could move about in her self-propelled chair
as swiftly as others could on their feet. This was the wheel-chair
we had tried out over a hundred years later. Anna had learnt to
fire a gun from it, which her father had taught her to do at an
age when most children's arms would not be strong enough to
hold one. She also fed and cared for her pet rabbits and puppies
from her chair. She was always a bulky child, yet she had an
amazing nimbleness of movement, except when staggering on her
heavily iron-clad legs. As a child she spurned chairs, except for
transport, preferring the floor on which she could roll freely,
reaching up for books and spreading herself out to read them.
She read with studious fervour all her life. When she was quite
small she was found with an Anglo-Saxon grammar under her
pillow. From it she taught herself enough to translate the Anglo-
Saxon Chronicles in order to read everything she could about the
old sea-dogs who scoured the coast she loved so much. She was
always begging to be taken down to Overstrand to watch the
terrors of the storms.

Kitty writes from Northrepps in November 1810, after a
brief return to Earlham. 'I am writing in Anna's room at
Northrepps while she is busy on the floor as usual. I very much
enjoy being here. I had a comfortable ride here on Sunday with
my Uncle and Aunt, and found Sarah and Anna very glad to see
me, and it has been a great pleasure to see both of my pupils
going on so well. Sarah now makes the study of the Scriptures

her first object, and besides this she is hard at work at Greek with Anna. I should never be surprised at her becoming a very superior character. There are no common materials to be turned to account in her. She and I spend two or three hours together in the first part of every morning, and I have scarcely ever enjoyed so much reading with anyone else, and in the latter part of the morning she and Anna and I have read something else together. I have scarcely ever had two pupils so rich mentally, or so interested in all our pursuits; it is quite a treat to me to be with them. It is a real comfort to me also to be with my Uncle and Aunt. My Uncle declines perceptibly and is in a sweeter state of mind than I have ever seen him in, for he is so contented under his infirmities, though fully aware of the decline of all his powers. My Aunt's conduct to him is quite an example.'

'Aunt Gurney', as Richard's wife was known by all the family—'Madam Gurney' or 'Lady Gurney' by the village—hurried about Northrepps Hall in her black silk dress and short white shawl setting things right before she put on her sombre shovel bonnet and went off to the village to nurse a sick child or an old person and to take little extras to the poorer cottages. She always came back with tales of further need, and would go to the cupboards in the study which were always kept filled with material for the poor, and would say to her gentle, self-effacing niece: 'Come Sarah, and bring thy thimble and scissors and we will cut and contrive.'

At the annual Sunday school treat the children were lined up in the backyard at Northrepps for her inspection. Aunt Gurney would speak kindly to the clean children and pass over the dirty ones so that the following year they would strive to be noticed. But however dirty they were, all received prizes alike—straw bonnets, white neck 'whisks' and long gloves coming well up the arms for the girls, and useful garments for the boys.

'I hope I shall never forget,' writes Mrs. Joseph Gurney of The Grove, after a bereavement, 'the kindness of Aunt Gurney whose feeling attentions were most delightful.'

Nobody in distress, or even discomfort, was free from her attention. For several weeks in the evenings she knitted easy slippers to relieve the feet of 'The Pedestrian', her stepson, Hudson's brother-in-law, Robert Barclay VI, of Urie, who was walking a thousand miles in a thousand hours for a wager of a thousand pounds. Part of the challenge was that he must walk a mile in each hour, so, to get the maximum of rest between each walk, he started twenty minutes before the hour was up and walked for twenty minutes into the next hour. As Aunt Gurney knitted, Dick, whose interest in any form of a gamble was excessive, brought excited news of his progress, which helped to cheer up his ailing father.

After successfully winning his bet, 'The Pedestrian' was so stiff after resting that he had to be lifted to his feet, but after seventeen hours' sleep he had completely recovered, except that he was two stone lighter than when he started, in spite of a diet of beefsteaks, mutton chops, roast fowls and plenty of porter and wine.

Later he won another 500 guineas by walking 110 miles in twenty-four hours, but probably his longest walk was for pleasure. He went out shooting at 5 a.m., walked after grouse over the mountains for at least thirty miles, then dined, set off for Urie, sixty miles away, which took him eleven hours, then attended to his ordinary business. He walked eleven miles in the afternoon, danced at a ball all night, walked back to Urie and spent the next day partridge shooting. Besides walking he could also run, lift fantastically heavy weights, beat professional prize fighters and breed shorthorn cattle. For all his great strength he was finally kicked to death by a horse.

CHAPTER ELEVEN

Vote for Gurney, Gurney, Barclay and Buxton

WHEN Dick was at Northrepps he still slept in the room at the top of the back stairs that had always been his as a child. It was next to the night nursery we loved best, overlooking the backyard. In Dick's day it was known as the Fawn Room.

He also now had a house of his own, Thickthorn, near Norwich, for he had left his uncle/brother-in-law's brewery in London and joined his father's bank in Norwich in which Hudson, his half-brother, had a partnership.

When their father died—quoting Shakespeare rather more than the Bible—he left Keswick to Hudson and Northrepps to Dick, though both were to remain in his widow's hand throughout her lifetime.

Except for the same piercing blue eyes, no two half-brothers could have been less alike. Hudson was slim, urbane, 'dashing smart'—as his sister Gatty said of him when he took to wearing a pink waistcoat—and loved London and its literary society on whose fringes he moved. He had married a grand but benevolent Barclay cousin and his early aspirations of 'London and Parliament' were already realised. He had a house in St. James's Square and had bought himself a parliamentary seat in the Isle of Wight to which, it was said, a condition was attached that he should not set foot in the place. But this was no hardship to Hudson who anyway conducted most of his affairs, even at the Norwich bank, from London. It is doubtful whether he ever quite realised his highest aspiration 'to write one good poem', for all his inability to resist transposing every passing thought into rhyme.

On perceiving a Chinese beauty he at once set pen to paper with:

'Soft in her palm as the flower she handles
Her smile and her laugh make her lover sigh
And lackered and black is the white of her eye.
The skin of her face like the tallow of candles
Her neck like a worm—eyebrows silk which is reeled off
Her teeth like the seeds of a melon when peeled off.'

Dick, on the other hand, was massive, florid of complexion, and loud in voice and praise of coursing, cock-fighting, wagers and country wenches. He hunted regularly with his uncle/brother-in-law, Sampson Hanbury's pack, and had his favourite horses' hoofs made into ink-pots.

He kept and raced his own greyhounds and fought his own fighting cocks, eggs from his special strain always being in demand. He bred his own prize oxen and had several horses in training. His racehorse, St. Francis, won the Gold Cup at Ascot, which magnificent and ornate structure, with other important trophies, reposed for many years in shame in the vaults of the bank. For it was Dick whose bust was eventually only insured for thirty shillings at Northrepps.

Melville, the sporting writer of the time, observed that Dick was 'one of the three heaviest men I ever saw ride perfectly straight to hounds'. He weighed nineteen stone. Sampson Hanbury weighed only seventeen.

In the volume, 'Hunting' of the Badminton Library, a drawing depicts Dick on his famous horse, Sober Robin, jumping a six-barred gate, with the incident described:

'Sir Charles led Mr. Gurney, on Sober Robin, over a gate such as a nineteen stone man has never yet jumped and never will again. The Pytchley had a fast thing from the gorse and ran to Nen, near Heyford, where there is a bridge across the river, and a six-barred locked gate in the middle of it. They were just running into their fox about two hundred yards ahead, when the baronet and Mr. Gurney reached the gate. Finding it locked Sir Charles turned his horse round and went over it, and to his amazement as he glanced back, the Norfolk welter and his horse were in the air. Fortune favoured them, and although Robin tapped it like thunder with every leg, they landed safely.'

'I wouldn't have done it for a bishopric,' observed the local sporting parson. 'Young Gurney has more guts than sense.'

To the astonishment of everyone who knew him, at the General Election of 1818, Dick stood for parliament as Whig candidate for Norwich.

'I heard today R.H.G. is standing. I cannot believe it,' Fowell writes in an astonished postscript to one of the love letters he wrote daily to Hannah when they were apart. Fowell was standing for the first time himself. Charles Barclay was also standing.

The 'bright morning star', Joseph John of Earlham, who shared Fowell's particular philanthropic interests, could not, as an active Quaker, stand for parliament, but he promised to back his brother-in-law wherever he could, and always kept his promise. After he left his tutor at Oxford, Joseph John joined the Norwich bank, rising at dawn to read the scriptures in Hebrew before going to work and running a ragged school after it. He and his youngest sister, Priscilla, had both now, like Betsey, turned to the very plain clothes of the more serious Quakers, and took the consequent teasing they received from the rest of the family in good heart.

Young Joseph Gurney of The Grove, having been brought up more strictly than his cousins at Earlham, could not get away quickly enough from the restraint imposed by his parents and, with his first earnings in the Norwich bank, shopped accordingly. Unfortunately his tailor's bill went, in error, to the other Joseph Gurney, known now universally as Joseph John of Earlham.

The account turned up years later.

'Joseph Gurney Esquire, to Andw Shear Dr.

		£	s	d
March 18th	Superf. Brown Coat, single breasted bound Buttons	4.	10.	0
	Buff casame. Waiscoat bound B	1.	3.	0
	Pair of Mixt. Mill. Casame. Pantaloons	2.	4.	0
June 9th	Superf. Brown Coat, Single Breasted, covered Butts.	4.	10.	0
	Superf. Brown Great Coat, Single Breasted	5.	3.	0
	Silk Sleeve-Lining		13.	6
	Fine White Quiltg Waiscoat	1.	4.	0
	Pair of Drab, Milld Casame Breeches	1.	18.	0
Aug. 19th	Pair of Drab, Milld Casame Breeches	1.	18.	0
		£23.	3.	6

At the foot of this bill, Joseph John of Earlham has added:

'Methought the letter, sure, was mine
Because "Esquire" was on it.
I read—and willingly resign—
Here, Joey, thou hast won it.
Won it by wearing casameres
And fashions most amazing,
With quilted buff from Andrew Shears,
Whilst all the world is gazing!
O Joey, Joey, silken sleeve
And Wellingtonian breeches
Had best be changed, e're "Goats" perceive,
For Wiseman's sober stitches!'

And Joseph of The Grove cheekily replied in schoolboy doggerel on the reverse:

'The title Esquire more belongeth to me
Than to a mere working Banker like thee;
For honour I've heard is a gentleman's trade
To possess which I'm sure thou canst not be said.

By reading a letter not thine, though wert clear,
Proves that with thee honour does not often appear.
So with simple Mister content thou must be,
Or what suits thee far best, with plain J.J.G.
Wear then threadbare breeches with gaiters below
Made by thy famed Norwich tailor, John Roe.
And coat that keeps on to the wonder of all
And looks as if hung on a pin on the wall.
Thank Roe, truly to him much merit is due
For now I request thee, my dear Cousin Joe.
To write to the firm Messrs Barclay and Co,
And Pray order them, when called for to pay
This Bill for coats, waistcoats, Casameres grey
For Andrew Shear tailors far far from hence
Of £23. 3s and 6 pence.
On account of J. Gurney, Junior, "Squire"
A title to which thou canst never aspire.'

Indeed, as a plain Quaker, as Joey well knew, Joseph John could not even recognize the title of Mr. or Mrs.

He, Rachel and Priscilla went abroad on many journeys together, preaching and comforting the sick. In France Priscilla's strange dress gave some the impression that she was 'Une Religieuse Anglaise' while others fell on their knees and prayed for her that she might be converted. Of one hospital she visited she writes: 'The nuns were kind to me though they always addressed me by the title of "Herétique".'

Her sister Betsey's would-be converts also suffered some confusion. Once on a return visit to a prison she was 'more amused than grieved' to notice a number of little leaden images of the Virgin Mary, and when she mentioned that they had not been there before, she was told that the prisoners had been so impressed by the importance of religion from her last talk that they had each bought themselves a Virgin.

At Earlham, the eldest brother, John, had languished on for a few years after Elizabeth died with a kind of psychological paralysis, 'his health and mental powers seeming to fail alike'. But in spite of the encouragement and loving care of his sisters, ending in one brief lucid burst of gratitude, he had died of what some said was a broken heart and others, judgment on defying the Quaker rule against marrying a first cousin.

Both Joseph John and his brother Samuel, the London financier, married more circumspectly, third cousins. Jane Birkbeck and Elizabeth Sheppard had played with the brothers as children when staying with their Uncle Bartlett at Northrepps Cottage. Both shared the same Hadduck great-grandmother from whom we are thus descended. Now, as master of Earlham, and married to Jane Birkbeck, Joseph John offered hospitality to all who needed peace, green lawns, a quiet river, conversation, sympathy and a good lunch. He was loved and respected by all who knew or had even heard of him.

When Dick asked him to speak on his behalf before the 1811 General Election, Joseph John agreed, hoping Dick's election would aid the passing of many overdue philanthropic measures. Both had high opinions of each other's judgment in the bank and, though Dick had long abandoned the Quaker faith in which he was brought up, and Joseph John had long abandoned sport— even fishing seemed cruel to him—he was able to introduce his first cousin and bank colleague as 'a highly popular and accomplished sportsman of great strength both of mind and body, full of sterling sense and kindly feeling.'

Dick was elected with an overwhelming majority, just before a scandal appeared in the local paper that, had it come earlier, would almost certainly have lost him many of his votes. Immediately following a court case headed 'Johnson for Murder' another was reported in full that had been brought against Dick by a neighbour for alienating his wife's affections.

The first witness in the case was this wife, Mrs. Muskett's, nurserymaid, who admitted that when her mistress drove her and the child to Norwich in the pony chaise, she now always went

round by a route that was half a mile longer, so as to pass Keswick
Hall where Dick was now living with his mother and sister
Anna. The defendant came out and leant on the gate and sometimes they walked together into a straw house with an open
front. 'Mrs. Muskett went in cool and came out rumpled. When
she came out she was warm and flushed and her bonnet was a
little bent down before.' The maid was sure the defendant had
some cobwebs on his back.

Another maid said that she saw him and her mistress sitting on
a bank; they passed by and when she looked back he was kissing her.

Other maids said that he rarely came to the Musketts' house
but once came in by the parlour window, which was hardly ever
used as an entrance even by the family and never by visitors.
There was no sofa in the parlour, but Mrs. Muskett shut the
door into the passage, so that anyone going upstairs could not
see in. Another servant said that she had seen Mrs. Muskett airing
a fine shirt which she usually only wore when she was going on a
visit; and then there was the incriminating umbrella left in the
hall after the defendant's visit, which, when noted, disappeared.

Another servant said that Mrs. Muskett got ready to go to
church, when Mr. Gurney, who had already been to church and
come out before the end of the service, called. She also said that
in election week she saw them walking together, talking earnestly
and frequently stopping. Another said that one day when she was
ordered by the cook to shut the shutters, she found them nearly
shut already, so that nobody could see in. All admitted that no
beds were tumbled.

Then another maid said that the plaintiff lay down on her (the
witness's) bed when she was in the room but she could not
recollect ever being alone with him.

With the defendant's name impeccable (had he not on the very
morning concerned, come on a visit to Mrs. Muskett straight
from church?) the learned sergeant said there was insufficient
evidence to·establish a case, when 'indiscretion was the most that
had been proved'. The Judge said that there were some suspicious

circumstances but 'with a child and a maid in day time, they could not be compared with a midnight assignation'.

The jury returned almost immediately with a verdict in favour of the defendant. And there, to the relief of his mother and other Quaker relations, the matter seemed to end without a hint of any impending recurrence. It was regarded by Dick's supporters as just a piece of electioneering bribery that had come too late to have any effect on his seat. It was well known that Norwich elections were conducted with a certain amount of loosening of the purse strings and the city expected it, and even later objected when attempts were made to pass a law against it. At the time of Dick's election it was said that 'while the meetings of the party leaders were being held in the bank parlour, gold from the bank cellars was flowing into the ward'.

Hudson himself wrote later: 'I have been making a calculation. My own seat has come to £1,200 per annum; R.H.G. at Norwich'—Dick—'averages £3,000 per annum.' Dick admitted later still that 'he had spent £80,000 on electioneering', though it was thought he far exceeded this. In return he was presented with a silver candelabrum which also went the way of the racing plate and ink-pots, until, in this more broadminded age, our great-great-grandfather's name may be mentioned again and his Ascot Gold Cup and horse's hoof ink-pots may be exposed with his candelabrum for all to read its inscription: 'Presented by voluntary subscription, raised by upwards of 1,200 citizens of Norwich, chiefly of the operative classes, to R. H. Gurney, Esq. in testimony of their regard for his universal benevolence and sincerity in upholding the just cause of mankind, and of their admiration of his inflexible advocacy in the Senate to obtain for his country a salutary Reform in the House of Commons.' Thus his votes had cost him round about £66 apiece.

It was said that Dick went into parliament on a whim, Hudson for the free franking of his daily letters from London to the Norwich bank, and Fowell out of a genuine, burning desire to uphold the under-dog—at first, *any* under-dog.

Fowell wrote to Joseph John twenty years after his first election:
'Before I went down to Weymouth I began to fear, for one of my
supporters told me that if I wished to secure the election it would
be necessary to open public houses and to lend money, another
name for bribery, to the extent of £1,000. I, of course, declined.
It might be or it might not be my duty to get into parliament but
it could not be my duty to corrupt the electors by beer and bank
notes.'

In a final speech to his electors he claimed never to have paid
any man one sixpence for his vote, and never, except in two
instances, was he asked to do so.

In fact by the time Fowell entered parliament he could easily
have afforded to buy his seat had he wished to. The Irish legacy
had come to nothing, but five years before the General Election
his grandmother had left him a fortune as well as her beautiful
home, Bellfield, near Weymouth. Though he was often in
Weymouth, he never lived at Bellfield, but let it to his eccentric
Uncle Charles, who moved in many of the same circles as Dick
and Fowell's other uncle, Sampson Hanbury.

Though of a generally sporting turn, Charles Buxton's main
interest was 'the keeping up of the habit of coaching'. There were
a number of amateur coaching clubs in London and he was
prominent among their members. He was President of the
Barouche Club and Founder President of the Four-in-Hand. The
driver's costume was a most elaborate affair with every detail
specified, down to the width of the blue and yellow stripes of
the waistcoat, the size of the mother-of-pearl buttons, and sixteen
strings and rosette for each knee of the corded silk plush breeches.
The boots had to be finished with broad straps which hung over
the tops and down to the ankles. The hat had to be three and a half
inches deep in the crown and the same depth at the brim—exactly.
Each charioteer had to wear a large bouquet at the breast, as did
the coachmen of the nobility on special occasions.

Though Uncle Charles happily poured out money for these
luxurious vanities his stinginess over such necessities as paying

his own doctor was notorious. He could hardly bring himself to unclench the fist that held the fee, and while furniture was sparse inside his house, a magnificent padded sofa stood in his stables so that he could admire his horses in the greatest comfort.

On one occasion, when the wife of a member of the Four-in-Hand died and her husband could not be at the funeral, Charles insisted on driving the hearse, while the other members drove the funeral coaches at a gallop to the churchyard.

When he became too old for active exercise, he took to drink, joined by his one-eyed wife. Together they gambled and quarrelled over their cards into the night, and one relation said she never saw either of them sober again.

Yet curiously enough, Fowell and his Uncle Charles were devoted to each other, though they had few interests in common, except shooting and Bellfield, which, while Fowell was abroad, his uncle once sold to a friend, and had to buy back again, on finding it entailed. When Charles Buxton was offered a baronetcy, he refused it because it could not be passed down by special remainder to his nephew, Fowell.

CHAPTER TWELVE

Rachel of The Grove

NONE of Uncle Charles' raffish ways brushed off on to Fowell, and although Fowell too worked in Sampson Hanbury's brewery, where Dick was said to have been 'exposed to circumstances from the effect of which he never recovered', Fowell, who was also exposed to Sampson's sporting, and gambling colleagues, always remained on easy terms with them without ever falling under their influence.

Hannah never felt at home with Sampson and Dick's set, in fact none of the Gurneys of Earlham did. The Grove made a point of keeping their young people away from them. 'Joseph (of the silken sleeve) has got a job at the Bank', writes his mother. 'What to do with him when we leave home is very puzzling, as constant unsettlement is certainly very undesirable for him. I have thought of Keswick, but there again I fear Dick's influence.'

Hudson found Dick's friends actually distasteful, though their father had always managed to disregard their more uncouth aspects, and had heartily enjoyed their, presumably toned-down, sporting conversation. Aunt Gurney let it all sweep unnoticed over her, attending only to the immediate comforts of the company, and Anna, even as a child, had such strength of character and breadth of outlook that she could mingle as well with a hard-bitten bookmaker as with a gentle Quaker missionary, leaving a stronger impression on them than either could ever leave on her.

But Gatty, who at nineteen had married into the sporting set, seems to have found their way of life—if not Sampson himself— harder and harder to bear, judging by her increasing efforts to keep away from them. The explosive rudeness in Sampson's letters preserved by his firm suggest that he was not always one of the best tempered of men. More and more Gatty's name appears alone in the groups of young unmarrieds who gathered at Northrepps, Earlham and the Grove. 'Gatty dined and slept with us' and 'Gatty here till third day' and 'Gatty went with us'. It is true that she had no children to keep her at home, but nor had her brother Hudson's wife, Margaret, whose name rarely appears unlinked with his.

In 1814 Rachel of The Grove confided in her sister in a letter from Cromer: 'Gatty looks better but she will not recover the wounds she received; to be sure they have been aggravated. The quiet of this place suits her, and she enjoys being with my father and mother.'

Whatever these wounds were she had certain sympathy from her brother Hudson, who said she was the best and most beautiful woman he had ever known. In fact they were both exceptionally good-looking, as portraits of them by Opie confirm.

'We dined at Keswick', Rachel goes on to write after discussing Gatty's troubles, 'and met most of the Earlham party. We spent a more cheerful day than is generally our lot to do there, for certainly the Keswick atmosphere is not propitious to gaiety.'

Rachel was now 'a lovely girl of seventeen with russet hair, sweet steadfast eyes, a rounded chin and plump rosey cheeks' and a tremendous zest for all the frivolities of a large family whose father found his seven pretty daughters and two handsome sons 'agreeably blooming'. No innuendo concerning the latest love affair escaped Rachel's discerning eye, and all was passed refreshingly on to her eldest sister. 'We think of having a sick ward in our house for lovers and to keep plenty of spirits of lavender and camphor julip, with a squirt to use when we see them going off into despondency. We do not think that one of our Beaux would be capable of doing anything but handling a little lavender water or Epsom Salts.'

Not long after this Rachel had a weird and frightening

experience with her father, returning through snow and storms from the north. It was not till they reached Norfolk that their carriage became snowbound and remained so for two days. At last they were able to get help. 'We left Swaffham,' Rachel afterwards wrote to her sister, 'preceeded by a waggon with seven horses and men in it with shovels to cut away the snow where it stopped us, which it did in many places. The scene was beautiful and curious; the masses of snow were immense, higher than the carriage in some places; I hardly lost the sensation of going through the drifts, one I never desire to feel again. E. Geldart (a friend) died peacefully on the first day. Jane said she had faith in our return when she heard this, as she knew we *could* not miss a Norwich funeral!' But for all Rachel's cheerful irony over the funeral, she had been badly disturbed and either this shock or, as her father said, breathing the sharp air as she walked through the snowdrifts, produced asthma from whose attacks she was soon rarely free.

Dr. Alderson, Amelia Opie the novelist's father, who had treated most of the Gurney family all their lives and knew what comfort they could give each other, thought of Hannah in London with her calm and gently reassuring ways, and so he suggested that 'the close air of the city' might help Rachel's breathing. And so for four months Rachel stayed in the house in Spitalfields attached to the brewery. 'The Brick Lane smoke has suited my fanciful breath thus far,' she wrote in 1814. 'I have much enjoyed being with Fowell and Hannah. They are truly kind to me. Their children are very well and in capital order. I really think they are quite an example. I enjoy playing with them very much. It has been a great treat to have so much of Hannah's company and a lesson to see her in her own family. There is a peculiar charm and steadiness about her that is very winning. The noises in the streets of every kind almost distract me.' But behind Hannah's smiling charm there already lay her first sorrow, which she never allowed to affect the smooth-running happiness of her little family.

After her third baby was born she was writing to her brother Samuel's wife, Elizabeth:

'I have so enjoyed my baby, and have set my mind on showing thee my darling. Thee cannot think how sweet and dear she is to me. I never felt so proud of a baby before, or so delighted with one. She is so flourishing and good, and I scarcely have a care about her. She takes so much notice that I almost fancy she knows me and is so bright and lovely that she is much admired. She has a sweet colour in her cheeks and in my eyes is very pretty.'

Five months later she was writing that the hand of the Lord had been raised to afflict her and he had 'taken to Himself my beloved baby. I have found it hard to resign her, but I pray that I may be delivered from a spirit of murmuring.'

Babies were easily lost in those days but to Hannah, whose capacity to feel was always great, it was an unforgettable bereavement. Now at Brick Lane three years later, she was still writing privately in her diary: 'Scarcely a day ever passes that I do not feel the vacancy in my little flock and picture Suzanna filling her right place.' But Brick Lane had a wonderfully happy atmosphere and Fowell was as delighted with his other children as their mother was.

'In the midst of his business, he would help his children to find their lost playthings, or go out himself and buy what they might want. Nor did they fear to interrupt his studies with the most trifling requests. During his hardest work in London he would often, on his way home, buy pictures and conceal them in his waste-paper basket to enjoy the delight of his younger children and their daily renewed astonishment at discovering them next morning,' one of them wrote later.

Rachel returned to The Grove in the spring and when there seemed no sign of her asthma abating she was sent to Devonshire, where she had constant visitors, regardless of the distances that her parents, brothers, sisters, aunts, uncles and cousins had to travel, when they wanted to visit her.

'Gatty came for a long visit', and then Rachel wrote with

excitement: 'You will have seen in the newspaper the neighbour we have had,' and she describes the commotion in Exmouth when Napoleon appeared, two weeks after his surrender on board the *Bellerophon* and friends had come in to tell her that they had seen him walking on the deck with the captain. 'They said he looked very sallow, black hair, turning grey and bald. He laughed to see the English coming to see him. The captain said he was a most fascinating man and won the hearts of both officers and men.'

Anna and her mother came with news of Northrepps and the winter's toll of wrecks off Cromer. Anna poured all her affection and sympathy on her cousin Rachel, for whom she could not do enough, fetching and carrying for her on her two sticks or in her own wheel-chair.

Rachel's spirits remained high and her pen lucid, as she pertly observed the doctors' barbarous treatment of bleeding and more bleeding with every attack of asthma, so that she grew weaker and pale with anaemia. As always, she refused to give way to any expression of sentiment.

'Mama is too indulgent,' she writes to her sister. 'Of course the subject of my disease is carefully warded off, rather to my amusement, for, after all, it is impossible to hide it from me. It appears to me that the chances of my recovering my strength or not are even, I cannot feel them greater. With this idea, perhaps thou wilt hardly understand me when I say I do not know what it is to have an uneasy thought about myself; I feel as if I had nothing to do with the business but to bear the present evil, and to leave the future. I suppose in due course I shall be bled again. Only think of David's making his appearance on Sunday night, to our great surprise. He most kindly came round from Ireland.' This was one of the Barclays who had first lived at Northrepps. Her sister, Lucy, was now keeping The Grove's youngest daughter, Emma, company. 'Dear Anna is so sweet, such a noble girl, her love for me is almost amusing: I tell her she will come to her sober senses on the subject in time . . . I am very glad you are at Cromer . . . Shall we ever all meet there again?'

Some did, but not all. Quite suddenly Henry, the younger of the two Grove sons, died within three days of becoming ill.

Rachel made what she called 'a suffering journey' home by packet to Guernsey, then after being becalmed at sea, to Southampton, then by road to Hudson's house in St. James's Square. She arrived at The Grove 'safe but breathing hard'.

Next Dr. Alderson ordered her to the South of France, and a new and even more painful journey to Nice began. As though Henry's death and Rachel's slow fading were not enough at The Grove, young Joseph followed his brother a year later, 'his system shaken by his brother's apoplectic seizure', it was said. Oh Joey, Joey Silken Sleeve! 'Whose death in innocence', his little sister Emma supposed, 'could not have been worse than witnessing the vice to whose temptations he might have yielded had he lived.' But even this thought could not comfort his parents.

It was harder than ever now for the family to write cheerfully to Rachel, who herself could only last a few more months. Yet write they did, telling of all that went on at home. Dan was in the bank now, and had found a cottage at Runcton that he was going to enlarge and settle into with his sister Rachel to look after him. Their sister Richenda was marrying a clergyman and joining the Church of England. Betsey was forming a Ladies' Society to help to improve the conditions of women prisoners at Newgate. But what Rachel liked best was to hear of the small things at home—wild flowers found on Cromer cliffs and shells and seaweed picked up on Overstrand shore.

Anna waited at Northrepps for replies, knowing that they could no longer be from Rachel herself but from her parents and sisters who were with her.

One afternoon when Anna was in her chair in the garden at Northrepps with her mother, a letter came from Emma, then aged sixteen, dated March 25th, 1817. It was to her Aunt Gurney.

'My dearest Aunt, Rachel has passed a very restless and suffering night. She hardly knows how to bear my dear Mother from her a minute when she is awake. She has every possible relief to her sufferings. Eiderdowns in plenty, and she cannot have less than 12 or 14 pillows about her!' Poor, poor Rachel—first the leech, and then the asthmatic's anathema—feathers! 'She takes a good deal of notice of the things about her, and seems interested in the flowers and insects any of us bring her; the fire flies have much pleased her. With my dearest love to Anna, I am, thy most affectionate niece, Emma Gurney.'

A week later came the letter that they knew must arrive.

'My dear Sister,' writes Rachel's father. 'By the late accounts you will not be surpris'd that this shou'd contain the intelligence of the close of our dear Rachel's short, and of late greatly afflicted race.' He describes the dawn in Nice on the first of May when Rachel slipped away, unable to muster enough breath to make some apt comment on the act of dying. The letter ends, 'It is a great stripping to us.'

Anna, heartbroken, turned to Fowell's sister, Sarah, for comfort, and presently transferred the adoration she had had for Rachel to this tall, gentle cousin who was waiting ready to be her slave. Their first achievement together was to get Anna's translation of the Anglo-Saxon Chronicles published. It appeared under the pseudonym of *A Lady in the Country*.

"Betsy", Elizabeth Fry, after her eleventh and last child was born on the same day as her first grandchild, 1822.

"The giant", Sir Thomas Fowell Buxton, first baronet, M.P., from an engraving from the water-colour by George Richmond. Fowell married Hannah Gurney of Earlham in 1808.

The dining-room in Hannah's day. In ours it was the library.

Hannah's drawing-room in 1862 and hardly changed in our day.

"Granny's room . . . was quite a sight of family portraits and the bed is noted for its immense size," writes Ellen Buxton of Hannah's bedroom at the time this photograph was taken, 1862.

The *Benjamin Bond Cabell*, Cromer's new life-boat launched in 1867. Most of today's life-boat crew are descended from this one.

"The sport". Dick (R. H. Gurney, M.P.) of Thickthorn, Keswick and Northrepps. Portrait painted posthumously 1855 by Sir Francis Grant

Northrepps Hall: white-washed to match "plain Quaker" Earlham.

The coal ship *Ellis* (so-named after the early seventeenth owner-builders of Northrepps Hall), unloading on Cromer sands beside bathing machines used from 1837-1939.

Hollow oaks in Shucks Lane behind Northrepps Cottage.

Catherine. Lady Buxton (nee Gurney), our great grandmother.

Catherine. Lady Buxton, at Colne House, Cromer, with some of her grandchildren. Lady Buxton was then seventy-six with another twenty-two years to live.

Our mother, Rachel Gurney, aged six, Chenda, aged four and baby Gladys in chestnut blossom time on the back lawn.

Our grandfather, R. H. J. Gurney, when High Sheriff in Norwich (1896), with the carriage that went to Rome.

CHAPTER THIRTEEN

The Hampstead Catastrophe

M EANWHILE, in the House of Commons, while Dick's
initiation passed off almost imperceptibly, Fowell was
soon making a brilliant impression, for which he had
unconsciously been preparing for years. He had belonged for some
time to a debating society, so was already an accomplished
speaker, and, with his many charitable works, also an experienced
committee man. At once he was taking part in debates over the
horrors of convict transport ships and prison discipline, with
Sam Hoare, who never wished to become a member of parliament
himself, sitting under the gallery ready to give encouragement
and advice afterwards for the next debate. Fowell was also on
committees concerning the abolition of the death sentence,
except for murder, and Indian widows burning themselves at
their husbands' funerals.

In 1820, with the death of King George III, Parliament was
dissolved. Dick, Hudson, and their cousin Charles Barclay and
Fowell stood again.

'Here I am continually in the air,' Fowell writes to Hannah
from his constituency of Weymouth, 'and have already found the
benefit of it. I rode this morning for two hours on the sands. I
have determined not to canvass, but to be constantly walking
about: the worst of it is, I do not know above a third of their
faces, and the names of about one in a hundred, so I am in
momentary danger of grasping a hand, and enquiring with
kindest solicitude after the welfare of the wife and family of a
man who never saw Weymouth before in his life.'

Hannah was by now at their new home at New End, Hampstead, where they had moved away from the smoke, smells and

129

noise of heavy drays next to the brewery to the country air near
Louisa and Sam.

'Our seven darling children,' Hannah reviewed them in her
journal, 'are a continual source of pleasure, the older ones
especially; my dearest Fowell', the eldest, 'is most sweet and
lovely in his conduct, though sadly idle and painfully backward
in his lessons. Priscilla is most promising. My darling Edward
and Harry are much pleasure to me, Edward needs some care, for
I feel that I am deficient in my pains with him'—this was the
baby Rachel had seen while still 'like a piece of clay'—'Harry
remarkably generous and noble, truly promising. My two little
girls Rachel and Louisa are, I fear, too much a source of pride, as
well as of particular enjoyment. They are a beautiful, black-eyed
pair, fat and healthy, and universally admired. My precious baby,
Hannah, a source of tender interest and pleasure, full of smiles
and activity, but not very handsome. I am not quite so wrapped
up in my babies as I used to be yet when fears arise for any of
my tenderly-loved treasures, how soon do I become sensible that
they are entwined very tight about my heart.'

Now Hannah awaited her next baby, her only 'valley' being
the prospect of her dearest little Fowell—lazy, beautiful and
affectionate—going to boarding school.

'How lovely he has been today in person and conduct,' she
could not help noting down a fortnight before he was to go. 'He
was employed this evening in driving Edward and Harry, who
were harnessed to a basket, in which either my little Rachy, or
Louie, rode while Priscilla played about with the other. The baby
on my lap in the window.'

But little Fowell only survived a few months of boarding
school. Just as the election was gathering momentum and his
father was most needing support at home, a rapid succession of
calamities occurred. No sooner was the new baby born than the
other children all broke out with whooping-cough. Meanwhile,
ten-year-old Fowell had already been sent home from boarding-
school, looking poorly but well enough to go riding next day

with his father who fetched him from his aunt's house where he was staying to avoid infection at home. Within a few days he had inflammation of the lungs and within a week he had died.

Hannah, who had already resigned herself to yielding him up when he went to boarding school, now conducted herself with serenity and even outward cheerfulness. But Fowell was inconsolable. 'Thus has left us our eldest son, the peculiar object of our anxious care—a boy of great life and animation, and a most beautiful countenance.' He tried to console himself with prayer. But his faith was destined to be more severely tried.

Hannah's outward calm, as observed by her brothers and sisters, concealed the anguish revealed in her diary during the next few terrible weeks. The children, already weak and pale with whooping-cough, were seized within a few days with measles which soon assumed a very serious character with one child after another causing anxiety. The three elder children, Priscilla, Edward and Harry, struggled through and the newborn baby never caught either infection. But now the three very small girls, Rachel, Louisa and Hannah, aged four, three and eighteen months old, were very ill indeed.

In an effort to prevent the disease spreading there was a constant changing round of beds and cots. While frantic efforts were being made to get steam kettles and hot compresses to relieve four-year-old Rachel's chest, little Hannah, who had seemed to be recovering from whooping-cough and measles, had a convulsion and attention had to be turned to making a warm bath to put her quickly into. She seemed to recover and was put for the moment into the warmth of Louisa's arms on the bed. Hannah reveals how entirely God was in her everyday life as she records how her baby 'was a little convulsed, and after coughing, her sweet spirit sprung to God.'

Now the mother wished that she too could follow her darling. But there was no time. There was so much nursing to be done. By the time Betsey was there to help to nurse, Rachel was considerably worse. Deciding that something must be done urgently, the doctor ordered the little girl to be moved to The Hill, Sam and Louisa's house where Edward, their second boy, was recovering from measles. They put on Rachel's flannel nightgown, stockings and nightcap and Fowell carried her into Betsey's carriage, leaving three-year-old Louie in the night-nursery—which her mother already found 'tainted with grief'. Rachel cheered up in the carriage and quite enjoyed the ride. Fowell held her up to look at the children and flowers they passed going up the Hampstead hill. At the Hoare's it was decided that she had croup.

Now Louie was taken up to The Hill too, and there was much passing of flowers and pieces of barley-sugar and toys between the two little girls by their brother Edward. Louie got the knack of making parcels for everyone and wrapped up an apple she had been given and sent it to her father as a reward for carrying her about to make her better. Hannah alternated between hope with every sign of relief in either child and fear that these two would follow the others.

After a bout of unusual crossness at last Rachel seemed to be easier and in a sweeter mood and her mother left her with relief to sleep with the nurse. At seven in the morning one of the older children came running in to tell Hannah to come quickly. She hurried to Rachel to find that 'her lovely spirit had just been set free'. Hannah then wrote: 'My darling Louie is now extremely ill. My heart sickens when I turn to her. Her breath panting—hot—and greatly reduced. I hardly hope for her recovery, and indeed feel just now, nearly indifferent to it, so marred is my flock, that another gone I see without astonishment', but the next moment Louie called her and she was at her side, all anguish renewed and nothing that she could do but soothe.

In a desperate attempt to save the last of the three baby girls, the young parents wrapped Louie in a shawl and hurried her on to Betsey's house—'although she looked dreadfully ill, and so altered, she could not sit up in the least. My precious girl was distressed by the ride, often asking "take me out". She took a little milk frequently. We went very fast, Fowell on horseback by our sides. I felt very anxious, but patient, still believing we had done right. Through the next day we were in so low a state we could hardly get lower.'

Perhaps whatever they had done would have made no difference in those days when there was so little that could be done. At least the children were spared the barbarous bleeding which had killed their cousin Rachel.

Louie, who had played a little with her toys before they moved her, now lay almost still, and then after convulsions her mother could no longer bear to stay with her. She looked into the room once and Louie was sitting up but when she returned 'her little spirit had instantly drunk deep of the fountain of life'.

Many gathered round the small coffins which were laid side by side in the dining-room ready to be buried together beside the other children's at Hendon, but Hannah could bear no more—to see again the graves of her other children was more than she could endure. Instead of going to Hendon she went and played with her sister Louisa's healthy children in whom she found some mild comfort.

That evening Fowell wrote in his diary: 'Oh, when one affliction flows in upon another, may they burst the bonds by which we are tied to the earth, and direct us heavenwards; may we, having our treasures in heaven, have our hearts there also. Oh, my God, be Thou the strong consolation of my beloved, my patient wife; break not the bruised reed, pour Thy balm into her wounds, and teach her that He who send this affliction, sends it as a blessing, that she is under the hands of the most gracious and tender Saviour.'

On the tomb of his four children who had all died within a month Fowell had inscribed the two words 'Eheu! Eheu!'

Fowell's prayer, poured into his journal, was answered. After the funeral he and Hannah went to Tonbridge and he was able to write: 'We came here with the fragments of our family, in the hopes that it may recoup the strength of my dear wife. She has during the whole time evinced a holy fortitude and a degree of resigned cheerfulness beyond my hopes, knowing how tenderly her heart felt for her children. May God give her every blessing.'

But while Hannah busied herself with her remaining children, the four others were never out of her mind, and then, too, she kept remembering little Susanna.

'I have had the most affecting business of clearing out my nursery of every remaining vestige of its late lovely inhabitants. To see their hats in a row bespeaking the departure of such numbers at a stroke was hard. I found my faith tried by it.' When the other children were poorly she felt 'sick at heart lest we should have sorrow still upon sorrow. It makes me live again my grief.'

Fowell decided to take Hannah away from Hampstead and make a completely new life in her beloved Cromer with their four remaining children. They were able to rent Cromer Hall from the Wyndhams, a picturesque old building surrounded by woods, which has since been rebuilt.

Once at Cromer, Hannah began to revive and took pleasure in pictures and toys and scenery she had enjoyed in her own child-hood, while still she could not help entering in her journal time and again what she had been doing a year ago, going to see her darling boy at school or travelling with her three lovely girls beside her in the carriage. 'I have been on the beautiful shore with my love, Prissy', her eldest girl, 'and the boys, deeply crossed in heart because my will does not conform to the will of my God.'

Hannah was determined to push aside all further thoughts of death, sickness and anxiety over the least little ills and lead a cheerful life with the children, full of hope and good health.

But alas, it could not be for long, for Prissy developed a painful and completely incapacitating hip complaint. Hannah consulted a doctor in London and word was sent that Prissy should follow by steamer, in the care of her uncle Sam Hoare, accompanied by his and Hannah's other children. 'As we began to descend the cliff at Cromer,' Prissy writes in her diary of the steep zigzag path down to the sea, 'I was terrified. I was lying quite flat, so that I could not see except upwards: I saw numbers of people staring at me. When we got to the boat they lifted my mattress in: I was extremely frightened. It was now full half-past nine, and very dark. I looked up at the sky and thought that God was looking at and caring for me. We had two miles to go before we got to the ship. Then there was the greatest difficulty to get in; the boat rose and fell so much.' It was a terrible night and they were all seasick in the one small cabin. But all Prissy could think of was 'how dreadful must be the sufferings of the poor slaves, crammed and crowded and not allowed nor able to stand or lie down'.

For months Prissy never left the sofa. So little hope did she have of recovering that, when she wrote of the three things she most wished for, she never mentioned a relief from pain but 'first, to draw beautifully. I shall not be content until I have aunt Richenda's boldness, mamma's foliage, and dear aunt Priscilla's exquisite softness and clearness; second, to write beautifully; and the third . . . to mend pens charmingly.'

Prissy made a complete recovery and asked to be sent to boarding school. Life at home was too stimulating to be able to concentrate on the education she felt she lacked.

Hardly had Hannah heard that her youngest sister, Priscilla, was in an advanced state of consumption, than she fetched her from Earlham to nurse her herself at Cromer Hall, where she believed that the sea air would help to prolong the already fading life. Besides, Joseph John's wife, Jane, was expecting her second baby at Earlham—with complications—and was not fit to have another invalid in the house.

Priscilla—La Religieuse Anglaise—lingered for a year and when her end drew near, all her brothers and sisters gathered round her, as was usual on these occasions. But it was Fowell, her brother-in-law, whom she wanted to see most urgently 'to speak about something of importance'. She had often discussed with him what she felt should be the first object of his life, but now when he arrived, she was seized with a violent fit of coughing which so completely exhausted her that she could only press his hand and whisper, 'The poor dear slaves!'

These dying words seemed to him like a sacred commission. Only a few weeks later, William Wilberforce, who had already noticed Fowell's success with home reforms, wrote to him a long and earnest letter begging him to devote himself to 'the blessed service for the anti-slave trade' and finally to succeed him as the leader in the cause if his own health, always feeble, should so fail as to forbid his further attendances in parliament.

For several years, thanks to Wilberforce's efforts, it had been illegal to import slaves to any part of the British Empire, but his dream was to see total emancipation of all the slaves already imported, and slavery abolished throughout the world.

Fowell was certain now what his life work was to be. He took a house in Parliament Street and dropped much of his work at the brewery so that he could concentrate on anti-slavery.

On Sundays he visited the Sam Hoares in Hampstead and whenever holidays were possible they returned with him to Norfolk. 'Cromer Hall', Hannah wrote later, 'was an escape after London and Fowell revelled in its retirement and leisure; he would wander about in the woods, alone in reflection. Prissy grew up to be a delightful companion to him and his two elder boys, Edward and Harry, were his constant object. He was ever desiring means for their amusement and took their part of asking for holidays, and forming plans of the pleasantest character for their occupation. He also took infinite pains with a class of girls— our youngest daughter Richenda, her cousins and others—for hearing and repeating poetry in which he would examine them. It was an interesting sight on these occasions to see him with his class, his careful consideration for each and yet his justice and impartiality; he rewarded them each with handsome prizes according to their deserts. He shared some shooting in the neighbourhood with Sam Hoare, and for some years Cromer Hall was in common between the two families, till old Samuel Hoare died and Sam and Louisa always went to Cliff House.

'Other families united much with us. Mrs. Richard Gurney who then lived at Northrepps Hall with her daughter Anna Gurney and Fowell's sister Sarah were often with us to draw forth his cheerful and playful mind. Mrs. Upcher of Sheringham and her children were also pleasant visitors.' The Hon. Mrs. Upcher was a young widow whose husband had started to build what Humphry Repton, who designed it, regarded as 'the culmination of his art'. Sheringham Bower, as the Hall was then called, was built in the beautiful wooded hills above Sheringham. Abbot Upcher died before it was finished and his widow, a daughter of the eleventh Lord Berners, and her son completed it. She and Hannah had much in common over their children and recent bereavement. They met through Fowell applying to rent the Sheringham shooting and being 'decidedly repelled'. However, Mrs. Upcher wrote after her first visit to Cromer Hall: 'Mr. and Mrs. Buxton are extremely sensible and very well informed. It was quite unlike a common dinner visit.' She and Hannah became devoted friends.

But the ties with Earlham were as strong as ever and Hannah, although she had two more baby boys herself in quick succession, Fowell (the second) and Charles, she took her share in going over to Earlham to help to nurse Joseph John's wife, Jane, in a long decline after her second confinement. When Jane died, the running of Earlham fell back into the hands of Kitty, who, as mistress of Earlham for twenty years, had merely stood back during her brother's marriage till she was needed again. Now she and her sister Rachel mothered Joseph John's two small children, Jackey and little Anna, as they had done their own younger brothers and sisters.

Rachel taught Jackey to read when he was four by giving him a Bible with large print and telling him to underline all the birds and animals in it. This not only achieved its object but also produced a lifelong interest in both ornithology and the Bible.

CHAPTER FOURTEEN

Jackey of Earlham

I T was Jackey, our great-grandfather, later known by his full name of John Henry, whose earliest memory was of plunging into the over-ripe giant gourd in the kitchen garden. All his earliest memories of his grandparents', which was also his parents' home, were as delicious as ours of Northrepps. He remembered the rambling old place full of mice, which he caught and skinned 'to clothe his toy soldiers in fur to go to the northern wars'. He remembered the feasts of fruit from the garden with slices cut by his aunts after dinner with a silver knife to guard against cholera. And most warmly he remembered, as we did of Northrepps, the backyard at Earlham with, among the main outhouses, the brew house where the household beer was brewed. High up among its dark beams a white owl lived, but one day it perched too long over the vat where the fumes of the fermenting beer intoxicated it and the owl fell in and was drowned. Jackey remembered a snowy day in winter when he could see from the drawing-room window the winding river and the small lake beyond the park where there were pike to be tickled, and the heronry beyond. It was a view he knew well. But now he saw a row of new palings which had been put up along the lake. He ran out to look at them and to his amazement saw the fence fly away in a long line of cormorants. One was shot and still stands in a glass case at Northrepps where for years it was to remind him of its origin.

Jackey was a quaint little boy with a twinkling smile and curly hair, and many were the stories that came from Earlham about him and his exceedingly pretty little sister, Anna.

Once he came home from Goats in his stout Aunt Kett's capacious carriage and nobody noticed him fall asleep deep in the

cushions and rugs. The carriage went to the stables and when his
Aunt Kett sent for it to return home, she climbed in and to her
dismay sat down on something warm and alive. It was Jackey.

When he was very small he was taken to Goats in a carriage
drawn by two horses, one a survivor of the four black horses
which his grandfather used to lend to the bishop to go to con-
firmations in state, while the Quaker John Gurney used the
bishop's brown horses to take his family to Goats.

But Jackey and Anna were by no means the only grandchildren
who spent long sessions at Earlham at this time. Samuel, the
financier, brought his family annually from Essex, with always a
few days by the sea at Cromer where his little girls, Catherine and
Rachel Jane, became special favourites of Hannah's children at
Cromer Hall. Once Catherine, not wanting anyone else to play
with her beloved baby sister Rachel Jane, shut her for several
hours in a drawer.

Catherine wrote of the memorable journeys to Earlham in their
father's coach 'painted a light olive green, with a box in front,
and an ample rumble behind for man and maid. Our own horses
took us to Woodford directly after breakfast, and then four
posters were clapped on in a very few minutes, at the sound of
"horses-on" from the ostler at the inn. Then the two postboys,
in high white beaver hats, blue jackets, red waistcoats, white
neckcloths, short white corduroy breeches, and bright topboots,
started off at a smart trot, which continued the whole stage up
and down hill, only stopping for a moment to put on a drag.
Our greatest delight was driving on the box. I remember my
astonishment as a child, at seeing my father pay away so many
gold pieces as the postboys came up to the window for their fare
at the end of each stage. We always slept at Thetford, in a charming old-fashioned inn, with large stables and a garden opposite
across the road; the same old footman warmly welcoming us
there year after year. Then how delightful was the arrival at
Earlham Hall, with the warmest of welcomes awaiting us. These
were refreshing times. The great comfort and luxury of the

coach, well lined with fawn coloured watered silk, the step made to fold up inside and covered with softest carpet. How quickly the hours passed—our father always bright and cheerful, our mother quietly happy, a variety of books and amusements for each of us.'

Betsey's children also came frequently, and two of them were more or less permanently at Earlham for several years.

Katherine, Betsey's eldest, wrote: 'Perhaps Earlham was never more charming, or in its zenith than during the five years in which our aunts Kitty and Rachel were our Uncle Joseph John's companions and mistresses of his house.'

The children all teased their Aunt Kitty affectionately for her many small eccentricities. There was much banter over her wearing, while ministering to the poor of Norwich, a 'very common stuff gown and petticoat got for the purpose—the petticoat with a great tuck not quite halfway up it', which caused her aunt at The Grove to prod her affectionately and ask her, 'Why didst thou put that ugly tuck *there*?' Kitty laughed and said some strange lady had also asked her if she meant to get fatter.

Jackey, when he was nine, wrote a long epic poem about the family at Earlham, referring to his Aunt Kitty's daily bath in the great tank beneath the perforated ceiling which she took before hurrying three times round the garden which, she said, made a mile.

> 'There is another good and grave
> Who ofte in a great tub doth lave;
> And when she's done, out she pops
> And round the garden merrily hops,
> And when she comes in her breakfast to get
> Says "my walks, my dear friends, I cannot regret."''

If one of the children, or a group of them, were lazy, naughty or over-excited, it was their aunt Rachel's lot to 'make judicious adaptations of the arrangements', which consisted of a mixture of threats and early bed-times or other mild punishments, with gentle pleadings for them to behave better.

The saintly Joseph John smiled benevolently at the children, always pleased to see more of them at Earlham.

'On second day morning I returned to this dear place', he writes, 'and found Rachel and the darling children at home. They were overjoyed to meet me. Louisa and her little ones are with us, very delightfully.'

George Borrow describes a meeting with Joseph John at this time in his novel *Lavengro*. The novelist had in fact himself been discovered fishing in the Earlham stream and gave the incident to his fictional hero. 'Close behind me stood the tall figure of a man dressed in raiment of quaint and singular fashion, but of goodly material. He was in the prime and vigour of manhood; his features handsome and noble, full of calmness and benevolence, though they were somewhat shaded by a hat of finest beaver with a broad drooping brim.' They discuss fishing, Greek, Dante and the scriptures and the Quaker asks him into his house.

'Our people,' the Quaker explains, 'have been compared to the Jews. In one respect I confess we are similar to them—we are fond of getting money.' 'The Hall of many an Earl', Borrow says, 'lacks the bounty, and the palace of many a Prelate lacks the piety and learning, which adorn the quiet Quaker's home.'

When faced with any emergency concerning the 'getting of this money', the quiet Quaker was surprisingly active. Amelia Opie describes in a letter to a friend an evening at Earlham 'spoilt by the sudden disappearance of the men. Dan went off suddenly to Lynn, and Joseph John and Samuel to London, leaving only a party of women. This is quite between you and me, but a report got wind in London that Gurney's and Barclay's had stopped payment. The consequence was a run on one of the banks—they knew not why—which led Dan's partner in Lynn to send all his money there—when lo, there came a run on *his* bank, and Dan was sent for *express*, being met on the road by the news that the Lynn bank had stopped payment. So it did for *two hours*—what a dilemma! Consequently Joseph John and Samuel, who knew where to get money, left *post and four horses* immediately for London.

The next day at five o'clock in the morning Fowell arrived and his men with *blunderbuss* and broadswords, with sixty-thousand pounds!'

Fowell, who was not even a banker, would nevertheless have been unable to resist an adventure of this sort.

Such were Joseph John's good looks and fortune that after his wife Jane died, many a cap was set at him again and none more jauntily than that of 'that excellent but ridiculous person, Mrs. Amelia Opie', as one literary reviewer called her. Amelia, now widowed, had remained a close friend of the Gurneys since the old Earlham days when she used to ride over with her assorted friends to excite them with her bubbling gaiety and enthusiasm for the arts. Her racy novels and flighty plays were even then causing a local stir. After her marriage to John Opie, in London, she became nationally known for her literary daring. In London even such a man of the world as Hudson Gurney complained about the morals of one of her heroines, 'making it impossible to read parts of the book aloud to ladies'. Hudson urged Joseph John to reprove her for her allusions to adultery, seduction and houses of ill fame. This Joseph John did with an unexpected smile.

Now Amelia was prepared to give all her writing up for Joseph John. She even became a Quaker herself, sweeping elegantly about in a splendidly cut Quaker gown of a fine silk of a subtle shade of grey, which material was ordered from Paris, where she had previously purchased her clothes. She had her visiting cards inscribed in the Quaker fashion without title or prefix but could not resist decorating them with a tiny circle of painted rosebuds.

Joseph John, although he was always fond of Amelia, never took her love seriously, for she was nearly twenty years older than he. When he made Mary Foweler, a strict Quaker girl fourteen years younger than himself, his wife, Amelia 'soon passed it off' and trekked across England to attend the wedding.

Great preparations were made for the new mistress of Earlham with much white-washing and dusting, but this was nothing to the changes she made herself, pulling down the fine old wainscoting and pictures let into the panels and burying them in a hole dug in the garden by the housekeeper, with, it was always said, many other valuable old masters. But what the family found most disturbing was her painting the house white, 'which it had never been before'.

Within weeks of the wedding, sweet attractive flaxen-haired Rachel of Earlham had fallen into a decline. At last the letter came she had waited for so despairingly twenty-eight years before. The lover who had ridden away wrote saying he had thought of her every day since. Next day she died with the letter still clasped in her hand.

The new Mrs. Gurney tried to win her step-children's affections but found it hard. She had brought 'many little Quaker prejudices and ideas hitherto unknown in Earlham' as the family politely called her revolution not only in the house and garden but also in the much more rigid behaviour expected of the young, which put a great strain on Joseph John's normally uninhibited children. Their most lively times were now spent at Cromer Hall, where their Aunt Hannah, who now had six children again, always welcomed them.

In the eight years there, Hannah, in her slow recovery from the Hampstead disaster, had found great comfort in the old house. But now the Wyndhams wanted it back to rebuild. Samuel had just bought Colne House in Cromer.

While the Buxtons were deciding on buying a house of their own, Dick offered to let them Northrepps Hall. They agreed at first to take it for a month, and in fact stayed for forty-four years. For over two years Northrepps Hall had stood empty, since the death of the much-loved Aunt Gurney. Dick, who had then owned it, had only used it as a shooting box.

Anna and Sarah had moved down the hill to Northrepps Cottage where they became affectionately known as 'The Cottage Ladies'.

'Here', wrote Dan, 'these two attached cousins resided in a beautiful abode surrounded by every comfort and dispensing to all around them with a profusion of kindness and Christian benevolence. Schools, life-boats, guns for preservation of ship-wrecked sailors, Bible and missionary societies, in short all that could benefit others, occupied their well spent hours. There was a cheerfulness and ease and intellectuality about it all, and a simplicity that showed itself in the love of animals, The Cottage grounds, swarming with rabbits, ducks, fowls and innumerable favourites of that sort. The cousins always referred to themselves as partners.'

They were now only half a mile from the sea and whenever there was a storm Anna would demand to be dragged down to the cliffs in her chair by her two menservants, Spinks and Stephans. She was already well-versed in Latin, Greek, Hebrew, Anglo-Saxon and Icelandic but now she took the trouble to learn additional modern languages so that she could speak to foreign survivors of shipwrecks and take them home and give them warm, dry clothes, and then assist them out of her own pocket, back to their own land.

Finding there was no school of any sort at Overstrand, Anna and Sarah, who had both taught in 'Lady Gurney's' Sunday school at Northrepps Hall, started teaching the Overstrand children daily themselves at Northrepps Cottage, till they could build a school for them in their own village. Each child paid a penny a week. The rules for this school were most carefully drawn up and still exist written out in Sarah's clear, delicate handwriting. Anna was extremely progressive and well ahead of her time, with a great emphasis on encouragement with sweets, rather than punishment. Every single duty of the junior teacher, whom they trained, was written out for her, right down to ladling out the last bowl of soup, cooked in The Cottage kitchen, for the children's dinner.

Anna was the last of her brothers and sisters to leave the Society of Friends. Soon after her mother's death she was chris-tened at Overstrand church, in which formal entry to the Church of England her brother Dick declined to join her. Anna, with

Sarah at her side, had already made one or two abortive attempts to convert Dick when he came to Northrepps Hall to shoot. It was not only the matter of his baptism that concerned the partners, but, respected Member of Parliament that he still was, there was again considerable talk behind fans about his romantic interests, and particularly the revival of interest in Mrs. Muskett, whose husband had already sued him once. Anna, who spurned both fans and local gossip, was nevertheless disturbed over Dick's soul.

But Dick was accustomed to being called on by lady relations with his soul in mind. When he had been ill once with an attack of his usual gout, his cousins, Betsey and Priscilla, had come quietly into his bedroom in their Quaker garb, with folded hands and downcast eyes, and there found him with his head out of the end of the bedclothes, urging on a main of cocks brought in by his groom to cheer him up with a fight on the floor.

Now, in self-defence, Dick had a sunken terrace dug in the garden on the Cottage side of Northrepps Hall, which, he told Anna, it would be impossible for her to cross in her wheel-chair when she felt like lecturing him. The clear glass on that side of the house was changed to the stained glass that is still there, to guard against her trying to admonish him through the windows.

Dick had another objection to make about Anna. He disliked the way she did her hair. Even Dan, who supported Anna in most things, suggests that it was a pity. For all the kindliness of her expression, wearing her hair cut short and uncurled gave her the look of a man. A drawing survives of her in her late twenties with her thick, slightly wavy hair cut in a short practical way that makes her look more athletic than masculine.

To the relief of both brother and cousin, she presently let her hair grow and wore it 'properly curled' under a cap tied with a bow at the side of her powerful chin.

Sarah, Dan writes, 'was tall and delicate-looking and more like her Aunt Gurney than her mother, with a great sweetness about her countenance'.

K

Dan came frequently to Northrepps Cottage, for he had already begun to write his *Record of the House of Gournay* and needed Anna's knowledge of ancient Norse history to help him in his efforts to trace his family back as far, if not farther, than that of the Earl of Erroll, whose daughter, Lady Harriet Hay, he had now married.

During Fowell and Hannah's move from Cromer Hall, they stayed at Northrepps Cottage for a fortnight in 'a season of gratification never to be forgotten', writes Sarah.

Hannah writes from Northrepps Cottage to her sister: 'My dearest Richenda, we are still in our passage from Cromer Hall to Northrepps and very comfortably sheltered at the Cottage, with dear Anna and Sarah, who are affectionately kind and attentive to us. We find the help of being here great, it is not only an important convenience, but much more cheering than to be in either house, in the confusion of furniture heaped in one, or emptied in the other.

'I have hardly felt leaving dear Cromer Hall, for my mind is now occupied by Northrepps which I very much like, and I am interested in getting it into order.

'We have no solemn parting from Cromer Hall, the family were so entirely occupied the last morning, that we could have no reading. Mrs. Upcher and her girls were with us, and we did not wish to make it a melancholy occasion, though we felt it deeply at heart.'

A week later Priscilla writes in her journal: 'Northrepps Hall. February 4th, 1828. Here we are! This day we have entered our new abode; begun that new stage and section of our lives here . . . Dearest Mama looks tired and I thought low when we went to bed.'

Now came a period of tremendous anti-slave activity for Fowell, in which he was helped and encouraged by The Cottage ladies from Northrepps and Sam Hoare from Cliff House, whose children continued to live as they had at Hampstead and Cromer Hall, almost as one family, with constant interchange of children and daily visits between the families.

Priscilla worked as her father's secretary both at Northrepps and in their London house in Devonshire Street.

Wilberforce was fairly often at Northrepps. Priscilla writes, 'Overstrand church was rather pleasant, Mr. Wilberforce's behaviour quite edifying, nice dinner and evening, Mr. Wilberforce most beaming in mind, I have never seen him brighter. He is altogether a glorious sight. The honour that encircles his hoary head, the brilliancy of his genius and the light of his mind contrast with the decrepitude of his body.'

Although Fowell now bought Colne House from Samuel, he never lived there, for he was 'entirely delighted' with Northrepps. When he was not shooting with Sam Hoare, he was organising boys' shoots, cricket matches and excursions with endless children from the various families carried in a variety of unconventional vehicles with many mounted on makeshift horses and donkeys. He was always able to find plenty of other energetic relaxations from the paper-work he brought with him from London.

He loved taking Hannah for a drive in his high phaeton if it was fine, or the brougham if it was cold, and this is when he would call from the hall when the horses were ready: 'Bustle, bustle, Mrs. Noah, the ark is at the door.'

He delighted in teasing Hannah, and would tell the most preposterous stories about her unlikely doings which brought forth frantic denials. He was extremely fond of horses and dogs and usually rode one of his favourites, Abraham—called after the gamekeeper of his childhood—or John Bull, for an hour or so on the cliffs before breakfast with his Newfoundland dog, Moscow, bounding behind him. Horses, dogs, woods and other parts of the estate were all called after 'his utmost interest at the time of their naming'. There are woods to this day called 'Rome', 'Niger', 'Fernanda Po', and 'Sierra Leone'—(pronounced locally 'Sarah Alone-y'). Fowell said the same was true of him as of Marsham, the Norfolk naturalist who wrote to White of Selborne, 'When you touch on trees, you touch on my mad string.' He made models on the lawn of each new plantation before work began on it. When part of the home wood at Northrepps Hall was flattened in one night by a freak blizzard that sprang up from the north-

north-east, Fowell replanted it with the fine trees that only reached their full splendour in our childhood.

His one sorrow was that Dick kept the Northrepps shooting. Dick stayed at Hill House for the purpose. He made the old house comfortable and built a delightful stable block on the edge of the wooded valley above Northrepps Cottage which is now inhabited exactly as he would have liked by the North Norfolk Harriers. The stable buildings were, and still are, roofed with a cargo of slates (an unusual sight in Norfolk where thatch or pantiles are the normal local roofing) that were all that remained, still neatly stacked and unbroken on Overstrand beach, after a ship had been wrecked and broken up by the same storm.

Gradually Fowell and Sam Hoare added to their own shoot by buying more and more land on both sides of Northrepps and Cromer till eventually it was 'Knocking at the door of two thousand acres.'

Fowell had already introduced capercailzies to the original shoot they leased together, but the birds had died out, as they had done in Scotland. With the acquiring of the new land, he sent Larry, his Irish gamekeeper, to Sweden to bring back new stock. It was a difficult procedure, procuring the birds, making crates and then trying to keep a dozen pairs of large wild birds alive for three weeks at sea, but Larry did it, keeping an almost hour to hour diary of the setbacks.

The capercailzies thrived and Fowell was able to send several pairs to a friend who had lent him grouse shooting in Scotland, in the hopes of their becoming naturalised again. The fact that these large unwieldy birds, when shot, taste like turpentine did not in the least deter him.

Among the notes that went daily backwards and forward between The Hall and The Cottage, as telephone calls do in Northrepps today, is one from Fowell to Anna: 'I have sent living capercailzie to nobles and princes, but I have reserved for you, whom I value above all the nobles and princes upon earth, a capercailzie fit for your table this day.'

CHAPTER FIFTEEN

Shipwreck Practice with the Cottage Ladies

THE Buxton children were constantly in and out of the Cottage. Chenda, born just before the Hampstead catastrophe and who was eight when they moved to Northrepps, went for advice on her pets, or to help Anna to tend hers. Edward, aged sixteen, was specially interested in the school at Overstrand which the Cottage ladies were building of exactly-matched small, round, grey cobbles from the shore. The partners' initials were interwined over the porch in white and pink pebbles which their school children picked out for them from the shore. Later, Priscilla, inspired by the Overstrand school, started an infants' school in the smaller hamlet of Northrepps in the kitchen of a 'Homely woman who could sing and read' and so could replace her when she was helping her father. Later she too had a tiny school-house built in Northrepps.

Fifteen-year-old Harry was a special favourite with the Cottage ladies for he and Anna had so much in common. He was an out-of-doors boy with, Anna said, 'A taste for so many branches of natural history and a peculiar quickness and accuracy of observation. Moreover, the touch of a book or a word makes him bound forward to distinguish himself, and he has a habit of accuracy unusual with so ardent a temperament.'

Another young naturalist after Anna's heart was Jackey of Earlham. Though he was only nine and Harry was nearly sixteen, they would go off together in search of rare birds and small mammals, which Harry shot and Jackey had stuffed for his collection. Already he had contributed to the Norwich museum, which items appear in its annals as one female sparrowhawk and a ringed dove 'donated in 1828 by Master J. H. Gurney'. Killing and stuffing birds was then the normal method of studying them. Jackey was already such an addict that he became known in the family as 'The Stuffer'.

Anna had a collection of fossilised bones of pre-Ice Age animals which she and Sarah had picked up at Overstrand after cliff falls. To these the boys added their finds. They rode their ponies almost daily on the sands, whatever the weather, getting off to scramble on the cliffs and poke about in the pools. Thus they witnessed some of the increasing number of off-shore shipwrecks that were worrying their elders.

Priscilla writes in their first December at Northrepps Hall: 'There was a great storm and the sea getting up rapidly. Harry was at Cromer, and he mounted his pony and rode up to Northrepps to tell cousin Anna and our father.'

And Harry writes himself: 'As I was going I saw the ship coming in at a terrible rate. Cousin Anna went off to Sidestrand, and my father to Cromer, when I arrived there the ship was ashore by the gangway. The crew were safe and hundreds of oranges were floating about.'

Cromer lifeboat station had already been equipped with a 'Manby gun' designed to shoot a life-line to a sinking ship, but it was an early design and besides being heavy was in other ways not entirely satisfactory. Fowell and Sam Hoare had been involved in several attempted rescues with it. Once they were shooting at Sheringham when a storm became so violent they gave up to go home. On the way they saw a ship driving on shore. They ran to get the gun, with tiles blowing off the houses round them. With great difficulty they dragged the gun along the shingle, trying to keep up with the ship which was striving to keep off the shore. When she was nearly under the lighthouse she struck. 'The life-boat was put out, but was quite unmanageable among the breakers and all but four men jumped out.' Fowell told his family immediately afterwards: 'I suggested that if we got in, others might follow and another man and I jumped into the boat. At that moment a wave took us out to sea. The men were sure we should all be drowned and I thought we were in the greatest danger, but I considered our only chance was to remain firm in the boat, so I put my hands under the seat and held tight. Happily the raging breakers threw us again on the shore. We left the lifeboat to try other means. The ship had thrown out a piece of wood with a line to it. I saw it on the top of the water and at that moment resolved "That wood I'll get or be drowned." I made a plunge at it and after a violent struggle with the breakers I obtained the wood and then the string went. If it had been fastened securely we could have established communication and the crew would probably have been saved. The waves increased in fury and the tide continued rising till we obliged to retreat to a ledge halfway up the cliff, against which the sea beat with such violence that we thought it must give way. We fired the gun but could not nearly get the rope over to the ship. The men were very much afraid of shooting, but I said I would take the responsibility. At length a huge sea burst over the vessel and she went to pieces, blackening the waters with her cargo of coal. "Poor dear hearts, there they go," one of our men said. Someone said, "Let us all make a rush and save some." We all ran in. The waves brought a quantity of planks and boards which dashed against our legs, and after being two or three times knocked down we saw a man coming in on the top of a wave. I made a spring at him and caught him, but the wave threw me down like a child and flung me over the man's body. The people behind dragged us out. The man was insensible and I was more dead than alive. I could not walk a step and was dragged up the cliff half drowned, unable to do any more. Another man appeared and was saved in the same way. The rest of the crew went to the bottom.'

Now Anna heard that Captain Manby, the Norfolk inventor of the gun, had produced a lighter and more effective one. She asked him to bring it for a demonstration at Northrepps Hall, where there would be room in the garden to try it with some of the Overstrand fishermen.

Captain Manby turned up, a small brisk retired army captain, who began by volunteering the information that he had been at school with Nelson. The party went on to the back lawn. Captain Manby said that since he was a subaltern in the Gunners he had been trying to find a means of firing a cannon ball into the teeth of a gale for 200 yards, but his experiments had always been greeted with ridicule. The chief difficulty, after discovering how to arrange the line so that it would pay out evenly and not break under the strain, was to prevent it being burnt by the blast from the mortar that fired the ball. He had got over that by using a couple of feet of plaited hide to attach the rope to the ball. He had now perfected the whole apparatus and mortar, cartridges, balls and line could be carried by one man on horseback. Anna was only interested in whether she could carry it in her wheel-chair. This she found, due to the enormous strength of her arms, she could do.

The demonstration was carried out, using the big silver fir in lieu of a ship. This was the fir we called the 'Rescue Tree' as children. Standing on the edge of the wood, it towered above all the other trees.

Captain Manby fired the gun up into the branches, and children and gardeners swarmed up a ladder to play the part of the ship-wrecked, riding down to 'safety' in a breeches-buoy slung to a small trolley-wheel on the line, which the fishermen, in their leather sou'westers and striped jerseys, held taut on the lawn.

Hannah made a sketch of the scene, which was at North-repps, with Anna looking like an enormous pumpkin, beneath a coloured umbrella in her outdoor chair (a kind of Greek chariot, almost certainly Silver-made) with Sarah, aghast, beside her and Fowell standing behind them egging everybody on.

Anna was so impressed she ordered a gun to carry on her knee to Overstrand where she could lead the fishermen in their rescues. She also helped to tide Captain Manby over while he expanded his inventions, for such rewards as he received from the government always fell short of his needs. He was then able to go on to invent the first powered lifeboat, a chemical fire extinguisher, and the jumping sheet for rescuing people from blazing buildings.

Joseph John of Earlham, watching Anna practising with her fishermen at Northrepps Cottage, became as interested as his coastal-dwelling relations and later designed an inflatable life-jacket which was exhibited at Cromer lifeboat station for all to copy. Meanwhile, Mrs. Upcher gave Sheringham its first lifeboat, *The Augusta*, named after her daughter.

Another coastal activity that was at its height at this time at Overstrand and Northrepps was smuggling. All the villagers took part in it as a matter of course. Anna said that they did not see the distinction which more refined moralists would, between this and other breaches of the law. Even she seemed almost to turn a blind eye. She writes: 'There was a great run about a fortnight ago at Overstrand. Howes and Harrison' (members of her rescue team) 'are clear, we have not ventured to enquire as to the others.'

'Old Summers' of the Northrepps foundry was the ring leader, and when there was a run he called out his allies, who took horses and carts from the farmers, and conveyed the goods—spirits, tobacco, silk and lace—to nearby hiding places, to be moved later, as far inland as possible. This was when the small Billy Silver—already a weeding boy at Northrepps Hall—drove a cart three nights running to Norwich. Anna writes again: 'On Friday the preventative officers and men searched the plantation—part of a keg of brandy was found, sixteen bottles of brandy and two of gin, nearer the Hill House than ourselves.'

Bartlett's trees had now grown up into thick woods that shrouded the hills and valley, making excellent cover for smugglers and pheasants alike. Behind Northrepps Cottage and Hill House the little-used sunken lane is an almost soundproof tunnel when leaves are on the trees, and an eerie place at night. It was easy enough to put around the fable that Shuck, the two-headed ghost dog, walked here.

Hill House still remained a rambling farmhouse with walls thick enough to harbour secret hiding places requiring years of living in the house to discover. To its back door, loads could easily enough be carried up through the woods from carts standing unseen halfway up the leafy tunnel. It was characteristic of Dick who had no need to evade the tax on his liquor, to take a sporting interest in these 'run goods'. Though Hill House was frequently searched by the preventive officers, it was always to no avail.

At the top of Shuck's Lane stood, (and still stand), a pair of lump and cobble cottages with a twenty-mile view of the country-side to the south of it. It is shown on a map of 1750 as belonging to Mrs. Sally Bean. The 'Mrs.' was by courtesy only, for although nine of her children are buried in the churchyard, she always re-mained the unmarried daughter of Mr. Bean. When she was old and nut-brown with age and tobacco-smoke, she still received her keg of gin for watching the distant lanes across her garden for the redcoats, and if she saw trouble, hobbling to the top of Shuck's Lane to warn the smugglers. Old Jocka was one of them. Billy Silver was recorded to have said, 'with a poney borrowed from my porr ole father, that only had three legs. But that could fly. As Jocka come up the lane the old woman hisses she'd see'd the riding officer a'coming an' he gave her the gin, an' away he goes as hard as that old poney could go. The riding officer he come up and goes in to transack the old lady's house, and there she squatted', as in cat, 'on her keg of gin with her skirts drawd down over that, and he never do find it.'

The children at Northrepps Hall found, among the many irreg-ular holes and corners and cupboards so admirable for hide-and-seek, several with secret doors behind them leading to deeper niches. When the house had stood empty with only an occasional visit from Dick for shooting, his estate workers had, not unnatur-ally, made use of the facilities offered.

Even the church tower was not immune. Long after the last run, ropes and pulleys for heaving the contraband up to the top were found still hidden there. Once there was a great seizure of horses and carts which were to be sold by auction at Cromer. One of the horses, a black one, belonged to Mr. Playford of Northrepps' who went to Cromer and called to his horse which promptly followed his master home. No sooner was it home than the animal was dredged over with flour and when the officers appeared there was no black horse, only a grey, so they left 'unable to do anything'.

But the most unfortunate run was after Anna, when watching the ships with Sarah from the cliffs, noticed a Yarmouth boat hovering off the coast. In the night they were woken by shots and shouts in Shucks Lane. The cargo had been landed at Overstrand and the preventive officers had got wind of it. There followed a bloody stand-to just outside the old entrance to The Cottage from Shucks Lane. Billy Silver said that two men were killed, others caught and imprisoned and only Old Summers the blacksmith got away. They followed him to the foundry but then only got hold of his coat-tails as he fled through the back door to live in the woods at Foxhall for several months, till the quest died down. Occasionally an old woman was seen in the village street, and once some child called out in broad Norfolk, 'Why that do fair like Ted Summers', but was promptly squashed by its elders.

As Fowell and Hannah had to spend more time in London, the Cottage ladies had a great deal to do now with supervising their children. Anna once said that 'the spring of 1829 was perhaps the brightest spot in our lives. Our boys were so spirited, and yet so gentle. Harry was so aspiring, and in a right sense, his mettle was up.'

On Sundays they always had supper together to read the letters from Devonshire Street.

Hannah writes that on their arrival home from London Harry was sitting on the gate to receive them, 'delighted and delightful he looked, well and happy. Thankful indeed are we to have our two blooming and flourishing youths together, and all we could desire.'

Harry was about to be baptised and took an enormous interest in the whole affair. Hannah wrote: 'I and my two lovely companions drank tea at the Cottage with Anna and dear Sarah who was still confined to her room', and she mentioned 'Harry's lively, tender manner to us all. My impression of him is all vigour, both of mind and body.' But it was a false impression and Harry had to put off his christening due to inflammation of the lungs. It left him with a cough, and feeling unusually listless.

Then at his sixteenth birthday party he over-exerted himself romping with the younger children, which started a violent fit of coughing, and he coughed blood. Poor Hannah! 'A death stroke I knew it to be. Our first care was to soothe and cheer him,' she writes, 'awful as the moment was, he told me afterwards that he immediately turned to God for help and that he was not much overcome.'

His father lay down with him and read to him until he was asleep—leaving 'with an almost broken heart'. But Harry was as usual lively, cheerful, playful, and full of confidence. He was kept in bed for a week or two and then only allowed out in good weather. Being deprived of active employment and almost entirely confined to the house, he turned his mind vigorously to the studies and amusement he was still allowed to pursue. Anna came up every day to read to him. She gave him a list of authors and they studied them together. The last entry in his own journal was October 25th, 1829. 'The thought occurs to me whether I shall ever see October 25th, 1830.'

His mother noticed his almost imperceptible daily decline. He went to stay with the Cottage ladies and, returning to the Hall, instantly caught a severe cold and became much worse for a time. He was well enough to pay a round of visits in the spring, for the old cry of 'a change of air' was still prescribed, with a long tiring journey to the Isle of Wight. All Harry wanted was to get back to Northrepps, but the journey home was almost intolerable. Once back, however, he revived a little and there were some pleasant drives on Roughton Heath and on the cliffs above Overstrand. But by the middle of October Hannah was writing: 'Harry was so weak that I took him from one room to another in Anna's wheeled chair. There never was the slightest resistance to any measure, that told a sad and mournful tale that he was stepping lower and lower into the valley. He always cheerfully, and often playfully, acceded to anything I proposed in these trials.' He did live to see October 25th, 1830, but only just. When he died, once again Fowell's chief concern was for Hannah.

In the ante-room the family gathered round for this 'wonderful' occasion, as Mrs. Upcher called it when she wrote: 'I have been to the Hall and Cottage today. I am not enthusiastic when I say Northrepps Hall is, as it were, the very gates of Heaven. It was like a visit to an angel, I thought, when I came out of the dear mother's room last night. Her weakness, great depression, wondrous exaltation, exquisite kindness and consideration for the feelings of every individual is the most splendid and touching spectacle in the world.'

A vault was made in the ruined chancel of Overstrand church, into which was sunk the 'earthly remains of this child of bright promise'.

A few months later Fowell wrote: 'I took the boys Edward and Edmund and the two Upchers to shoot at the Warren Hill, opposite the coast. The ground was covered with snow, the sea was dark and fretful. I went along the town side and turned up one of the most distant hillocks, and there I placed myself. And then in a moment a picture burst upon me, which made this one of the most melancholy moments of the last melancholy year. On that same hillock about the same day two years ago I stood. Nature seemed as if she had not changed, the same surface of white beneath my feet, and the sea bearing the same blackening aspect, the game-keepers and dogs in the same hollow, and the boys exhibiting the same eagerness—all was the same, with one sorrowful exception. Dearest Harry was nearest to me on the former occasion, his quick eye perceived a wild duck sailing near the sea, and we observed it alighting on a pond near the farm below us. I sent him, full of life and alacrity as he was, to secure the bird in his hand and the pleasure I felt at his pleasure, and now I see nothing but the church yard where his bones repose, dear fellow. But there is comfort, he has gone to eternal security and peace.'

This was the hill, the Warren hill, on which a hundred years later my cousin Tommy would watch the wild duck sailing near the sea, with gamekeepers and dogs in the same hollow, and boys exhibiting the same eagerness. This was the heath near his home, the Warren, of which Tommy wrote as the same, still then incurable, illness began its listless course:

> 'I do not think the heath will blossom so
> At the next meeting
> The flowers are older now, the trees less straight
> Than they were wont to grow.
> Nor will the same brown bird
> Carol a greeting.
>
> There is a presence now about the place
> A sting of sorrow
> A dim-drawn wistfulness that the next spring
> Will never quite efface.
> Leaving its yesterday
> To haunt tomorrow.'
>
> T. F. Barclay

CHAPTER SIXTEEN

The Apocryphal Book of Dan

FOR all Anna's efforts, Dick had been unable to keep out of trouble and on December 26th, 1829 a new case had been brought against him by Mr. Joseph Salisbury Muskett. It was said in court that Muskett was the son of a gentleman possessing considerable landed estate in the county of Norfolk. A short time prior to his marriage with the lady of whose seduction he complained, his father had settled an estate on him in Norfolk. Mrs. Muskett had been a Miss Jary, daughter of a most respectable gentleman residing about eight miles away. She was married in 1812 when she was eighteen, her father gave her five thousand pounds, and Mr. Muskett's estate was settled on her issue. For four years they had lived affectionately and harmoniously. They had one daughter. Mr. Gurney was well known by name as a banker and he represented the City of Norwich in Parliament.

He was the owner of a landed estate and mansion at Thickthorn and also lived a great deal with his mother and sister at Keswick and at Northrepps. The plantation attached to the Keswick estate adjoined that of Mr. Muskett, who had not known the Gurneys before his marriage.

They had met in 1817 at Holkeham, home of Mr. Coke, M.P. for the county. Mr. Muskett soon noticed some little alteration in his wife's manner. He passed it over. Every Sunday evening he went to see his father. Once in 1817 he did not go and Mrs. Muskett became greatly flustered. She went up to her room and would not come down. An old friend, Mr. Nash, who used to enjoy bringing flowers to the house and arranging them, called and stayed to dinner but Mrs. Muskett refused to come down. She was found writing notes and after a scene her father was told and she was made to go to his house, Burlingham, until investigations were made. Although there was no proof that she was not innocent she was never allowed to go back to her husband's home, Intwood. This was evidently to guard the Muskett thousands from reaching any non-Muskett issue.

When examined, Mr. Muskett's sister said that he and his wife always seemed affectionate. The schoolmistress of the Ladies School where Mrs. Muskett—then Miss Jary—was from eight years old until she was sixteen gave her a good character. Then Mr. Jary's groom gave evidence. 'I am in the service of Mr. Jary, father of Mrs. Muskett, as groom. I was there before Mrs. Muskett was brought there by her husband in 1817 and have lived there ever since. In the course of that time the defendant has visited there for eight years. He sometimes slept there, sometimes dined and went home in the evening. I think he oftener stopped than went home. He used to ride out on horseback with Mrs. Muskett and I attended them. They appeared to be on very good terms. I have been in the habit of carrying letters from Mrs. Muskett to the defendant and from him to her. In October last year Mrs. Muskett appeared uncomfortable. She sent me with a letter to the defendant. He read it while I was there and said he knew all about it. She was with child by him and that he would take her in his care. I took back the note to my mistress and told her what the defendant had told me.'

She was missed from home about eight days after that.

When cross-examined he said he was constantly at Mr. Jary's the whole time from Mrs. Muskett's coming from her husband's and had remained there ever since. It was four years after her being brought home, before Mr. Gurney ever came to the house. For some time after he came backwards and forwards only when there was company there. During the four years that he did not come, Mrs. Muskett, who was not allowed to see her child, lived there constantly, and was never absent. Mr. Jary's groom never carried letters between them before the last five years. The visits were all open and known to the family. 'I have seen them together in the home, and never observed anything particular in their conduct to each other.'

James Tanner, the Northrepps coachman, then said: 'I was coachman to the late Mrs. Gurney, mother of the defendant, and I am at present living with himself. That is at 54 Montague Square, London. I have been living there with him for a fortnight or three weeks. In October last I drove Mr. Gurney to Burlingham —Mr. Jary's house—it was Tuesday, the fourteenth of October. Mr. Gurney told me he was going to take Mrs. Muskett away from Burlingham. Witness said that when Mrs. Muskett joined Mr. Gurney they arrived at Burlingham at night. They then drove to his house and from thence came on to town and are now living at Montague Square.' He admitted she was well advanced in pregnancy.

It was summed up as a most unusual case, one that could never be brought to court in any other country. But after half an hour it was found that Richard Hanbury Gurney had lost the case with damages for two thousand pounds.

In 1830, two months later, Mrs. Muskett was brought to bed of a daughter, Mary Jary, whose illegitimacy had been established in court and who, since neither Hudson, Gatty nor Anna were likely to have any children, became sole heir to all the estates left by their father and cousin Bartlett, including Keswick, Northrepps, and the Hadduck property.

Mrs. Muskett was at length divorced from her husband by Act of Parliament and Dick was able to marry her that year but the laws were still such that Mary Jary could never become legitimate, and Dan said that behind fans it was even suggested, particularly by those who might otherwise have benefited, that there was some doubt as to whether she even was Dick's daughter. One glance at her portrait and then at his shows these doubts as unfounded. Both are remarkably alike.

Mary Jary was brought up very quietly at Thickthorn with ponies and dogs as her chief companions. She was a pretty, lively child though given to tantrums, probably because, as an only child,

L

she was spoilt by both her parents. There is no indication that she saw much of the other children in the family of her generation when she was small. If she came to Hill House with her father, she must have bathed alone at Overstrand and played alone in the woods. Her mother, used to staying in during her long semi-captivity at her father's house, appears to have continued to stay very much at home after she married Dick. Few, if any, of the family seem to have made a habit of visiting her, probably more from her wish than theirs. No actual words of hers either in letters or in diaries survive, and so she remains a shadowy character much loved by her husband and daughter but rarely mentioned by others.

But one thing seems clear. The Dick Gurneys were an extremely affectionate and faithful couple and though Dick certainly strayed before marriage he apparently never did after it. He was returned to Parliament once more but at the next election he was too stout for the chairing through the streets of Norwich, when the candidate was borne by sixteen bearers, standing on a small platform in front of a chair, highly decorated with party colours. Every hundred yards or so the rider was thrown three or four times in the air with nothing to support him as he came down but the top of the chair back. Dan, who was still slim and agile, took Dick's place.

Dick was not re-elected, and Hudson did not again seek election and simultaneously withdrew from the bank. Dick who was a very much shrewder banker than his elder half-brother, had been less and less able to agree with the unbusinesslike investments Hudson made, often without due consultation. After a final disagreement Hudson agreed with his often haughty wife that anyway the ignominity of business was not really gentlemanly and he handed his partnership over to his cousin, Samuel Gurney, who had already proved himself a great businessman. Hudson had a fine income and no family so now devoted himself to planning a new and immensely grand Keswick Hall, which he later built half a mile away from the old Hall. This was the mansion with the great windows and water before it that had so awed me as a small child when I visited it with my grandmother. It is now a teachers' training college. The old Hall, which had almost doubled its size since Hudson's great-grandfather bought it to accommodate at one time two complete Gurney families, was let to Birkbeck cousins for nearly a hundred years. It is now the home of my own first cousin Dick, who inherited few of the characteristics of our great-great-grandfather of the same name except the ability to bank, breed prize cattle and ride straight to hounds.

During the winter of 1830, Betsey's eldest daughter, Katherine, stayed with her uncle Dan to help him finish his *Record of the House of Gournay* which he had begun when he was little more than a boy, and which was now ready to be published.

It was compiled from 'manuscripts in the British Museum, records in the Tower of London, and other public offices in London, as well as from manuscripts preserved in monasteries in Normandy'. But for many years this large, thick folio volume remained almost entirely in Katherine Fry's handwriting, with her original drawings and renderings of hundreds of coats of arms. Dan had hoped that it could be published by subscription and that Hudson, as head of the family, would give it his blessing as well as taking a generous share in financing it. But Hudson, with his mother and his wife both of undisputably ancient Barclay lines, was content with his Gurney ancestry being traced no farther back than to the Norwich Cobbler/Merchant Prince. With what some of the family called 'critical sarcasm', he referred to the book as 'The Apocryphal Book of Daniel' and composed one of his cryptic rhymes for its fly-leaf.

> 'The tadpole he dropt his tail in the mud
> A frog then crawls forth he
> And an ox stood quietly chewing the cud
> And an ox the frog would be
> But in this his ambition was cruelly worsted
> For he blew himself up till he bursted.'

Hudson's reply to the letter written by Katherine on Dan's behalf was as irritating to Dan in its manner as it was in its content.

'My dear Miss Fry, when a deputation went from Norwich to old Matthew Kerrison to ask his consent for Sir Edward Kerrison being proposed candidate for the City, his reply was, "I do not mind the £10,000, but I should not like my son to be made a fool of." Now, I do not think the expense of printing Daniel's book of the Gurney family would be matter of deep import. But the family existant being "made fools of" and that staringly and egregiously, is more than I could face.

'By presenting such a target as this to the Bitter Battery of Mockery would make both Cross and Pales fly endways, and never Fish would plunge headownwards into a Blacker Bearing.

'All families, be they who they may, have more to hide than to tell of, and when people rising from shop keeping into the jungle of a few halfpence (which they may possibly keep, and probably lose) will rejoice themselves in a Morris Dance to their Copper Music, let it be done in their own house, and not parade the streets in a Chimney Sweeper's Garland.

'Daniel's collection is well for the amusement of solitary vanity. Let him, if he can, prove the links which attach Beggary and Commerce to a Line of great Feudal Power and High Antiquity in Normandy.

'The sequence of the goings on of a *name* through all the varieties of Rank and Fortune would give a view of life and manners which it would be well to write, but it must be one to show what pretentions *are* and not one *of* pretentions, but still never to *publish*.'

The 'rise from shopkeeping' jingled to a tune of something more than a few halfpence according to a note in Hudson's diary twenty years later.

'In looking over papers for reference' (for a life of his cousin), 'I certainly find in my own case what is most singular.

John Gurney, 1670, was a thriving merchant of Norwich worth twenty thousand pounds.' (This was the Cobbler.)

'John Gurney, his grandson, died 1710, worth one hundred thousand pounds.

And I, the grandson of the last, wind up, 1850, with eight hundred thousand pounds.'

Dick was now, in the eighteen-thirties, only to be seen in London at Lord's Cricket Ground and fatstock shows, and Hudson only in the more elegant drawing-rooms. Fowell, however, became more active in Westminster than ever. In his whole-hearted attempts to ameliorate the appalling slave conditions in the British Colonies, he came under fierce attacks, not only from the planters but also from members of the government with interests in plantations, several of whom were Fowell's personal friends. When at last a resolve was passed that it was even desirable to improve conditions, the negroes themselves were excited by exaggerated reports which could not be kept from them, and fancied that the King of England had personally set them free and many of them refused to work. Soldiers were called in and a hundred slaves, who had not lifted a finger to hurt anyone, fell before their fire. Forty-seven were executed and ten were flogged to death. Fowell, of course, was accused of causing it all.

In 1832 came the Insurrection in Jamaica. The slave-holders tried to throw the blame on the missionaries and proceeded with acts of violence and cruelty against them in every possible way including torture. The government, for political reasons, were unwilling to take up the question. But Fowell was still determined to press his motion for the abolition of slavery, though every effort was used to prevent him from bringing it forward. His own friends said that he would only injure the cause if he persevered and they and other individual members of the government pressed him to withdraw it. He had over a hundred applications of this kind from different M.P.s. One of them went to see him four times and then sent a series of notes up to him, 'Immovable as ever?', 'Now don't be so obstinate' and 'You will only alienate the Government.' He said it was like a perpetual tooth-drawing. But he remained unflinching. He was, of course, in a minority but it was a larger one than he expected and deeply and painfully did he feel his unpopularity. For days afterwards he used to come home and mention with real grief that one or other of his former friends 'would not return his bow'. But he had done what he thought right and in 1833 the Bill for the Abolition of Slavery at least received the royal assent.

Fowell had a happy art of imbuing all those around him with his own feelings and inducing them to give him his most strenuous aid. Now he used it to persuade many influential and industrious ladies to work towards trying to sway public opinion in favour of pushing the bill through. Among his most vigorous supporters were the Cottage ladies at Northrepps. Thus, more than ever, daily notes passed between the Hall and Cottage—interspersed with the serious memorandums, frivolous little pencil scrawls of encouragement and gratitude appear: 'My ladies dear . . . What think you of having saved a nation? What think you of a lady's talent and industry being successfully dedicated to such a work?' and, another time: 'I must tell you a piece of news which has made me sing ever since I heard it. It is nothing short of this. The hand of the proud oppressor in Africa has been, under Providence, arrested by Miss Gurney of Northrepps Cottage, and a whole nation doomed by the one to exile, ruin and death has been delivered by the other and restored to a degree which surpasses all our dreams.' And again: 'The slave trade is uppermost in my mind, but let me give you, Miss Anna, a great lecture. I hear evil things of you, namely that you are so inveterately industrious that you are working yourself to death. Pray be more moderate and self-merciful. Such desperate efforts do not answer.'

But Fowell himself showed no self-mercy and often lashed himself into a state of utter exhaustion when he would stretch himself out on the specially long sofa in the drawing-room at Northrepps Hall and wait till he recovered. If he could be read aloud to, so much the better. And yet, however tired, he seemed to be ever watchful for opportunities for heaping kindness on those he loved.

His schoolboy son, Fowell, wrote in his diary: 'I cannot help being struck with the exquisite tenderness of heart that my father always displays, his unwillingness to debar us from pleasure, the zeal with which he will make any sacrifice or take any trouble to gratify us. One little example today—he being really unwell was lying nearly asleep on the sofa, and seeing me on another with my feet hanging over the side he quietly got up, placed the chair under them and then lay down again.'

Priscilla, who herself worked extremely hard as her father's secretary, writes from Northrepps: 'My father is uncommonly bright and Anna seeks to work with a kind of intensity which is most interesting to see. We all sit round like ostrichs' eggs outside the nest to look on and give our assistance from time to time.'

Thanks to a huge female following, Fowell was able to present a petition bearing 187,000 signatures from British women in favour of the abolition of slavery. The roll was so enormous that it required four men to lay it on a table in the House of Commons.

Priscilla wrote to the Cottage ladies: 'After this letter I think I must burn my paper and pens and give my poor tired wrist, which is nearly worn out and always aching, some rest. I am tired, most utterly tired, of writing and everything connected with work. As for petitions I only wish I might never see the face of another. What a bad mind you will think I am in.'

The following June she became engaged to Andrew Johnston of Fifeshire, M.P. for St. Andrews, whom Fowell described as: 'A dear fellow, who will not bother with such delicacies in the country as a hat.' He, in turn, found Fowell 'a delightful chief to work for—so stimulating, yet so indulgent, and so ready to pay with lavish liberalities every effort, however trifling, made.'

At the end of the next month Fowell was able to write in his journal: 'On Friday next slavery is to cease throughout the British Colonies.' While Priscilla looked forward to the same day in hers: 'Here is the eve of my wedding-day, I am going to lock up my desk and close my single life.'

CHAPTER SEVENTEEN

The Literary—or Waste-Paper basket— Society

PRISCILLA wrote of how on her wedding-day she had helped to adorn her lovely bridesmaid and sister: 'I felt so bright, I let them all come into my room and, in glee, I was dressed in my bridal white satin. The girls were a sight, one no more beautiful than another; they were in fairy white, and all wore natural flowers, mostly in their hair. The scarlet geraniums in Kitty Hoare's shining locks was one of the most lovely pictures I ever saw. My shoes pinched me dreadfully, but the girls only laughed at my cramp. By the·altar sat Aunt Sarah and Anna Gurney. My father made a great muddle, and would hardly let me get to the rails, and after all settled himself on the wrong side. "I will," said Mr. Johnston, in so sturdy a manner and so broad a Scotch accent that I (inwardly) laughed.'

She went on to describe the combined wedding reception and celebration for the triumph over the slaves. 'After sufficient loitering the party gathered and my father took his place by the table in the drawing-room. He read several passages and his prayer was noble—most bold and steadfast—first for the slaves and, to my comfort, he found words for me but with a faltering voice.' Priscilla wept when he said: 'are they not more to me than silver and gold?' and her father came and comforted her on the sofa while everyone sang a hymn. In then came her cousins bringing the silver salver on which is inscribed 'To Thomas Fowell Buxton Esquire M.P. presented by his nephews and nieces, August 1st, 1834, with the humble but earnest desire that they may be enabled to act through life upon those high principles which have led him with undaunted resolution to pursue the noble object, by the blessing of God this day accomplished, in the abolition of slavery throughout the British Dominion. Tu ne cede malis sed, contra audentior ito.'

Now it was Fowell who burst into tears and everyone had to go out into the garden for a breath of air to recover for the lunch at which fifty-two guests were seated, with Priscilla presiding, flowering myrtle and pomegranate in her hair. There was champagne and toasts, and afterwards several people took it in turns to read poetry, some of which was their own, written specially for the occasion. Priscilla changed into her dove-coloured silk, blue bonnet, white scarf and veil, took leave of her precious mother upstairs with many tears, and was almost carried downstairs by her father who could speak to no one else. All the world was gathered at the drawing-room door. Priscilla kissed the front row, and the Cottage ladies in the dining-room, and off she went with her Scotsman.

Fowell immediately sat down and wrote to Mrs. Upcher, a pillar among his workers, who was unable to be there. 'Aug. 1 4 o'clock My dear Friend, the bride is just off. Everything has passed off to admiration and there is not a slave in the British Colonies! Mark the seal "safe and satisfactory".' The set of seals bearing these and other useful recurrent tidings still exists.

Anna wrote to Priscilla from Northrepps Cottage to tell her how things were going after she had left home.

'My dearest Priscilla, It just comes into my mind to give you a little sketch of our state and condition. I wish you could just now see us in our very quiet life, at this moment my partner playing some gay tunes while I am writing—door open into the drawing-room—I often long to record the happiness of these days, but you might as well try to bottle the fragrance of the furze-blossom, and after all there is the shivery sense of its not lasting. So far we are very comfortable and tolerably prudent. My partner has just given up coming down to family reading, so I have found Jeremiah for myself and Randle, etc. We have perched up a new gallery in the church at Overstrand, it is over the tower door, and the organ is to stand there. It was not, however, finished yesterday but the church was so full, we were glad to tumble up my boys into it sailor fashion, a feat they enjoyed performing for the benefit of our eyes. There were fourteen of them, and a diadem they were to our congregation, not above two of them asleep, and the others far too delighted with their perch to think of absconding. I really am as pleased with my converts as St. Paul could have been with his saints that were at Ephesus, and gave them much the same advice, viz. to let all clamour be put away from them.

'I hope you will not think me in a naughty mind, for I am in a remarkably good one. I have had two days of fishing—a few soles that would make your father sing for joy; no curiosities, but one nasty creature that I felt bound to preserve for Charles, and so I bundled it into my tract case, and he is such a monster that I do not like to look for him, and take him out. Do not let your father forget that if he wants any Dutch books or papers overhauled, I can do it for him, and with great glee, if he will employ me.'

The organ arrived, a small barrel-organ almost more really in the nature of a musical box. This instrument could play twelve tunes, and all was ready for it to be played on Sunday. The congregation sang through the first hymn until the end but not so the organ, which went through the second hymn and as nobody could remember how to stop it, it had finally to be lowered from the gallery and carried out into the churchyard where it was heard playing out the remainder of its repertoire.

Sarah writes later from the Cottage: 'My Dearest Niece, In this storm I will write to you. Perhaps a gale without may sober down the hurricane of my impetuous feelings within, and I may be able, under the bustle of the morning, to slide in easily a letter to you.

'The wind is blustering at our windows, the boughs and even the stems of the trees, rocking to and fro. Wamba asleep on the chair, one puss on one sofa, and Spot on the other, a primrose in the dormer window and one little stand of glasses for Hyacinths in another but the green buds scarcely show themselves yet. I have no desire for January's blossoms since my flowers are not here to admire them. My eyes are towards the cliffs, and I write to you by snatches, I run to the kitchen to make sure that we have hot water, soup and fires. We have had no reading of the family and scarcely any sleep from anxiety and before six we heard that a crew of nine men had left their sinking vessel in their little boats and had reached the shore, off Cromer, in safety. Soon after seven, Anna started in her pony-chaise with Hannah Roper and William. She returned alone half an hour since, the little boy'—the house-boy—'only following her. She looked distressed but could not wait, or I, to face the wind in our porch. Stephen jumped in to return with her and her little hand-gun, with its lines, etc. I made another messenger scamper to The Hall and very shortly "The Chief of Ten Thousand" on John Bull, with coat-flaps flying, galloped by. I can only gather that there is another vessel off Cromer in peril, striving to come in. Oh! May the lives be spared! Another report— the vessel has struck and with glasses, from our coast, some poor creatures were seen getting into the boat, and they were lost. And our watchers say they can see some still on the vessel; and at this moment I conclude your father has joined Anna and they are labouring to save them.

'Anna now home—sullen with cold and pain, she is taking off her things; and I shall hear more when she can bear it, you know how her heart writhes under the tortures of a calamity—hope quenched and five lives lost before her eyes.'

This kind of scene was almost a common occurrence in winter. Hannah Roper, the maid, and even the faithful menservants, Spink and William, did not always set out in quite the same spirit of enthusiasm as their mistress did, as they heaved and pushed her rather cumbersome chair, particularly as she was putting on considerable weight. Stephen, according to a note against his name by Anna was 'aged fourteen and engaged by my partner. She *lost* her footman on his first excursion to The Hall behind the carriage, but he came to hand again before church and attended me there exciting much reverence amongst the men and boys of Overstrand on his first appearance in livery.'

The loss of life at sea was a constant worry to Anna and she was determined to use what knowledge she had gained to try to bring down the numbers with continual letters to Trinity House.

She said that within the last four or five years the wrecks had increased owing to the natural filling up of a passage which brought vessels in a new direction on to Happisburgh sands. She thought that a floating light at the north end of Happisburgh sands could prevent many accidents. As there was no possibility of sending assistance from the shore, twelve miles or more away, she also thought a small lifeboat should be attached to the floating light. She had noticed that vessels frequently went to pieces in twenty minutes after they struck the sands.

Such was the effect that Trinity House placed a lightship off 'Hasebro' as the fishermen called it, which was always known as The Gurney Light. Fowell congratulated her: 'My dear Anna, Long life to the new light and to the determination (some people call it obstinacy) which extracted it from the reluctant brethren of the Trinity House.

'I hope that it will save fifty lives every year, and that every first of January you may feel cheerful and happy in the consciousness that you have done some real good to the mariners.

'The ladies are talking so loud and so fast on the subject of indiarubber shoes, which seems to engross their minds this first Sabbath of the year, that I can say no more, except dearest love and my best wishes to Sarah.'

The Belfry School at Overstrand was complete, a small rectangular school-house which now forms the kitchen of the Overstrand Primary School, but then was the whole school. Anna and Sarah went down to teach the children there every day, though the soup was still made in the Cottage kitchen and brought to the school by the so far uncomplaining Spink.

During the Easter recess Fowell went to Northrepps alone, but the Hall was cold and lonely so he stayed at Northrepps Cottage. He writes to Hannah: 'After a cheerful breakfast I lounged with a book to The Hall. It looks brighter than I expected, the day so fine, the flowers so abundant, and the birds so happy. I am going to sell the sheep, so there is an end to that sagacious speculation. Anna called for me there and took me first to a cranio-logist, who spent an hour over my head and told me strange news of myself; some hitting the mark and others far from it. Then we drove to Trimingham where we looked at fossils and the calm sea and the land which I am to have for shooting. We got home about two o'clock and she read to me till a quite lively dinner, everything vastly agreeable. Moscow', his Newfoundland dog, 'was allowed to come in and dine with us. After dinner, reading and a trifle of sleep and so on till now. The only take off is that I am quite out of my element, hardly knowing what to do in the country at this time of year.'

The next wedding with Northrepps repercussions was between Fowell's nephew, Edmund, who, since his father's death, had lived so much with Hannah and Fowell that he was described 'of Northrepps', and Mrs. Upcher's eldest daughter, Charlotte. The day before, Anna gave a party for them at Northrepps Cottage. The Cromer blacksmith, Curtis, brought his cannon to fire in their honour, as was his custom when attention was required to be drawn to shipwrecks, fires and particularly joyous occasions. This eventually far from joyous occasion was reported in the hand-written *Cromer Telegraph* under 'Express from Northrepps Hall'. 'As a cannon was firing this evening in honour of Mr. E. Buxton's intended marriage with Miss Upcher of Sheringham, it being too hard loaded, burst, and the unfortunate blacksmith who was firing it was shot and fell down dead instantly, leaving a wife and five children to lament his loss.'

The Coroner's inquest is reported, with a verdict of accidental death followed by a formal announcement of the marriage.

Fowell and Hannah's eldest boy, Edward, was next to fall in love and no objections were raised when he became engaged to his first cousin, Catherine (who had shut her baby sister in a drawer).

'I take it very kind of Providence to give me a new child,' Fowell said. 'Just the person I most like. Just the person to make Edward happy.'

Catherine's father, Samuel Gurney, was happy too but could not, as a Quaker, attend the wedding and stipulated that it must be a quiet one, with no wedding bells and only such carriages as were really necessary. Less on religious grounds than those of his own wealth, he also said that none of his young nephews and nieces' wedding presents were to cost more than ten shillings.

Samuel remembered what it was like to be on a small salary from the time he had been in his brother-in-law, Joe Fry's counting house as a boy. He had subsequently invested his wife, Elizabeth Sheppard's fortune—she was a co-heiress of Bartlett's and the daughter of a wealthy mast-maker—in the firm of Richardson, Overend and Gurney and Co., which for forty years was said to be 'owing to the extraordinary sagacity, courage and prudence of Samuel Gurney, the largest and best conducted money business in existence, lending so much to other houses that it was known as the Banker's Bank.'

The two families—the Fowell Buxtons and the Samuel Gurneys —had much in common, including an ardent love of animals and birds; very tame kangaroos, peacocks and cockatoos were at large in the gardens and parks of both homes. The parents of both families were strong supporters of the Anti-Cruelty Society for the Protection of Animals, which Wilberforce, Fowell and Betsey had helped to launch.

Catherine's childhood at Upton was not so unlike Edward's at Northrepps. 'Our father,' she wrote, 'however tired after a long day of business in Lombard Street, was always ready to preside at our occupations as we gathered round the great table. He often had a good play with the younger ones before we settled, swinging them in the curtain or romping on the floor in the greatest merriment with a parrot or kitten while the mother cat lay on the rug at our mother's feet. Then he generally had a map spread before him which he would study if not wanted for a moment, or a book of good prints, or in his unique style he would read aloud some delightful book whether light or important. He was very fond of science and we all remember our great amusement at what we thought the fantastical ideas about steam. He laughed and we laughed at the idea of his going to Lombard Street up Whitechapel Road at ten miles an hour behind some form of boiler.'

The wedding was to take place in London and the bride was to be given away by Hudson, who had just finished his term of office of High Sheriff of Norfolk and was still struggling to write his one great poem. He saw Catherine off to the church but did not go in her carriage, saying he would follow. When she arrived neither bridegroom nor guests were there. She waited for an hour in the vestry, as did the guests and Hudson in another St. James's church, till Fowell, guessing she must have driven to the wrong church, went off to find her.

Sam and Louisa Hoare's thirteen-year-old daughter, Kitty, who had been a much admired bridesmaid at the last wedding, describes this one to her younger brother Richard, in much the same style as Louisa's own uninhibited writing at the same age.

'We, i.e. Papa, Mama, Miss F and myself started from here. Gurney and Joseph on horseback. Altogether a very respectable turn-out, though Joseph's waistcoat was rather old and Papa, except for the white gloves, looked rather more as if he was going to a funeral.' She describes the confusion of the lost bride at length and then, on the way home in one of the carriages, 'it was my sad lot to be turned out, all but at the door, to go to the Frys, only. Fancy the tantalization! However, after a little walk around the garden with Uncle Fry, Aunt ditto pityingly ordered me some luncheon. I walked a little way with her and in this way met Uncle Gurney who said I might go to the breakfast. If you can imagine anything of excessive delight think of me at that moment!' (By Aunt ditto she meant Betsey Elizabeth Fry and by Uncle Gurney she meant the bride's father.)

'I quite forgot to tell you that we were greeted at the church with a most merry peal of bells which rang for Catherine under the pretence of ringing for another wedding.

'In we went—it was a most *beautiful breakfast*, most pretty it was. The bride and bridegroom and thirty two people, this "quiet" wedding—mobs, bells ringing and 32 people at the breakfast.'

She describes every mouthful and ends:

'Pray *don't send this anywhere*, if you do I will never write to you about such *things again*. I wonder whether I shall have to write an account of your wedding. A beautiful sandwich box enclosed in an elegant basket trimmed with white satin ribbons was your present, dear Richard—under 10s.'

Only a few months later their mother died, of grief, it was said, over her own education theories failing with one of her other sons, whose behaviour at school was temporarily not of the best. But it was not like Louisa to grieve and it was more likely that some undiagnosed illness caused her to worry generally. She was only fifty and had always been very close to Hannah, both before and, as the survivors of the 'Three Dear Pairs', after marriage. Hannah took two of Louisa's children, Kitty and Richard, back to Northrepps and Richard remained in her care till he grew up.

Besides the home party of children of Chenda, Fowell and Charles Buxton and Richard Hoare, the other Hoare children were frequently at Northrepps as were Jackey and his sister Anna of Earlham. They were all within a few years of the same age and led by Jackey they formed a Naturalists' Society for which they were to write essays and give lectures. Jackey, then sixteen, had lately been to a Quaker Meeting where his father was preaching and on the way killed a weasel and put it into his hat for safe keeping. There was an unexpected collection and innocently his father announced, 'My son will take his hat round,' and Jackey, forgetting the dead weasel in it, straightened his shoulders and holding his head erect, set off with it round the congregation.

Affectionately, this story circulated the family, with some amused sympathy for Joseph John. But for Jackey, skinning and stuffing was a serious business, too serious for the rest of the Northrepps party as it turned out, for gradually the Naturalists' Society tailed off. However it was replaced later by the Northrepps Literary Society, which met in the presence of the entire household, above and below stairs, to read scientific and literary essays. It started off with titles of great distinction with such beginnings as: 'In tracing the commercial history of the world we may observe . . .' Fortunately for the audience the high level of these meetings sank and more cheerful evenings were had, in character somewhere between Bible Meetings and Family Consequence. One of the members who had been invited to contribute a Logical Statement, offered:

'A logical proof that young Fowell, by bringing dirty shoes into the drawing-room confers a great benefit on Lizzy.

'If no dirt came into the drawing-room, the drawing-room could not become dirty.

'And if the room did not get dirty it would not require to be cleaned.

'And if the drawing-room did not require to be cleaned, Lizzy, would, of course, not be wanted to clean it.

'And therefore Lizzy would not enjoy her present honourable situation of housemaid to Mr. Buxton.

'And therefore she would be obliged to gain her livelihood by some menial employment, as for example, getting married.

'Therefore, those who bring dirt into the drawing-room confer a benefit to Lizzy.

'Still more, therefore, Fowell, who brings dirt into the drawing-room at the rate perhaps of a cartload per anum confers a great benefit on Lizzy, quod erat demonstrandum.

'Corollary. Fowell confers a great benefit on Lizzy, therefore Lizzy being grateful, pats Fowell's head and calls him a dear boy. But Lizzy threatens Fowell with the broomstick if he ever brings dirty shoes into the drawing-room again. Therefore Lizzy is an ungrateful hussy.'

Their father referred to the society as: 'a revival of the old *Cromer Examiner*, which had always been known locally as 'The Wastepaper Basket'.

Hudson's poetry was too serious to him to allow him to take part but Joseph John turned up with Jackey at one of the meetings and wrote to order a few verses on Chenda.

M

'Until some gentle swain and true
Shall find his heart well smitten,
My husband is a cockatoo,
My bosom friend a kitten.

On a single wing my cockatoo
From house to house was tripping,
Some fifty other maids to woo
I cured him with a clipping.

My kitten too in water clear,
Deserves a deadly sousing,
For oft he leaves his lady dear,
And skips away a-mousing.

Alas alas what shall I do?
With such perfidious rovers?
Avount my kitt, my cockatoo,
Henceforth I scorn all lovers.'

In a round childish hand remains, as a reminder of many
evenings:

'AN EVENING AT NORTHREPPS HALL
Says Charles, "Who comes, Mamma, tonight?"
"The Cottage Ladies, dear," "That's right."
The smaller folks all stand aghast
To see the Giant striding past.
He marches on, and there he stands,
By horses's measure, twenty hands
At least in height, Compar's to us
Goliath as to David was.
No books for pleasure them he seeks.
But lays him down—the sofa creaks—
Miss Gurney comes and brings a book
All idle works are then forsook.
For what? Because this great man deigns
To read of deaths, and hear the pains

Of negroes, slaves, poor helpless men
"They have no mind," some say. "What then?"
But to return, Miss Gurney reads
A sentence. Says Mrs. B "Who feeds
The stork when Charles is out?" "My dear,
We're reading what should draw a tear,
Of starving men, not birds. Go on
Miss Gurney, we shall ne'er have done."

  Miss Gurney reads. 'Twas not for long
The Ladies held their slipp'ry tongue.
They talk, they whisper. "I will go."
Says Mrs. B "You chatter so."

  That silenced them, for to appear
To wish him gone they greatly fear.
He sleeps—but lest we should mistake
His sleep and carelessly should wake
His pleasant doze, he tells us plain
By snoring o'er and o'er again.
At length the tea-time comes, and he
Is snoring more complacently.
"Come! Come!" says Mrs. B "my dear.
"Wake! Wake! 'tis time, the tea is here."
"I'm wide awake, my dear, I am."
"I'm not quite sure of that. Hem! Hem!"
He snores again—His tea gets cold.
Poor Esther knows that he will scold
To find it so. At length a cry,
Which she does hear most joyfully
Of "Spectacles—a boy—a boy
"What are you made for—to employ."

  His tea is cold. His temper hot.
"You've put no water in the pot."
The tea is almost done, when Lo!
In comes the Hoares. "How do." "How do."
Pass quickly round. "You're very late.

We've just done tea—we could not wait."
The evening's spent in merry talk.
The Hoares go home—some ride—some walk.

The cottage ladies disappear.
The supper comes with ginger beer.
When all sufficiently are fed,
They leave the room and go to bed.

Thus ends an evening at the Hall.
I've mentioned many great and small.
Some well, some ill, but all I've served
Just as their character deserved.'

Fowell delighted in being cheeked by his youngers and as he was perpetually sweet-tempered, heartily enjoyed allusions to his pseudo-gruffness. Hannah, however, evidently did not approve of the idea of her dearest Fowell being said to snore for each 'snoring' is crossed out and 'sleeping' substituted.

CHAPTER EIGHTEEN

Spink and the Pope

THE year Queen Victoria came to the throne, Fowell wrote
to Samuel Gurney's wife to comfort her after visiting her
dying mother.

'I this day saw our youthful queen, surrounded by all the chief
officers of state, herself wearing a crown of diamonds and arrayed
in royal robes, the house of lords filled with all the great ones of the
country. She delivered an admirable address to parliament with the
utmost sweetness of voice and most exquisite grace of manner; and
yet this spectacle left a less lively impression on my mind than the
sight which I had yesterday, the pleasure of witnessing an aged
Christian refined and purified, her world completed, waiting in
patient cheerfulness the will of her Lord. That is a sight full of
instruction and consolation.'

The same summer, after constant warnings from his doctor, he
was writing to Hannah: 'Well my dearest wife, Your wishes are
realised. The troubles and worries of parliament are over with me;
and now we must be as happy, as healthy and as long-lived as
possible. I am perfectly satisfied with the result and view it as a
release from a vast deal of labour.'

That summer Joseph John set off for three years to America to
preach, with the gospel, anti-slavery and restraint from war. Once
again he was a widower, for his second wife who had tried to
change the face of Earlham had nursed young Anna with scarlet
fever and died of it herself. Kitty, who was all ready to step back
again into her old place, endured no small trial in seeing Joseph
John's deceased wife's sister put in charge of Earlham instead while
he was away. Anna of Earlham, now fourteen, found herself forced
to write out a list of rules to remind herself what her duty should

be to her two very different aunts who were both to live at Earlham.

Many of Joseph John's admirers went to see him off from his ship, including Betsey, who, when she went to his cabin to arrange flowers, found the other admirers and was unable to resist bearing them off to buy books to set up a ship's library. As a niece of hers once remarked: 'It is droll to see how our aunt makes *all* work, who ever they may be.'

Little escaped her attention. A few weeks later she went to speak to prisoners at Plymouth and was heard in a most kindly and persuasive manner pointing out to the fishermen how they might kill lobsters to prevent the cruelty of boiling them alive.

Fowell writes to Joseph John on his way to America: 'I had fully resolved, had I continued in parliament, to have sent you a kind of journal of notable events, but in my present non-effective condition I am not likely to have anything more interesting to tell you than the history of the pigs and poultry at Northrepps. As I leave parliament for health, I do not by any means intend to defeat that end by dedicating myself to any other objects. I mean, for conscience sake, to ride, amuse myself and grow fat and flourishing'.

He writes from Northrepps to his ancient Uncle Charles:

'I take shooting very easy this year, having always a shooting pony with me; he is a wonder, has as good action as your old leader and is as handsome; quiet as a lamb; strong enough to carry, and sometimes does carry, Sam Hoare and myself together; eats bread and cheese; drinks beer; is a particularly good judge of porter and prefers ours.'

And to his eldest son Edward:

'I have again made an alteration in my gun stock contrary to your advice. I have shot execrably all the year and could stand it no longer so I employed a Holt carpenter to hew me a stock according to my own fancy out of the trunk of a tree. It is in its primitive simplicity, and is so wide as to "contrive the double debt to pay" of stock while shooting and table at luncheon; but rough and awkward as it is, I shall, I trust, take the conceit out of the young men with it.

'I have been calculating that since Parliament closed I have ridden 500 miles and walked 1,500.

> Better to hunt in fields for health unbought
> Than fee the doctor for a nauseous draught,
> The wise, for cure, on exercise depend.

So sang Dryden, and what he preached I practise.

'I shall send you a basket tonight as proof that my log of a gunstock can do execution. We are very happy here. If you catch influenza, lie up at once.—principiis obsta.'

Great preparations were made for the following Christmas when Priscilla and Andrew Johnston were to return to Northrepps for the birth of their third baby. They sailed from Dundee and after a buffeting thirty-hours passage reached Cromer and, like the coal at that time, were landed directly on the sands for the usual want of a sound pier. 'They drove up to Northrepps but fearing too sudden a surprise, for they had been unable to give any warning of the day of their arrival, decided to stop by the pond. Andrew crept in by the backyard and found the party all reading. In a few moments Chenda and her father came tearing out and, amid acclamations of all kinds, the party were got into the drawing-room.'

After a tremendous Christmas gathering with all the family, Prissy retired to the ante-room with the five doors, where she gave birth to a son.

The bad weather set in and Hannah had a succession of colds. And so began much talk about spending the next winter in Italy. Anna, who had been abroad several times with Sarah, had a scholar's yearning to go to Athens, and suggested she and Sarah should first visit Greece and then join the others in Rome. Elaborate plans were made about how they should travel.

Fowell wrote from the brewery in London during the summer:

'My dear Ladies, I have received your magnificent packet today and mean to read it with the party tonight. If we do meet at Rome this winter we *will* enjoy ourselves, "We'll never do nothing whatever on earth" and if that is not pleasure, what is? I'm sick of turmoiling.'

But alas, only a week before they were to start, their plans were sadly frustrated. The Cottage ladies had gone to stay for a few days at Clifton and while they were away, first their beloved footman, William, was drowned while bathing at Overstrand, and a few days later a 'letter-summons' arrived at Northrepps at two in the morning from the doctor at Clifton, telling Fowell that his sister Sarah was seriously ill. It was decided that Fowell and Priscilla should go at once and by four o'clock they were off. On their way they were stopped in the road and told by a passenger in the down coach that all was over.

All Sarah's schoolchildren attended the funeral—the boys in black pinafores, the girls in black frocks—as well as fishermen without number, with long flowing hair and weather-beaten faces.

Harry's vault in the ruins of Overstrand church was opened to receive the remains of his aunt, on whose coffin Anna leant till the end. Richenda of Earlham's clergyman husband leapt on to a grave and, unrobed as he was, preached a combined funeral service to cover both Sarah and her drowned footman.

Anna also preached a sermon, beginning: 'Oh Lord, now that my partner's lips are closed, enable me to implore thy blessing on all those she so dearly loved.' A marble scroll unfolds forever over an arch in Overstrand church to Sarah Buxton 'inscribed by her sorrowing relative and partner, Anna Gurney'. Another beside it commemorates 'the sisters and partners in the love of the Lord'.

Dan said that 'although she had frequent intimate friends staying with her, Anna never again had what she used to call a "partner".'

It was decided that the journey abroad should still be made, but Anna would put off starting till Fowell was able to go, when he had finished writing his book, *The Slave Trade and its Remedy*.

Hannah left with a bunch of children and their tutor, on the day arranged, only three days after Sarah's funeral. She writes from their first stop to Fowell who was unable to see them off.

'We had a very sorrowful departure from Northrepps, there were many tears from all but the two Ashantee princes, who stood amazed at the scene, staring with their black faces. We hope to sail from London tomorrow.'

The Ashantee princes were two of the many dark-skinned visitors who stayed at Northrepps, some of them ex-slaves and one of them an ex-slave bishop. In our day a favourite guest was a bishop we called in the nursery 'The Chocolate Biscuit'.

On November 3rd Fowell wrote to Hannah from Northrepps Hall:

'I have been working hard during the week, but yesterday we had our hardest day. With the exception of a few minutes in the garden, and a run to the Cottage, and dinner, I did not stop from breakfast till past one o'clock at night, and what is more extraordinary, I had seven capital secretaries at work, and many of them during the whole day. We got on famously; till then I had been very doubtful whether I should not be obliged to stay a week longer'.

A fortnight later he climbed into the carriage outside the front door, in which Anna and young Fowell were already settled, and gave the order, 'To Rome'. The specially curved trunks, made by Billy Silver to fit the roof of the carriage for the journey, still lie at the back of the coachhouse. The main baggage cart, with Anna's chair and Spink and the maids, had already started for the London docks.

At Northrepps Hall, great 'improvements' were to be made during the family's absence, both to the house and grounds.

Fowell wrote to Priscilla next day from London:

'My book is finished; there it lies in the bag; a precious tug it has been to get done. I do not think I have worked so hard since I left college; day after day, from breakfast till two or three o'clock. I quite wonder at my capacity for exertion.'

And from Montreul, near Le Touquet the day after:

'Since I left London I have spent four hours in sailing, some time in meals, a few minutes in chat and reading, but my great business has been *sleeping*, which I have effected with laudable energy.'

It was a tedious and dangerous journey during which, Fowell said, they 'were in the carriage, and moving, at a quarter to four in the morning, and out of the carriage at twelve o'clock at night. The last two stages were rather awkward ones to pass in the dark, we had a continued succession of precipices on one side of the road. On seeing a light straight down an immense way below us, Anna said: "There is a star, only in the wrong direction." '

Fowell writes from Rome to his son Edward:

'I picture to myself your arriving at Northrepps on Monday and you and your party hugely enjoying yourselves during the week; and I fancy I know precisely where you shot each day, if not the exact number of the slain. I thought you had an especial nice party. I suppose that Edward Hoare was at the top of the tree? I hope you took decent care of yourselves, age and wisdom being absent, I at Rome and Sam Hoare at Lombard Street. You may well suppose that I am "un peu fâché" to be absent for the first time for more than twenty years from my humble task of attending to the wants and promoting the sport of a rabble of boys. I resolved, however, to console myself as best I might and I accomplished this so effectively that I am ready to back the Pontine Marshes against all Norfolk.' He then describes a snipe shoot with three Italian pointers, Spink and two other guns. They had already been shown the blood in the road of a man who had been murdered the night before with a little cross stuck into the hedge to commemorate the event. Spink, who had heard there were more robbers and assassins here than anywhere else in Italy, had borrowed a small single-barrelled gun. They shot a few snipe, but there were not many so they had a picnic and started back to the carriage. But 'Spink was seduced by a jacksnipe someway back, went after it and killed it. No sooner was his gun off than, from a broad almost impenetrable hedge crossing a swamp, out rushed two fellows, one seized his gun, the other his collar and kicked his shin, and out of his side pocket drew his long knife. Could any situation be more forlorn?

We out of hearing, his gun discharged, his knees knocking together, his head turning round and round, his heart in his mouth.
I use his own expressions. What did he do? Why, exactly the right
thing. He let go his gun, he put his hands in his pockets and produced from each a pistol, loaded, capped and cocked. The state of
affairs was suddenly changed. The robbers, who a moment ago had
jabbered so loud and kicked so hard, turned tail, dropped the gun
and dashed into the hedge, and Spink remained master of the field.
But not for long. "I did not know where I was," Spink told us,
"nor anything about it; I ran through a pool up to my waist and
never stopped till I fell from fright and want of breath, then I
loaded and fired my gun as a signal." We of course who had waited
nearly half an hour for him thought it very cool to be following his
sport while we kicked our heels. "Why the man must have got a
charm," suggested the *cacciatore*, "he has had more shots than any
of us put together." Little did we dream the poor fellow was in
the extremity of distress, not knowing whether his road lay to the
right or to the left. When he fired again it occurred to me he might
be making signals so replied, which shots he never heard, probably
because he was lying down in a kind of swoon, I began to haloo as
loud as I could and at length he heard me and came running after
us.

'I was just beginning an oration on keeping us waiting when I
saw his face pale as ashes and looking most strange and bewildered
so I gave him brandy instead. Then followed his most graphic and
natural description of his exquisite terror; his conviction that
neither he nor his mistress would ever have been happy again if the
blood of the men had been on his hands; his deep detestation of
snipe-shooting, marshes, Rome, and the Romans; his solemn
resolution never to quit my side if he had the misfortune to go a-
shooting ever again, and his anxious enquiries whether we thought
there was any chance of our getting back to Rome without en-
countering a fresh gang of *banditti*, beguiled our way home.'

The next letter to arrive at Northrepps is of a rather different
experience.

'Today I have been in the house of the heir to the Caesars and the successor of St. Peter. The Pope is a civil, lively little gentleman. He was very inquisitive to know what I thought of the Roman prisons. Baron Kestner, the Hanoverian Ambassador, who knows neither English nor Italian, interpreted for us, and I heard said for me rather more than I liked, "*contentissimo.*" Having praised wherever I could, I gently intimated that the Roman jails in general *wanted a good bit of purification.*

'I told him of the satisfaction his Bull had given in England and he seemed not a little proud of what he had done, saying: "Thanks to me, if you please." Having disposed of my own two pets, prisons and slave trade, I felt constrained to put in a word relative to some atrociously cruel practises here, such as the treatment of lambs to the butchers. He hardly seemed ripe for this, but our interpreter stuck to it manfully and I gave the Pope Anna's paper on the subject and he promised to give it his consideration.'

While Anna and the children pushed on to Athens, Fowell nearly died in Rome of 'previous overwork' but managed to avoid being either bled, or moved on elsewhere. He even seemed to extract some pleasure out of it all. 'I enjoy to have Hannah fidgeting about me all day and all night. I recreate myself in watching her and in thinking of the goodness of Providence in folding up in one person the general characters of nurse, tutor, friend, chaplain and wife and giving the prize to me.'

When Anna and the children returned from Athens, he said, 'Anna is my glass of champagne. I send for her when I want to be brightened up and she never fails.'

The party returned to Northrepps to find all the alterations carried out. As they came up the drive, there were the newly built stables modelled on Dick's at Hill House, with the cobbled loose boxes, stalls, coachhouse and coachman's cottage built halfway round the cobbled yard, and a cobbled wall of the same neatly matched egg-sized stones round the rest.

Round the pond the cobbled wall had been built with steps down to the water. On the other side of the house the old farm buildings had been pulled down, all but one wall of the barn, against which creepers were already beginning to grow.

What had once been the herb garden was now the Italian-inspired *parterre* round which countless grandchildren were from then onwards to totter. What had been the horse-pond beyond it was grassed over to make the sloping lawn down which they would roll.

Inside the house, the drawing-room was made longer and higher with the french window opening on to the rose-garden, with a little boudoir above it. A banksia rose had already been planted to hide the almost imperceptible join in the square-cut grey flints.

In the back yard new larders and a laundry were beginning to form the present enclosed cobbled square.

The family had only been back from Rome a few weeks when the Prime Minister, Lord John Russell, sent for Fowell and said, 'Now, Mr. Buxton, I want to put a question to you. Will you give me a candid answer?' Fowell, having so often to represent the interest of others, hesitated and said he must know what the question was first. 'Would you like to be made a baronet?' It was a laughable change. They discussed the matter and eventually Fowell said slowly that he would like to leave a strong anti-slavery anti-slave trade memorial to his family, though it meant little to him, 'only to call Hannah "my lady", that I should like'. He discussed it with his children but kept it a secret from Hannah. The children decided that he should accept it, and even the members of the family who were still Quakers felt it would be right.

Soon afterwards the Ministry seemed likely to go out and Fowell smiled to Edward, his eldest son, who had been the least keen on acceptance. 'An uncommon good end to the baronetcy!' But the Ministry remained and when Hannah heard about it at a dinner-party she refused to believe it. Fowell confirmed it in the carriage going home. 'And then it burst upon the family as a pleasant thing,' he said. 'We went to the Sam Hoares at Hampstead and there it was so enjoyed it gave a new tone to it.'

The Northrepps Literary Society welcomed an excuse for a

revival of the family joke over Aunt Kitty of Earlham's confused
dress sense, of Aunt Betsey Fry's casual mingling with her crowned
heads and her daughter's 'worldly' visit to the Hudson Gurneys in
St. James's Square. Edward Hoare and others were the authors of:

'A rumour spread both up and down
The Baronet had come to town
To stay awhile—not only he
But Chenda came and Lady B.
No sooner come, from far and near
The family did all appear
Gurneys, and Johnstons, Hoares and Frys
With listening ears and wondering eyes.
For they had heard they came to town
To pay their homage to the Crown.
"Catherine dear," said Lady B.
"I want a little time with thee.
Thee knows some clothes must soon be bought
In which I may appear in court.
My gown, my feathers and my train
I wish to be both *neat* and *plain*.
T'would be a pity dears to spend
Our money on a worthless end
So all must help me, and suggest
What each would think to be the best."
"I'll settle that," Aunt Catherine said.
"Thy neat grey gown and shawl of red
And tidy cap upon thy head
Will surely do; for who could bear
To see smart feathers in thy hair.
I would not wear them, that I know
For all the Queens that reign below.
I only wonder Hannah can
Ever thought of such a plan!"
"I quite approve, my sister dear,"

Aunt Fry rejoins "thy coming here
And shall be truly pleased to see
Dear Fowell at the court with thee.
I, to be sure, when I did mean
To go and see our dear young Queen
Did only neaten up a little
And wear my first day gown I whittle
But yet I cannot quite repine
With dearest sister Catherine
For I have always felt it due
To those who kindly honour you
To show respect—e'en in your dress
And do the *proper* thing, nor less.
My daughter Katherine, she would know
In what costume her aunt should go."
To which her daughter quick replies,
"I really hope I can advise.
I'm often in St. James' Square
And know so well what people wear
And I confess, dear Aunt, I think
A velvet gown and train of pink
And ostrich feathers, I should say
Set in some brilliant head array."
"By some artiste from France's shore
(By far the best is Isidore!)"
Betsey suggested that her Tobe
Might do instead of drawing-room robe
And others hinted though in vain
A nigger boy might bear her train
'Twould show how Lady Buxton smiled
On poor oppressed Afric's child—
At last arrived the expected day
And all the Court in bright array
Assembled round the throne as gay
As singing birds in month of May.

At length arrived within the door
A pair there never seen before.
"Pray who is that?" 'twas whispered round
"Full eight long feet above the ground
Of giant mould, and bearing high
Stooping to greet the passers by?
And then that lady, who is she?
Such sweetness it is rare to see
So mild, so gentle, is her eye
And yet there's humour lurking by
So truly ladylike her mien
Though so unlike this giddy scene
Her whole deportment of a kind
That clearly proves no common mind
Who can they be? Sir Fowell he
And that's his wife—my lady B." '

This was the year in which Caroline Fox of Penjerrick, grand-daughter of Robert and Rachel Barclay who bought Northrepps Hall originally, came there for the first time and pronounced the characters droll, irregular and unconventional.

Our parents' triumphal route from their marriage in Northrepps Church, 1908.

Bridesmaids at our parents' wedding: sister Gladys, and Dorothea Moore, Jessie Tredwell, Margaret Bond Cabell, Meg Gurney, Peggy Barclay and sister Richenda. The pages, in red Peter Pan tunics, were Vaughan Hawker and Hay Gurney.

The rose garden today, unchanged for a hundred years. Pen and ink drawing by the present rector, David Ainsworth. It shows the nursery windows, overlooking the front court, on the left.

"Miss Gurney's wedding costumes", from *The Queen*.

Earlham Hall, 1908, signed by Richenda Gurney with touches by her teacher John Crome. Earlham is now part of the University of East Anglia.

The first eleven of our granny's eighteen. Back, Rhalou, Dick, granny (Eva Gurney, née Buxton) holding baby Ned, Ruth, Hugh. Front, Eve, Erroll, Joe, John, Verily, Merlin. Hugh and Ned were killed. The rest are all married with seventy-eight grandchildren between us; but this is only granny's first eleven. There were still seven more to come, Lorema, Pamela, Rosemary, Gurney, Jack, Anthony and Jim.

Rhalou and Merlin in the rocking boat made by Billy Silver

Merlin in 1911, showing the school-room wing.

Rosslyn Bruce, our father, Rhalou, Merlin, Rachel (née Gurney), our mother and Erroll, with Verily and Lorema in front

AFTERNOON.
Half past One O'clock.
Scriptural Instruction.

All reading the same portion. The Governess, her Monitors & the III.rd class reading together; And a good Monitor & the II.nd class reading together in the Gallery. On the general questioning afterwards, the Governess must encourage all to join audibly in the Answers. See Rules. Scriptural Reading.

For an Hour in Summer

Half past 2 O'clock.

Monitors Writing especially those who were engaged in Teaching in the Morning. —
III.rd class Reading and Working

For an Hour

Half past 3 O'clock. GALLERY.

Monday and Wednesday } The Monitors and the III.rd class are joined by the III.rd class of Boys to receive a lesson from the Governess on Singing Hymns and Chanting, & afterwards in Summer if permitted, they read some useful Book & go on with their Needle Work. See Rules H "Singing".
The II.nd classes take the Small Room, unless detained by the Governess.

For an Hour

Half past 3 O'clock.

Tuesday and Friday } The Monitors & the III.rd class go into the Small Room to join the III.rd class of Boys in working Sums.

For an Hour

Half past 3 O'clock. GALLERY.

Tuesday and Friday } The II.nd class of Girls are joined by the II.nd class of Boys to receive a lesson from the Governess on Singing Hymns and Chanting, especially the Services for the Sunday following, & afterwards some few approved Songs already learnt by heart. The Highest Draft of Infants unite with these II.nd classes —

For an Hour

Lessons over by half past 3 in Winter, and half past 4 in Summer.

School Rules.

CHAPTER NINETEEN

Valleys over Africa

FOWELL'S next project was to raise interest and funds to fit out an expedition to explore the River Niger with a view to making treaties with native chiefs to abolish slavery and also to establish lawful commerce. H.R.H. Prince Albert attended the first meeting in 1840 and continued to back the venture though it was fiercely attacked by the leading newspapers. Three iron steamers were fitted out under Captain Trotter. Inevitably funds ran short when such extras as special ventilation were found necessary. The government refused to help and Fowell was forced to ask subscribers for more. Hannah's brother, Samuel Gurney, whose annual charities amounted to an average of £20,000 a year, nevertheless knew how to say 'No.' However, such was the impression his brother-in-law made on him that Samuel replied to his request:

'I leave it to you to put down my name for the sum you think right. To tell the truth I had thought of being very mean in my subscription. In one way and another Africa has cost me a good round sum and on this ground I felt myself justified in subscribing only £1,000. But if you think the smallness of this will discourage other people and do mischief, put me down for two, or three or four thousand. I am very glad to think that Africa has a friend like you, more able and more willing to give.'

Fowell was certainly willing, and though he had 'wealth in profuse exuberance' was not anywhere nearly in the same financial class as Samuel, who was described as 'one of the richest commoners in the country' and nicknamed 'The Quaker Rothschild'.

Prince Albert reviewed the three steamers that had been prepared for the expedition, arriving in state with his suite, which included Major Keppel, late M.P. for Norfolk. The prince examined everything very closely, and Fowell told Anna in a letter: 'He was specially delighted with a buoy fixed ready at the stern of the ship to be let down at a moment's notice. It contained a light which (at least they said so) water merely inflamed. This was for the purpose of saving anyone who might happen to fall overboard at night. I said to Keppel, not intending that the Prince should hear me, which however he did: "I wish His Royal Highness would order one of his suite, yourself, for example, to be thrown overboard that we might save your life by this apparatus." The Prince took up the idea and seemed half inclined to set Keppel a-swimming in order that we might have the gratification of the salvage.'

The inspection ended in them all, including the prince, nearly being set a-swimming. They had stepped into a small boat which was caught by the tide and, with the wind blowing and the tide rolling, was dashed with considerable violence against a yacht at anchor. It became entangled with the ropes and as lifeboats were hurriedly lowered, a cry was raised, 'Lie down! Or you'll be dragged overboard!' 'Down went his royal highness, flat to the bottom of the boat and without ceremony we all bundled down too, with the rope only dragging across our backs. However the prince sprang up laughing and told them he had already had one ducking that year when he fell through the ice.'

At first news from the expedition was good. The ships sailed 320 miles up the river, calling at villages and towns where the inhabitants were friendly, ready to consider treaties and most anxious to do trade.

Then came news that Fowell read with anguish in the woods at Northrepps. 'White Man's Fever' had broken out aboard first one ship and then the other two. Captain Trotter ordered the ships to steam back as fast as possible to the open sea where he hoped the cooler air would save the men. But the sickness spread and presently Captain Trotter and all the engineers were too ill to work. Fortunately the geologist found a scientific treatise, from which he and the already overworked doctor and one white sailor were able

to manage the engines and conduct the ships down the river. They
reached the open sea but forty of the men had perished, though, to
everyone's surprise at that time, all the Africans aboard recovered.

Now Fowell was attacked with a fresh outbreak from the newspapers which accused him of causing the catastrophe.

Prince Albert sent for him immediately the news reached him
and Hannah went with her husband on this 'sudden flight to
Windsor', which they made 'quite easily by rail-road', Queen
Victoria's Windsor line being one of the earliest. 'At this grand
hotel', Hannah wrote, 'we had a poor expensive lunch, a much
better one would have been had at home.'

They hired a fly and drove in The Great Park, and Hannah
admired the sights while Fowell went into the castle.

Prince Albert was in favour of pressing on with any advantages
left from the wreck of the expedition. Somehow the interview
ended more happily than Fowell had expected, with a comfortable
shooting gossip about the capercailzies, a pair of which Fowell had
presented to Prince Albert. But it was only when the chaplain of
the ill-fated expedition came himself to Northrepps with the as-
surance that the sacrifices had been worth while that Fowell was
able to rest.

In the summer of 1840 there were great family gatherings to
welcome Joseph John home from his three years in America, where
he had attracted an enormous following, the Gurneyite Orthodox
Friends sect having formed itself as a result of his visit to New
Jersey, and Earlham College, which still flourishes in Richmond,
Indiana, having been started at his suggestion for Quaker children.
So lavish was the hospitality wherever he went that there were
always remains left over from the feasts, which became known in
the parts of America he visited as 'Joseph Johns'.

Anna of Northrepps Cottage, who was staying with the Samuel
Gurneys when her cousin returned, adds an excited postcript to
Hannah at Northrepps Hall, written on August 17th. 'P.S. Joyful
news now come! That our beloved precious Joseph John landed
yesterday. Sam says to see the ship sailing in with him on deck was

the most interesting sight he ever saw; he arrives here tonight at about seven, What a mercy!' By 'interesting' the family meant always emotionally moving.

In the ship, on his way to America, he had met Eliza Kirkbride, a Philadelphia Quaker Minister, and friend of The Grove Gurneys. While she was in England she had been shown over Earlham by Betsey and had told The Grove that she thought it quite a 'place'. Now she became Joseph John's third wife, acquiring the care of it with Joseph John's nearly grown-up children, Jackey and Anna, along with 119 other Earlham grandchildren.

Eliza was very much liked by everyone, having the happy faculty of drawing out the latent power in others. Her conversation was 'rich with the ripened fruit of her large experience'. She had no wish to make any alterations to Earlham and was not as fanatically plain a Quaker as her predecessor.

The family gathered early by the sea that year, to make friends with Eliza who, with Joseph John, stayed at the Cromer Grove. Betsey, Richenda and Priscilla Johnstone and her children stayed at Northrepps Cottage with Anna. All went almost daily to North-repps Hall where 'never was such a welcome seen on any human face' as on Fowell's when he came delightedly out to meet them.

Priscilla wrote from the Cottage: 'The family and neighbour-hood are in commotion this morning about the public meeting which they have fixed to have in the drawing-room and hall. We hear hundreds are coming and expect to have to adjourn under the silver fir on the lawn. "All the wisdom" has gone to settle it'— meaning Anna. 'We dined last night at the Hall, a busy evening, like thousands before.'

And Betsey wrote in her diary: 'I was brought into very near and tender love and unity in my visit with all my dear ones. Indeed it was like days that were past when a large party of us took a beau-tiful drive and walk on a fine bright day by the sea, over the fine healthy land upon the little hills. Surely the sun shone on us in every way and the next day at Northrepps Hall we had a glorious Meeting, and truth flowed.'

Eliza was fascinated by it all, and wrote home: 'We very much enjoyed our stay at Cromer, especially the daily intercourse which it afforded with our precious sister Elizabeth Fry, who was our near neighbour. She, as you know, is always engaged in endeavouring in some way or another to benefit her fellow creatures, and very sweet it is to be able to be co-workers with her for a season in her "labours of love".'

Eliza described the casual way in which the family would stroll along the cliffs, and finding fishermen with, because of the season, nothing to do, would ask them back to Northrepps Hall or the Cottage for a meeting of what Fowell called 'Bible and Water'.

Eliza attended a revival of the Northrepps Literary Society of which Priscilla said, 'We had such a bright evening over the essays! They were most capital! A great party, nearly forty in the evening and all the servants.'

Betsey wrote her essay for it during the night and such was her admiration of her sister that she could not stop for a full stop till the end: 'If you wish to be treated with good cheer, unbounded hospitality, true liberality, constant kindness, sympathy in your afflictions, good nursing in your illnesses, and to see in your landlord the strong man, the Christian, the philanthropist, combined with the simplicity of the child, and in your landlady the adorning of the beautiful ornaments that decorate the female character, grace being so poured forth, that in meekness and wisdom she fills the place as wife, mother, sister, friend and hostess, go to the house of Sir Thomas Fowell and Lady Buxton at Northrepps Hall, and do not leave it without your prayers being raised that in the fulness and freedom of the Saviour's love, they may long continue to be blest, and through the blessings of their children's children and to all around them and the world at large, particularly in bondage and affliction.'

Soon after the newly married couple returned to Earlham, Joseph John decided that Earlham, which for years had been famous for its hospitality and the excellence of its home-brewed beer which was supplied not only to the servants of the establishment but to labourers employed on the estate, was to cease to brew and dispense it. It was not that the beer was extravagantly used but that their master believed that it was the source of considerable mischief.

Joseph John was accustomed to take a little wine and beer with his meals for the enjoyment of good health and so being in a rather low state at the time found it difficult to set an example of total abstinence. He believed that the use of these beverages was necessary for health, as did his sister Betsey who once wrote, as a nursing mother, that she could not get through the day without her glass of porter. Indeed when journeying abroad there were family jokes about procuring Aunt Fry's steak and porter before all else. 'With Uncle Buxton's bottles as carnal, and her Bible as spiritual food, she might travel over the Arabian Deserts,' one of Samuel's daughters said teasingly. Joseph John's daughter Anna wrote that: 'Papa was a great deal troubled in mind about making arrangements for the servants having no beer, a plan that was difficult and disagreeable to execute. We had them all up in the drawing-room in the evening. Jackey was away and I hid my face behind a screen while my father told his servants that he had ordered a coffee tap to be opened in the hall, with a plentiful supply of hot coffee and bread to be kept for all who chose to partake.'

There is no suggestion that Eliza had anything to do with this change. But there are indications that she was behind the gradual extraction from Thickthorn of the now fourteen-year-old Mary Jary.

Mary wrote many passionately expressed and outspoken letters to an older and evidently understanding friend, referring to them as a 'secret correspondence' to 'E————'. Some of these letters were published several years later in Philadelphia, suggesting that Eliza Kirkbride, who came from Philadelphia before she married Joseph John, was the kindly sympathetic outside influence in this lonely child's life. Mary recalls in a letter a violent outburst at this time.

'E————, you remember me at fourteen; the time we returned from the visit to Wymondham; you remember how, repulsing the cold influences overcoming me in spite of myself, I dashed down in the carriage the plain bonnet they had asked me to wear that day, and stamped on it, and let all my hair fall down upon my shoulders, and said: I am free. And then, at last, when the carriage reached the house, how we threw ourselves into each other's arms, and I had no more courage, and feared to avow the act, telling them you sat down on it—and you were still; and then how I cried all night, that I denied the truth of my nature.'

Mary Jary must have been persuaded to put it on again for a miniature exists of her wearing a charming delicately tucked Quaker bonnet, showing a lovely oval-faced girl with red-gold hair and determined blue eyes.

But who were 'they' who had asked her to wear the bonnet? Jackey and Anna, though members of the Society of Friends, were unlikely to have pressed a Quaker bonnet on their cousin.

Anna, 'the Flower of Earlham' as she was called by the villagers, was presently married to John Backhouse. Priscilla writes: 'A picture of her rises before me as I saw her on her wedding-day. Her pale elevated look when she first entered the Meeting House, her happy smile afterwards, her charming demeanour through the day, thoughtful of everyone, full of feeling, perfectly herself, the stay of all others.'

A year later Anna wrote happily of her return to Earlham: 'Jackey's most welcome voice greeted us at the Norfolk Hotel and we were soon bundled—baby, maids, luggage and all—into the Earlham carriage. Happily the baby awoke as we drove up to the door and was in an excellent mind and ready for the seizure which ensued, three or four maids quarrelling about him in the hall and everyone calling loudly for him as soon as we got upstairs.'

Next time Joseph John and Eliza went to Northrepps they found Fowell immersed in his new plantations and wrote of what lively pleasure it was to accompany him over the hills and dales of Runton and Trimingham while he pointed out to them the exquisite views of the sea already rendered more lovely by the young plantations in the foreground.

A friend told Fowell, 'Your plantations will some day be the pride of the country.'

Hannah's artist sister, Richenda, describes the day as 'brilliant, the country in perfection, with all the glow of rich in-gathering harvest. As we approached, we were charmed with the brilliant colouring of the fine purple heather, yellow bracken, and dark green of the oaks, while a perfectly blue sea was sprinkled with many ships. The little villages and churches lay at our feet. Really enchanting was the scene.'

Next day Fowell wrote to his son-in-law, Andrew: 'Our party here, although very small, with a touch of the lonely, is very cheerful and comfortable. At least ninety families have been supported during this hard weather by double trenching my plantations, earning, I am happy to say, on average about 2/- a day. This last snow has beat them and they can do no more at present.

'All Earlham came here yesterday to dinner and have been riding with a large party to see the new plantations and we are all greatly delighted. Love to all.'

The small parties at Northrepps were now more and more often by Hannah's design, for she had noticed that Fowell, though rising magnificently to each occasion, became increasingly tired afterwards, 'his ideas and enthusiasm quite outstripping his physique'.

Priscilla, too, noted in her journal: 'The other day I met my father, in London, going for a long round, so knocked up and unequal to it, that I dare not let him go alone, so I went with him in a cab, a most characteristic round—about his will, to his doctor, then to Dr. Lushington, his Hatter, two or three gun-makers, a horse-dealer, etc. He was restless to give me a present and at last relieved himself by buying me a ten-guinea boa, a charming print, and caps for my boys.'

Even Fowell himself wrote at this time:

'I do not think my motto *Do it with thy might*, and I square well together nowadays. I have no might nor energy nor pluck, nor anything of that sort, and this kind of listlessness reaches even to my two pet pursuits, negroes and partridges.'

Betsey, too, had been suffering from ill health and overstrain and Sam Hoare lent her Cliff House for the summer, where, in daily contact with Northrepps Hall and the Cottage, she could recover quietly in the care of her sister, Kitty. Whereupon, being kept awake by the beams of the lighthouse, she promptly got up from her sick bed to organise libraries for lighthouse-keepers, and later started to work on the training of matrons for women convicts.

Betsey was soon sufficiently recovered to return home and entertain the King of Prussia to lunch in her own home: 'The meal was handsome, not extravagant but *fit* for a king!' She presented her eight daughters and daughters-in-law, her seven sons and sons-in-law, some of her brothers and sisters and twenty-four grandchildren. Fowell was well enough to be, with Hannah, among the guests. For this, and attending a Lord Mayor's banquet for King William (who referred to her as 'my favourite saint' and would not let go of her arm except to eat), Betsey received a 'strong and painful judging letter' from the Quakers accusing her of worldliness, even though she had asked that there should be no toasts because of her Quaker principles.

The family felt it was most unfair, for nobody worked harder for the cause. As well as her religious tours in England, Scotland and Ireland, Betsey went abroad on a number of tours in the Channel Islands, France, Switzerland, Belgium, Holland and Germany, and so magnetic was her voice that she could hold an audience without its knowing a word of her language. They would listen intently while she read a psalm, and then burst out into warm laughter, in which she joined, at the oddity of the words, which would then be followed by a solemn prayer.

Soon she went lumbering off again round France, Switzerland and Germany with Joseph John and Eliza. But Fowell had a bad winter at Northrepps, in languid feeble health and, he said, 'under decayed spirits' though he still rode round the estate on his cob with his gun and visited his plantations.

Betsey came home exhausted from her tour, planks having had

to be put across her carriage to form a bed for her when she became too weak to sit up.

Both families were now observing that Fowell and Betsey's hard work was beginning to tell on them. One day, stirred up by news of government activity in Sierra Leone, Fowell started to write a long and urgent appeal to Lord Stanley, but even though dictating, he kept sinking back, exhausted, in the middle of a sentence. He finished it and no trace is revealed in it of his debility, but afterwards he was quite overcome by the effort. Then, one evening, a well-known and most able missionary brought his exciting and adventurous African reports straight to Northrepps, but Fowell was unable even to take in details which hitherto would have excited and fascinated him. 'His family could not but feel that the blow was struck, and the solemn gravity of Fowell's own manner showed that he too was aware of it.'

Early in the spring of 1845 Fowell's second surviving son, Thomas Fowell, married Rachel Jane. Thus, two Buxton brothers married their first cousins, daughters of Samuel Gurney. But Fowell was not fit to go to the wedding. In a few days Joseph John was writing: 'Last week we were at Northrepps and deeply interesting it was to be with those there, and to unite in watching the sick, probably dying, bed of our beloved and honoured brother. There was nothing which could fairly be called suffering, and as to his mind, his sweetness, amiability, cheerfulness, and good humour were really delightful, especially as it is accompanied by a lively sense of, and firm hold on, the love of God in Jesus Christ.'

Three days later he sank into a quiet sleep, in the 'parents' bedroom over the drawing-room.

Priscilla wrote to her aunt asking that her little boy should be sent for and told—'Let him fancy the scene. My mother, Richenda, Edward and Charles on the far side of the bed. My brother Fowell and Rachel Jane and Anna Gurney at the foot; Andrew lying by him on the window side and I kneeling next to him.'

'No death was more still and solemn and gentle,' wrote Joseph John. 'So fell the forest oak, but truly without a crash.'

A pencil note survives, sent in the evening from Northrepps Cottage to Hannah. 'I do, dearest sister, desire with prayer and supplication that you may be granted peace tonight,' writes her cousin Anna.

Fowell was buried beside his sister Sarah and his schoolboy son Harry with a simple village funeral in the crypt of ruined Overstrand church which was later rebuilt over them. In London a subscription was started, headed by fifty pounds from H.R.H. Prince Albert, to place a full length statue of him in Westminster Abbey where it now stands next to that of his old friend Wilberforce. Meanwhile the freed slaves erected a bust of him in Sierra Leone.

At Northrepps, when Priscilla and Andrew Johnstone had to go home to their children, they left their baby behind to try to cheer up the household. Hannah wrote: 'The whole house, dearest Priscilla, feels thy being gone and the maids, too, take it regularly to heart. The baby is a pleasure and occupation to them as well as to us, and I think, it thoroughly answers to Chenda to leave it here as a consolation.'

Now Betsey felt she too was dying. Several of her grandchildren and her beloved eldest son had recently been fatal victims of scarlet fever and she was in a very low state of mind. Her one earthly wish was that she might see once again the scenes of her childhood, which normally she only visited later in the year. She went back to Earlham for a few weeks and then on for ten days to Northrepps where Hannah was mourning her darling Fowell. And yet it was Hannah who wrote of Betsey: 'I am struck by my sister's heavenly patience and forbearing spirit.'

Betsey saw again the scenery connected with her childhood and 'thoughtful month at Northrepps just before marriage'. She returned to her own home satisfied and died early in the autumn.

CHAPTER TWENTY

A Hasty Match

FOWELL and Betsey were mourned, not only by their own age, but also by the younger generation who were just coming up to take on responsibility themselves. None was more cast down by the 'two staggering gaps in the family life' than thoughtful, affectionate Jackey, now twenty-six, who, in his spare time from the bank and his many ornithological interests, helped his father with working men's clubs and even sometimes spoke in a boyish way himself at Quaker Meetings.

Eliza had now persuaded the Gurneys at Thickthorn to allow Mary Jary to stay at Earlham where, under her loving and sympathetic guidance, she hoped she could help her to channel her passionate spirit towards some useful end. Mary was seventeen and prettier and more vivacious than ever, though in many ways she was very young for her age. She seemed quite unable to take any part or interest in the dedicated life of philanthropy and prayer at Earlham. But she adored horses and dogs and, though she found Jackey's scientific approach to them as a species of mammals dull, she found Jackey himself—tall, charming, attentive and perhaps the first eligible young man she had had much contact with—easily the most entertaining object at Earlham.

To everyone's amazement, Jackey fell irrevocably in love with her and within weeks had left the Society of Friends and joined the Church of England in the hopes of persuading Mary Jary to be his wife.

They were married in London shortly afterwards, at All Soul's, Langham Place on June 5th, 1846.

Jackey, now known more often by his full name of John Henry, bought a beautiful house not far from Earlham, Easton Lodge, and

there these two extremely good-looking and immensely rich young
Gurneys should have been ecstatically happy. But Mary afterwards
wrote that 'the first few months of my married life I was truly not
happy'. And 'After the interesting grief on his part at the death of
his Aunt Fry and our Uncle Buxton, John Henry brought about
his marriage with me, both of us the great grandchildren of the
same pair—I, a thoughtless girl then staying at Earlham, and he
nearly twice my age. But I don't blame them. Heavens knows, their
ignorance of my nature, and the utter want of congeniality in
everything between him and me.'

John Henry being nearly twice her age was untrue, though
possibly he had pushed her into it. He was nine years older than
her. His father, shrewd man of business as he was, and great as the
combined fortunes of the two heirs of these two main branches of
the family were, would never have encouraged his only son to do
anything that entailed his leaving the Society of Friends.

Mary Jary's own parents would of course have had to give per-
mission for it but would hardly have been likely to press for it, for
neither showed much respect for the Quaker faith or for any of
Earlham's plain ways.

Mary next complained to E———— that 'Jackey had solicited
members of his family to go with her to visit her mother as though
as an especial favour.' She went on to uphold her mother as being
just as good as they were, in fact 'above them in every instinct of
the soul!' And so was her father. Mary certainly bore them no ill-
will for causing her illegitimacy, of which she once said she was
always conscious. Though perhaps there was a touch of bitterness
in her referring with a flourish to herself as 'I, their child, and the
only one that blessed their union, then nearly a year old.'

Jackey's family gave her no cause to feel affronted, accepting her
with appreciative affection, and including her in all activities that
she was willing to join.

Anna, her sister-in-law, wrote of a day at Earlham during those
first few months: 'I never saw my father more delighting in Earlham, in its flowery beauty. One day particularly, Jackey and Mary

were there—the latter in youthful glee, her dog Keeper and my
Johnny gambolling by her on the lawn, and my father walking
about in his cloak and cap, his beautiful hair blowing about, really
taking pleasure in this dear girl, and delighted to be able to do so,
while everything glowed with sun and beauty.'

And then came a spate of deaths that plunged the whole family
into a recurring state of distress and 'tended to check my free
indulgence of thought', wrote Mary Jary.

Three days before Christmas, her father-in-law Joseph John had
a fall from his pony in the rough streets of Norwich, and the
following Sunday he was setting off with his family to Meeting,
when he heard of the death of his brother-in-law, Sam Hoare. He
went on and preached as usual. When he came back he could only
speak of Fowell and Betsey—and now Sam. 'We four were so
closely banded together in benevolent objects for so many years,
and I, who was the most delicate, am now the only one remaining.'
His old nurse, who had lived in the park for eighty years (in whose
cottage he, as a little boy, could always be found when lost,
sitting with her own children round the scrubbed table for a meal)
had just died and he wandered down to her cottage and stood by
her coffin, and said with a sigh: 'Poor old Nurse! She seems to
have passed away most peacefully. Oh, what a favour! May it be
so with me when my time comes.'

The very next day he was 'failing' and, almost without suffering,
grew weaker, till, at the end of the week, he turned to his wife and
said: 'I think I feel a little joyful' and fell into a sleep from which
he never woke.

Eliza, who in her six years of marriage to Joseph John, had become so deeply loved by all his family, wrote to them all herself to
break the news. Hannah set off for Earlham at once and a note
remains, from her, written from Northrepps a few days later.
'How are thee, my love, to be greeted this morning?'

For a week after Joseph John's death the shops in Norwich were
half closed and, particularly in the poorer parts, the darkened
windows showed the feelings of the inhabitants. Everyone had

some story to tell of the saintly Quaker's kindness and the endless trouble he took to help the apparently most unimportant people. Then 'it was as if the whole population of Norwich followed him to the Friends' burial-ground, The Gildencroft.' This was the Flemish name for this meadow of golden buttercups.

John Henry and Mary Jary had only just settled into Easton Lodge and Mary had no wish to move to Earlham. So Eliza and Kitty continued to live on there for a while, trying to keep up the charitable spirit of the old place, with the usual visits from children and grandchildren.

Mary writes dramatically of one the following autumn when Anna was also there with her little Johnny and her new, extremely delicate baby.

'I remember the date and the appearance of the country well. I shall never forget either. The fields were undulating with their golden grain. Costessy Park was in its fullest verdure. Everything seemed rejoicing in the coming harvest—the happy maternity of earth. And so we reached Earlham.

'The first object I saw was Anna's child. It impressed me profoundly. I took him in my arms, and as I looked at him everything grew dark about me. I had been before the toy of ceremony; I was now a conscious wife. Beautiful lawn and woodland, summer breezes, kindness, marriage rites even, what can they avail against the first awakening consciousness of a crime against nature?'

Then follows a list of the current cousin marriages in the family with a frightful catalogue of diseases she had read were to be found in 'Hospitals, Asylums for Feeble-Minded children, and Institutions for the deaf, dumbs and blind' resulting, Mary said, from 'blood-kin' marriage.

If Anna's baby was feeble-minded or blind, she certainly does not show it in the charming drawing of him as a small but pretty baby nestling in the arms of the stout and redoubtable Johnny, then about four. Moreover his parents though connected more than once were not blood relations.

But already Mary Jary, though she may not have known it, was pregnant herself, and exceedingly healthily so.

Anna, however, was very far from well and was feeling her father's death with unusual despondency. Before her new baby was born she had written in her diary:

'I have of course a deep thankfulness that my husband and my child are left to me but it is impossible for words to describe how the zest and pleasure of every constituent part of my whole life is fled. The child's feats are so useless, the beauty of my home so valueless now that I cannot show them to him.' And now she added: 'Oh, the faint, sick feeling of that arrival at Earlham. Still it was more a crushing than a sorrow. Dear Jackey met me at the door.'

Anna's husband decided, for her health's sake, to take her and the children to Italy for the winter, but there, at Pisa, her baby died.

They were at sea off Palermo when the Sicilian revolution broke out and they had to leave their boat for the already overcrowded H.M.S. Bulldog. Johnny's nurse found she would have to sleep on the floor and their maid, Mary Ann, was never brought aboard at all. Anna had been 'very nicely the day before', said the nurse, 'but going on deck to enquire after Mary Ann in another vessel, she complained of shortness of breath and asked to be laid on deck.' Mary Ann was located and came on board to find her mistress lying there, with three doctors round her. Now whiffs of ether replaced the leech as a cure-all and one doctor proceeded to administer them. This, the nurse said, made her mistress happy and ready to die—'I did hope to have a more quiet end but this is a very public one,' she said. 'It is a strange place to die.' Indeed on board a man-o'-war with nine of Napoleon's navy anchored near, Mary Ann agreed she was right. One of the officers rubbed her hands amid a roar of cannon and ringing of bells ashore. Though Anna insisted she was dying her husband said no, she was not. 'Yes, I know I am, you'll see,' she said determinedly, and she kissed her little son Johnny and told him to be a good boy and he would go to Heaven.

and said she was going to Jesus and to her dearest Father, and quietly and sweetly breathed her last. 'How like her life her death had been', it was observed.

There was a cease-fire while Anna's body was rowed ashore and buried at Palermo. Her remains were afterwards moved to Leghorn and placed by those of her little child.

At Earlham, Eliza told the servants she would read the news from Palermo in the evening. 'When we went into the ante-room to my surprise I found it filled.' Between fifty and sixty persons from the Hall and villagers had come to hear the unusual details of the death of their flower.

Now Eliza and Kitty felt that the ties of Earlham had been sufficiently loosened to abandon it for younger tenants. The furniture that had been in the house since it was first rented by Kitty's father, over sixty years before, was put up for sale and Samuel bought it all, including the grandfather clock, whose ticking at the bottom of the stairs at Northrepps Hall later so impressed us as little children on our way down to Family Prayers.

Earlham lay empty for a while and then Samuel's eldest son John, who had married a sweet, gentle daughter of a canon of Norwich cathedral, came with their children and the welcoming hospitality continued as before.

Meanwhile Eliza went to live with the Grove Gurneys where the family continued to visit her. She writes comfortably from The Grove: 'Cousin Anna of Northrepps dined with us yesterday very agreeably, and I invited Lucy, Amelia Opie and the Foresters to meet her, which answered very nicely. She came at three o'clock, on purpose that we might have a nice private chat together before the others arrived, and most sweet and affectionate she was. What a treat it is, in this little minny-minded world, to meet with a large-souled, generous, noble creature of whom you approve entirely! Just such is Cousin Anna. I never was more deeply impressed with the greatness of her character than during our intimate conversation yesterday. What a splendid Friend and minister she would have made, notwithstanding her lameness! Indeed, I think

o

her very helplessness would have added to the effect, giving an emphasis of interest on the whole. But alas, not many rich, not many mighty, not many noble seem to stumble into our path, or rather, I should say, be willing to be led into it.'

Kitty meanwhile joined her sister Richenda and her clergyman husband at Lowestoft and she, too, was frequently visited. Priscilla Johnstone writes that 'Aunt Kitty is very, very infirm. But Aunt Richenda was surprising and more delicious than ever, her drawing-room like a fairyland of pictures, flowers and pretty things. Her garden delightful, she skimming down the ninety steps many times a day. She herself a sunbeam, brightly dressed, brightly looking, brightly speaking, singing and drawing.'

Richenda was the eldest of The Four Girls of the younger group of the Gurneys of Earlham. It was Richenda who experimented with deliberate rudeness on the road and who liked to stop off in her journal to survey her last meal. She had had no children and her husband was permanently lame after being thrown out of a carriage, yet her temperament being of the happiest, theirs was a good life. 'Her drawing was admirable, and incessantly kept up, as well as her music,' Dan once said. 'Her sketches show great merit and form a sort of illustrated journal of her life. Up with the lark, Richenda was to be seen with sprightly step descending her gay hanging gardens at Lowestoft and so to the shore and would frequently effect before breakfast as much as other people in a whole day.' 'I love to spin about,' she said.

When asked if she ever saw any evil in anybody, she looked up from her drawing, a little amused, and smiling said: 'Why, yes, dear. I see it, but I like to shut one eye, and open the other, only a very little way if anything is wrong, because I like honey so much better than poison.'

'There was a constant flow of primitive hospitality at the vicarage which was adorned throughout with her sketches and drawings, and various charities abounded. She frequently paid morning calls on her neighbours and sometimes to save time would take a drawing with her and pencil on during her visits. It was all in sim-

plicity and absence of ostentation. Everybody loved and delighted
in Mrs. Cunningham,' Dan said, 'though it must be admitted
there was a mixture of peculiarity in all the proceedings. It was
amusing to see her management of her husband's curates. One
named Rump she forced to add an F to his name,' though it was
never recorded where, 'as she thought he might be less useful
under the original appellation.'

Having already observed that she was 'weaned from life', Kitty
died in this delightful home in a burst of heavenly vision in 1850.
Shortly afterwards Eliza felt free to embark on a visit to her
native America, which she had put off while Kitty still lived.

That summer at Northrepps, though Hannah and the current
'Aunt Chenda' gave the visiting grandchildren the usual warm
welcome, the now sixteen grandchildren were causing such a crush
that drawers had to be pulled out for the smaller ones to sleep in.
Priscilla had six children. Fowell and Rachel Jane so far had four,
and Catherine had six boys. Now she gave birth to the seventeenth
grandchild in the ante-room at Northrepps Hall and, to everyone's
delight, it was a girl.

Edward decided it was time for his family to use their own
house by the sea for holidays, and he bought Colne House (which
is now a hotel appropriately specialising in families with children)
just behind Cromer church, with a huge garden stretching right
back, then, to the woods. Catherine then went on to complete
their family of eleven with four more girls.

Hannah wrote to Eliza in America of one of the many joint
picnics shared by Northrepps Hall and Colne House.

'This is my birthday—sixty-eight! . . . The day I was twenty I
remember we assembled a very large party to a picnic in Sheringham woods. At this time, how did youthful energy and spirits
abound! Now how changed—I alone at the head of another party
of children and grandchildren at another picnic on the cliff at
Trimingham. Everything made it most interesting to me, though
now surrounding my life and prosperity rather than sharing it.
A lovely sight it was today above the bright blue sea, Edward and

Fowell with their guns, dogs and keepers. Catherine, Sarah, Richenda, the boys' tutor and six children all congregating for the luncheon under a sheltered hedge. Thee, dearest Eliza, can fancy it, and how much I have to be thankful for.'

Catherine's parents now came often to stay at Colne House to enjoy their grandchildren by the sea. Catherine described Samuel and his wife as: 'beautiful radiant grandpapa leading a troupe of boys, or conversing in kindest interest with the elder grandson just emerging out of the boy but too shy to be quite the man, and the dear grandmother sitting on the lawn in the sunshine watching the pretty quartet of girls. One scene especially comes to me which I see, her in her wicker chair carriage, with the baby Evelyn in her long white clothes upon her lap, and three others clinging on behind; grandpa with his bare white head and beautiful tender look of interest, leading the shaggy pony that drew them.'

A charming portrait in an oval frame remains of 'Baby Evelyn' with a wreath of convolvulus in her curly golden hair. Later, as a child, she is referred to as 'bright-Eva', 'shining Eva' and 'Eva the little mother'. It was Eva who became our Northrepps grandmother whom we too loved so much.

CHAPTER TWENTY-ONE

Chequered Shade

THE next few years brought for Hannah 'sorrow upon sorrow', and yet, as always, she remained outwardly calm, showing nothing but love and thoughtfulness for those about her.

So far Priscilla had been at hand to support her mother in her many losses ever since, as a little girl, she had called her mother to one of her dying babies during the unforgettable Hampstead tragedy. Now Hannah was appalled to see that Priscilla, her 'beloved sister-like-child', who had always had such a 'surplus of keen energy' was almost daily, as her father had before her, losing it. Though Priscilla said she could not be spared from her children for the prescribed change of air, yet spared she had to be, for soon Hannah 'felt the darkness thicken', and her eldest and closest child died, surrounded by her children, husband and servants and mother.

Now Andrew left the children at Northrepps more often than ever, and, even with Colne House absorbing part of the usual quota of grandchildren, it was clear that more rooms were needed at Northrepps Hall.

After a series of storms, Billy Silver brought up from Overstrand beach enough wreckage to start building the North Wing over the outhouses on one side of the backyard. This was at first known as the Charles Wing, after Hannah's youngest son, who helped to fill it till the grandchildren numbered twenty-seven, only three of whom did not marry to produce more—and more—they to produce more—among whom, besides the inevitable bankers, preachers, masters of hounds, J.Ps., D.L.s, politicians and educationalists, there gradually began to emerge such variations as archbishops and artists, brigadiers and ballet dancers and now television tycoon and pop singer.

Hannah resigned herself to what she could only feel was a brief respite, while her youngest daughter, Chenda, tried to replace her elder sister, and stayed at home and helped to entertain the grand-children.

Chenda wrote of Northrepps during this time:

'The place is in great beauty, the flowers in rich abundance. The honeysuckle on the wall is still in flower and so are the white Banksia roses on the gable; the annuals are overflowing their beds —a brilliant sight in the bright sunshine. The scarlet Lory flew down to his stand opposite the drawing-room window the moment we arrived; the other parrots and cockatoos were flying about in great glee. A pair of cockatoos are sitting on their two eggs in a box against the dining-room chimney. The young cockatoos are de-lighted to follow us about the garden.'

Later in the summer she wrote: 'Our hay is going on so we sent for the school children to play in it, and an express to Cromer for plenty of strawberries and milk for their supper. This was spread on the lawn and, as usual, quickly attracted the parrots, who promptly stole the bread and butter from the children.'

Of Priscilla's children, she said:

'In the early morning it was pretty to see the little girls reading on the terrace and the two cockatoos pecking at their feet.' 'The little girls are now crowding round the cistern of water while Francis is eagerly pumping, and a cockatoo is sitting on the edge of the tub drinking.'

And now dear spinning Richenda began to 'feel the cold', but still 'Her comfort in music was truly a blessing. If restless nothing was like going to the pianoforte, and if the maids came in to sing she was sure to be relieved. It was a most soothing resource.'

To cheer herself up, she also took lessons in the new, to her, medium of drawing with charcoal.

The doctor shook his head and ordered Nice, and Hannah took Richenda there. 'But,' Hannah wrote, 'we had an extremely rough passage and my sister could not, on coming down, get across the cabin and sat down on a dressing box by the door. There she sat and sang in a low voice very sweetly, "When the Stormy Winds doth Blow".'

Richenda immediately brightened once they arrived. 'To my sister Richenda any place seems a garden; no spot is barren for her; there is no wilderness in her life; her mind's eye sees flowers everywhere.' All the same, she was very grateful to be back in time to die in her own home and her last words were full of delight in a rosy future.

When Dick died, just before her, he left no heavenly glimpses of the hereafter for the onlookers gathered at his bedside. Instead he left his mother's fortune, said to be a million sterling, to Mary Jary, with Northrepps to go to her also after the death of his half-brother, Hudson, who was already eighty. Certain regular payments were to be made to other young persons dotted about Norfolk, who, though not actually bearing his name, bore a striking likeness to him.

Unlike those of the more pious members of the family, Dick's funeral is not to be found described at great length in any of the letters or journals.

So plentiful were the funerals at this time that Hannah's sons, Edward and Fowell, and her daughter-in-law, Catherine, can perhaps be excused for extracting a little unexpected pleasure out of the funeral of their Great-Uncle Charles' widow at Weymouth. She lived to be ninety-five, outliving by seven years Uncle Charles who 'despite his intemperate life, did not die till his eighty-eighth year'.

Edward had already inherited Bellfield from his father, and most of his Great-Uncle Charles' own possessions went to him too. Catherine wrote from Bellfield:

'Well my dear sons, I will begin a letter to you in this old drawing-room—while your father and the three Mr. Enderbys are lingering at the desert-table. Here I am, lady of the old house!

'When the will was read I was frightened lest the cocoanut

sugar basin should be left away—but no, it was not mentioned, and "all" that was not, is for her nephew Sir Edward North Buxton'—Catherine's husband—'so the said sugar basin shall be Fowell's as far as I am concerned.

'After the will—your father, Uncle and I took a long walk. I doubt its being quite seemly, but as the latter was going off by the afternoon train we could not resist a blow together. Getting over the muddy meadows, along snow drifts, lanes and over numerous stiles and fences, did not quite agree with my handsome new mourning and their flowing crape hat-bands flying in the wind.

'On turning back we found two boys and two donkeys in great distress with a cart of sand, entirely stuck fast in the *deep* mud road up from the shore. We had quite a scene, we would not allow the donkeys to be beat, and they refused to move, they really could not *stand*, so your father and uncle went behind making one boy join and pushed with all their might, their crape bands flying, at least your father's, for Uncle's had come off with the wind—it was quite a picture. When Papa was quite beat, he drove and made the second boy push, and I supplied shoves when they rested, or made the boys do it, for I was too devoted to my new silk dress in the mud to be of much use. We ended by giving the boys sixpences not to beat their donkeys again when they could not move.'

The following year Chenda of Northrepps, now aged thirty-six, married Philip Hamond at Northrepps church.

That summer was Samuel's last at Cromer. 'His appearance on the sands was very striking when surrounded by the clusters of bright young faces, listening to their eager talk and promising fishing-nets to one, and scientific apparatus to another with an interest which beamed from his face.'

Even Samuel had faith in his doctors when they sent him abroad to Nice, and allowed himself to be borne off by several of his family, where they had a serious carriage accident from which he suffered least of any. But when he realised he was dying from other causes, he started urgently for home, though after an arduous journey with his children only reached the splendid, but still

unfinished Hotel Du Louvre, in Paris. Poor Samuel! He had
longed to die in the peace of his own home, but instead, his faithful servant wrote: 'The clanking of hammers and other noises are
incessant and we can't stop them. I went down after twelve at
night, they promised it should cease, but as soon as it was light
they began again.'

'Peace be still!' were Samuel's last words, murmured,
repeatedly, but without, for a while, avail.

These many deaths affected the survivors variously. Anna and
her half-brother, Hudson, with twenty years between them, had
never had much in common when they were young but after their
father's death were drawn more closely together as the sole survivors of his children, for Gatty had died not long before their father.
Anna wrote to Hudson from Northrepps Cottage in the spring:

'The trees are burst forth, but the brake hill still shows quite a
contrast in colour and the white rabbits sitting manifest at the
mouths of their burrows are a great amusement to me. I have a
Noah's Ark set of creatures and coops in the grass!' and: 'Grenville
Chester'—the archaeologist—'opened two burrows on Roughton
Heath the other day and found in both cracked vessels, bones and
ashes, in one four jet beads and a large round stone such as we
sometimes pick up on the beach, a very different weapon from a
British sling.'

Anna's collection of stones, flint arrowheads and fossils was said
to be 'the most informative in the country'. She was the first
woman member to be elected to the Royal Archaeological Society.

Eliza was not the only one who believed Anna could have been
great in one particular bent. Archaeologists also claimed the same,
and it was said she could have made a great banker, then unheard of
in a woman. The papers she prepared for Fowell, when he was in
parliament, are enough to show the clarity and magnitude of her
mind, yet all are introduced with the lightest, simplest and often
most humorous touch which must have made working with her a
most stimulating delight.

Anna now fairly often stayed at Keswick with Hudson, and, in the spring of 1857 she went for a visit from which she was destined never to return. 'She was seized with a strong and rapid attack of bronchitis and died on June 6th. By her express desire she was buried in the chancel of the same ruined church at Overstrand where lay her attached partner, and Sir Fowell Buxton and his son.'

Among Anna's bequests were generous legacies to her faithful servants, without whom she could not possibly, as increasing lameness and bulk lessened her mobility, have lived such an amazingly active life. In her will, also, the comfort of all her animals and birds was assured for the rest of their lives.

Exactly a year later, again in June, Hannah was called upon to bear further terrible losses. Her eldest son Edward, who was only forty-six, died at Colne House, leaving Catherine with her eleven children and, 'wonderful to relate'—meaning she had been quite prepared for what was to come—his sister, Richenda, died four days after in the Bow Room at Northrepps. 'The double funeral was inexpressibly touching, the procession from Northrepps coming down the lane to fall in with the one from Cromer, the two coffins abreast each followed by its own chief mourners to the ruins of Overstrand Church.'

The repeatedly bereaved mother wrote to her brother Dan: 'Last night I lay awake counting the deaths touching me in the last thirteen years—my husband, three children, nine brothers and sisters, young Anna at sea, Anna Gurney—' This, on top of her earlier nursery losses! And yet her faith never wavered. In fact, miraculously, it seemed almost strengthened by every blow.

Now Chenda's little boy, Charlie Hamond, came to live permanently with his grandmother and when Andrew Johnstone died, two of his daughters also made their home at Northrepps, from which they were eventually married, cheerfully dispelling, with other grandchildren who came in the holidays, any feelings of gloom that might otherwise have pervaded the place.

'On Wednesday we had a very pleasant dance in the drawing-room which—minus its carpet—made a glorious place for it,' wrote one of them.

'Tea under the trees in the field and then the boys had a game of cricket. Mary and Bessie showed us what they could do on the stilts. They hopped and danced a polka to grandma and walked up the steps.' wrote another. This was Ellen, daughter of Fowell and Rachel Jane whose journals, illustrated in the jaunty and characteristic manner of the family in all generations, are filled with delicious allusions not only to our favourite spots in the house and garden and woods, but also to the very toys we played with.

'We found the coachman, and he got us ready the donkey cart so we drove in it through the lanes near and found plenty of honey-suckle. We caught a young partridge that was in the road but let it go again and then drove part of the road way to Joy's Mill and home by Cromer.'

How we, who later knew those lanes and saw them from the same donkey cart, could smell again the honeysuckle, feel the salty wind from the sea and hear again the clip-clop of the donkey's little hooves on the sandy lane!

'We got a good many blackberries, and then went on to Shucks Lane and there we found more.' Blackberrying in all the places that we knew and loved! Shuck's Lane, the Pit, the Warren, the Cottage Woods. 'We put them into a saucepan with plenty of sugar and boiled them. Then we poured them into eight pots and grandmama came up and tasted it.' And how the smell of black-berries stewing in the nursery comes back! And the feel of the baskets, stained with juice, from under the front stairs! And of the small squat pots we too used for our home-made jam that used to stand on the shelf in the same nursery pantry.

'After breakfast we walked into the Cottage woods. First to the reed house, the summerhouse in the woods that has a very pretty view of Overstrand church and the sea. When we were at North-repps last year the boys and I built a little hut of ferns and sticks close to the reed house, and when we looked for it this year we found it as strong as though it were only built yesterday.'

'This afternoon we took the donkey cart down to Cromer and filled it with a quantity of bricks and then brought them up again to Northrepps and emptied them out in the woods near the lawn. The next day we dug a foundation and began to build a little house five feet square. The ground was very hard so it took us a long time but great fun afterwards putting the bricks in.'

'There not being room in the donkey cart for all, two rode in the green cart, tied behind it.' What 'trucks' were tied behind the donkey cart, behind bicycles and eventually the little car in those woods!

How many houses of sticks and ferns must have been built in that wood?

Hugh, of our generation built a little brick hut in the wood too and we all helped him.

And then the mice! Ellen describes the ancestors of the ones that tore round inside the walls in our day too.

'The mice at Northrepps Hall are most amusing. I do not think there is a single room in the house that you cannot hear the mice in the walls, generally at night but very often in the day.

'There is one particular room at the top of the stairs which swarms with mice and immense rats—this room goes by the name of The Mice Room'—It was the old Fawn room—'The night nursery is crammed with mice. The maids are really afraid to sit there in the evenings because the mice are so impudent that they come out across the floor and sit up with their ears pricked up, and look at the maids. They have races all round the rooms in the walls and make the most furious noise, far far more than anyone could have expected. I have seen rats almost as large as leverets running about the garden. Even in the middle of the day the rats come out and look at the children when they are dressing but as the night nursery is extremely old, by far the oldest part of the house, this is why there are more mice there than in any other part.'

Hannah wrote herself of the holidays: 'We are still in a good current of engagements. There are cricket and riding going on daily, nearly. It is a comfort that I can bear the tumult of grand-children, I had six in my room for an hour I think, some at least as long before breakfast. I go into the nurseries at seven o'clock, I begin with Charlie Hammond, by myself first before seven, and then they troop in as they are dressed, for play and coffee.'

She always rose at six in the morning and in the afternoon had a chair placed in front of the drawing-room door as a hint that she was resting 'though not really sleeping'.

It was not till November that she could write:

'I am this day left without either child or grandchild, having been full of them in succession since the latter part of July, to my great comfort. Fowell and Rachel's large party of eighteen are now cleared off, and my married grandchildren and their little girl all went off this morning.'

After Christmas Hannah was very ill and her two remaining sons were sent for by telegraph. Ellen was lucky enough to be chosen to go with her father and they dashed off together to the train. 'We had the carriage all to ourselves the whole way. About half past five it began to grow dark, so Papa lighted his lamp, and we read and worked by its light till we arrived at Norwich. There was a fly waiting for us. It was a very dark night so we lighted our lamp inside.'

At Aylsham they changed to another fly and arrived just before midnight, to find the grandmother still very ill. But slowly she recovered and Ellen stayed on long enough to find the first primroses and violets and then the rest of the family joined them for the Easter holidays.

'We all went on to the shore and dug fortifications and stood in them and let the sea come round.' And the next day it was a pond with rivers into it and the same shrieks of joy and excitement when it was filled up and they suddenly let all the water out.

The summer came round again with the stables and paddocks as full as the nurseries. Ellen, now fourteen, describes 'such a delicious journey. The five ponies, Garry, Granca, Cowslip, Star and Derry were led to the station and there put safely away in the boxes to go to Norwich. The two horses, Dalham and Venice, went in the carriage to Stratford Station and there they were put into the train and the carriage too. Then Papa's riding horse Delhi was put into the train with Aunt's beautiful pony. Aunt's children were already there. Then the carriage and ponychair were filled with my Father and Mother, Johnnie, Arty, Geof, Alfred, Timmie, Janet, Barclay, Effie and myself, and drove off to Stratford Station. Soon the train came up, and it was the greatest interest to us all getting into the saloon carriage. It certainly was most comfortable and *beautifully* fitted up. There was a table in the middle, two nice easy chairs, a sofa fixed to the wall at one side, and two seats at the other, there was also a little carriage opening into this big one, which we called the nursery and there was a wash hand basin with plenty of beautiful water. Then there was a Second Class carriage attached to this First Class, also a place for the luggage. The babies were most good and charming. About twelve o'clock, we spread out our beautiful luncheon on the table, and were a long time eating our dinner. Effie thinks herself too old to take the bottle now, so she will not have it, but she will eat her dinner just as the other children do.

'About one o'clock we arrived at Norwich. We stopped to see the horses taken out of their boxes, which was very amusing, little Derry looked perfectly self-possessed and as though nothing surprised him, but I suppose he was never in a train before. Then the ponies were all led to a stable to eat and drink and the carriage was packed full of different things. I put on my habit and we rode 22 miles. My mother, the little ones and some maids went in the carriage, and my Father, Johnnie, Arty, Geoffrey, Alfred and I rode on to Aylsham. It was not a very long ride, about 11 miles, and when we got there we got off for ten minutes to feed the ponies.

'At Aylsham Grandmama's carriage met my Mother and all the rest so they changed carriages and went on in it, and left our carriage to see if any of us who were riding would like to get in, Arty and Alfred were tired and they got in and the consequence was we had to drive their two ponies, Cowslip and Derry before us. Derry was *excessively* naughty, as vicious as he could be. If we tried to hunt him the right way he was *sure* to turn down the wrong road *on purpose* to tease us and sometimes he would stop altogether, and then as soon as he saw us coming back to hunt him, he would gallop off back again for a long way and would not turn till one of the boys got off, went and hunted him on foot.

'Derry was just like a pig but so clever he knew perfectly well which way he wanted to go and he would slip between us and run back a long way, and then look pleased with his own cleverness.

'But at last, at one particular corner, he became so *unbearably* wicked that we took Geof (who was ten) off his pony, Star, and put him on Derry without stirrups or bridle and so Derry found out that he had a master on his back. Geof guided him with his whip and let his own pony run. And so at last we got to that lovely old house, but I think that if we had not put Geof onto Derry we should never have got home that night. As it was he delayed us three quarters of an hour, after the time we had appointed.

'When we arrived we found Mother and all the babies had arrived long before us, and then we had a nice dinner but were rather sleepy after it.'

And no small wonder.

CHAPTER TWENTY-TWO

Dear E — — — —

MEANWHILE in 1854, John Henry and Mary Jary had moved to Catton Hall, a house almost identical to the one that Bartlett never, after all, built at Northrepps, with grounds laid out by Humphry Repton exactly matching his water-colour sketches in the Northrepps Red Book. In fact Repton's first commission was to landscape Catton. It is a serenely beautiful place, now an eventide home for the aged. Traces still remain of John Henry's aviaries and animal pens in a walled corner of the park. What is now the village hall was built by John Henry to house his stuffed birds with which he later helped his cousin, John Gurney of Earlham, to turn Norwich Castle into a museum.

Among John Henry's magnificent collection of books in the library at Catton were his huge volumes of flattened birds, whose skins were arranged in pairs on the page to show their full plumage. When, as children, we turned the heavy pages, the 'squashed birds' seemed even more dead than those standing over their stuffed, doubly dead prey in glass cases with red paint oozing from their wounds.

John Henry had specialised in birds of prey, ever since his agent by mistake bought Raptores instead of the birds he had ordered from a sale.

At Catton Hall, one small only son, now aged six, and bearing his father's name, looked down from the charmingly bowed nursery window on to the terraced garden and park below.

In the drawing-room hung portraits by Richmond showing John Henry as warm, handsome and friendly, though perhaps, for all the fashionable cut of his clothes, lacking a little in dash, while Mary Jary, whose colouring was as lovely as when she was a child, had developed in her searching blue eyes a certain kind of business-like shrewdness. Richmond was said, when discussing the truth with a fellow artist, to have agreed: 'Yes, the truth, but lovingly told'. Certainly in these two portraits both sitters appear as exceptional charmers, as does Anna of Northrepps Cottage, who was painted at about the same time. In her portrait Richmond emphasised her charm and humour almost to the exclusion of the strength of character that is so noticeable in other portraits.

John Henry was a director of 'the banker's bank' of Overend, Gurney and Co., which firm his Uncle Samuel had made so profitable and renowned. Most of John Henry's money was now invested in it. He had been elected a Fellow of the Zoological Society, and was a member—in some cases also the founder—of almost every ornithological and naturalist society in this country besides some in America.

He had several papers and manuals published and was already working on a book of the magnitude of some of the great bird books of John Gould, son of Queen Victoria's gardener, whose brilliantly accurate and beautiful plates continue to illustrate many modern bird books. John Henry was a friend of Gould's and they often lunched together to discuss the book John Henry was preparing.

Now, the year he bought Catton Hall, he was elected Liberal member of parliament for King's Lynn, 'filling,' Mary Jary wrote, 'Walpole's chair, or at least the edge of it.' For a while Mary enjoyed the 'honour and praises' of Jackey's new rank, but later listed the members of parliament in the family rather in the same derogatory manner with which she had listed those likely to produce disease and insanity in their children. Mary now decided that 'all this foolish member of parliament business was but a palpable sham.' The fact was that Mary Jary could not be persuaded to take more than a surface interest in politics or any of John Henry's other pursuits. Nor would she throw herself into the diversion of the philanthropic works other young wives in her position followed outside their own homes. Though 'constantly anticipated in her

P

lightest wish by a husband who knew no will but hers', she did not appreciate it. In every way Jackey showed her the greatest tenderness and love, while patiently waiting for her to grow up.

She was now twenty-five, and expecting her second child, yet with a mind that was still as full of schoolgirl passions as when she first married.

At last Dan's *Records of the House of Gournay* had come out, and been well reviewed as a serious contribution to history. But Mary Jary—to give Dan credit for something he had never intended—read it as though it were one of Amelia Opie's spiciest romances, identifying herself with some of Dan's medieval mistresses and comparing gentle peace-loving Jackey most unfavourably with the more bloodthirsty of the crusaders.

'I had my inner life and my outward life,' she wrote later to E————, 'what, I doubt not, other women have had as well as this poor one at Catton. I drummed, in the old schoolgirl way, into my husband's ears the set tunes for the piano, utterly unobservant of the music. I dressed in the same mechanical way to receive his relations, and thanked God when they were gone.

'But when alone, *immured, away from every one, I lived my fullest life*, my imagination went away boldly, admiringly, lovingly, to other men. They were not objects of jealousy, dear E————, for they were dead.

'I lived with the memories of the founders of our family, men who never sat upon the clerk's stool, men with strong arms and stalwart frames, making their deeds of knightly prowess known in a hundred battles—with the memories of Hue, and Walter, and Anselm, and Gerard, and Reginald, and Matthew and John, who in the Holy Land fought at Prince Edward's side.

'I lived with them too at the tournaments, held on the very spots where I daily rode.

'I admired their splendid force, their brains not emasculate with such education as I saw around me, nor hampered with narrow trade tricks. I wondered what work they would be about if they were living today. I tried to imagine how any of the family could

have got down, step by step, generation after generation, to studying Greek verbs, or calculating percents. Hue alive, I knew well,
would not be a praying banker, but abroad in the free air.'

Mary Jary's second son, Richard, was born at Catton and,
almost as though she had brought it upon herself by her earlier
harping on the dangers of what she called 'blood-kin unions', he
was an exceedingly delicate little baby. Forgetting the axe she
had liked to grind, Mary was intrigued by his pale face, fair hair
and light blue eyes and said admiringly, 'I shall call him my
white baby.'

For a while the baby's delicacy absorbed her attention. Then
she grew bored again.

'Under a conjugal yoke of continued kindness,' she wrote to
E————, 'I was undergoing a slow death. My early passion for
horses and dogs proved then my consolation,' she explained away
a sudden renewed interest in the stables. 'It would be impossible
to admire a horse more than I had always done,' or, as it turned
out, a groom.

William Taylor, whose parents had lately moved to Catton
and whose duty it was, as one of the grooms, to escort his mistress
out riding, was exactly as she had imagined the Norman crusaders,
'with strong arms and stalwart frame. I loved him almost before
I knew it; and he I felt, moreover, loved me, though not a word
was spoken between us.' She poured it all out to E————. 'When
the expression of it could no longer be controlled, it came first
from my lips. He was riding beside me, and did not reply to
me. He said out into the air, into the heavens: God has given me
too great a joy. Then he turned to me and said: I have loved you
from the first day I saw you.

'Dear E————, he was so beautiful, so noble, then, in the
expression of that love so long concealed. The earth whirled
around me, and his arm caught me falling unconsciously. When
I came to myself I was resting on his bosom, confident of its
strength as of a breastplate of iron, though I saw his eyes dim with
tears.

'We rode homewards in silence. There was a beauty in the very stones beneath our feet. The wayside flowers had an odor too exquisite to the scene. The air and sky were filled with an influence too beautiful for earth. I was very, very happy. Could this feeling have rested in me, I had been content—faithful to my duty, as I had been taught—to have lived ever so. But my heart was now craving constantly the repetition of that moment. It could not be satisfied but in his presence.'

Then came the autumn when they usually went to London a week or two before the opening of parliament.

'If I went to London with my husband in any hope of escaping the feelings that were mastering me,' Mary Jary explained afterwards to E————, 'I knew well that on my return this life of passion would only recommence on the sight of its object. If I remained alone I believed I would have strength to overcome it. I remained therefore at home.'

Having steeled herself not to see William, she insisted 'it was only at the last moment, on the very brink of my husband's return that I sent for him. I cannot describe what passes between lovers sundered by a social law,' she said, but nevertheless, she did, at great length with barely a fluttering of an eyelid left unrecorded.

'I have brought you to me, I said, because I can see you no longer.

'A moan of agony came to his lips.

'He looked up at me; the intelligence of his face was gone; his eyes were dim; the despair that was in me changed his face to stone!' and so she covered four pages of uttered sighs and unsaid avowals.

When Jackey came home and learnt of the situation he quietly decided that it would be wisest for Mary Jary to leave England for a time. 'I was to travel,' she wrote disgustedly. 'A change of scene they prescribed for the invalid of the heart. They would have me enjoy Paris, Rome. They would substitute the splendour of the Vatican for some little flower that might perchance come from his hand should I remain at home.'

And she refused to go, insisting that it was her duty once more to stay at home. 'I had preserved the honour of my husband, and the reputation of his children and was about to submit myself to his embraces without love.' Referring at length to this as 'prostitution' and, should there again be a blood-kin child, as 'voluntary matricide', she then contemplated the alternative of the convent doors, suicide, or, better still, leaving her husband, home and children while, of course, she said, 'sacrificing my great love'.

'Not a tear came to my eye when I told it them; not a pulse stirred in my breast. How inconceivable to them all this agony.

'My husband was even still solicitous to preserve the form of a union, now no longer possible in reality. One of those formality doctors of the soul was sent for—his uncle Francis—the lame old husband of his late spinning Aunt Richenda.

'But how weak and idle to me were his words about theological sin and social infamy. They fell on my ear, in constant repetition, meaningless as the dropping of the beads of a rosary.

'He told me I was imperilling my soul, and he left me with some formal expression of pious horror, when I told him I would willingly incur that risk.'

What Mary Jary had not told them was that she was already pregnant. But when John Henry found out, though it went very heavily with him, he offered to let it be supposed that the child was his. By then Mary Jary had broadcast her plight and Jackey's family were emphatic that he should take a firm line. But firm lines were not in Jackey's nature, and his gentle attempt to assert himself only ended at Catton in Mary Jary slipping out of the garden gate with her lover, to leave the country, and write later, almost in triumph:

'I have silently asked myself in his arms, when I dared not soil our lips with their utterance, about these words—groom and adulterer. Yet well I knew that they had no relation to our love.'

In the hopes that she would soon tire of her life of comparative discomfort and would come home, John Henry delayed bringing divorce proceedings. Mary Jary, with a considerable inheritance from her father, preferred to settle in Sussex at Hankham, near Pevensey, with William Taylor.

When their baby was born, Mary Jary called him Anselm, after one of the romantic crusaders in Dan's family history.

John Henry's family were sympathetic and discreet and none more so than Hannah at Northrepps, where he frequently took his elder boy, Jack, to stay. Richard, his younger son, was rarely fit enough to join the huge parties of grandchildren and stayed behind at Catton where his lonely childhood was enlighted by Anna Sewell, the author of *Black Beauty* who lived nearby and came to give him lessons. He adored his father and they wrote to each other daily when they were apart.

'I saw a fox while shooting,' his father writes to him in January from Northrepps. 'In the evening we came in for a dance at Northrepps Hall. There was a party of forty-eight and Jack took his share and enjoyed it very much. One dance was called Sir Roger de Coverley in which Aunt Buxton', Hannah, now over eighty, 'joined.'

'Northrepps is much less scorched by the drought than Catton or Keswick,' he writes on another visit. 'I have got a very good grey wagtail for the bird skin book before breakfast from a flock which were by the pond near the gate here.'

'When we were riding on the shore, Alfred was galloping through a rather large and deep pool,' Ellen writes of Northrepps at this time, 'and wicked little beastly Derry stopped short and sent Alfred over his head, head first and legs up in the water. He went entirely under the water and was of course drenched through.' Ellen's accounts show that it would all be much too much for poor asthmatic little Richard.

'We had a most exciting day, a huge party of us riding from Runton, several others came in the carriage bringing the lunch with them. We had a picnic on the beautiful Runton Hills, and enjoyed ourselves extremely and about two thirty remounted and started to meet Fowell and Victoria.' Fowell, Hannah's grandson,

had just married Lady Victoria Noel and they were returning to
Colne House from their honeymoon.

'So we had a charming ride through Felbrigg to Roughton and
came out near the church. We knew we were too early so we all
got off our horses and went and saw the beautiful old church.
Then we remounted and as they did not come we rode slowly
towards Northrepps over Roughton heath. We stopped at the
big pond near the school and there the fresh carriage came. It was
an open carriage and they were going to draw them into Colne
House.

'At last we saw the carriage coming and it stopped. They got
in to the open one and we all galloped behind them till they came
to the bottom of the steep hill where were heaps of people prepared to receive them. There they began to take the horses out,
and tied rope to the carriage and pulled them at walking pace till
they came into Colne House garden. The road was ornamented
with quantities of flags and near the gates was a triumphal arch
made of evergreen with Welcome written on it. The road was
lined on each side with people.

'Of course we all followed on our horses but they jumped about
and did not like either the flags or the people or the band or the
guns which fired often. When they got into the carriage they
pulled the carriage as fast as they could run till they got up to
the front door where there was another arch put up and lots of
other people

'But the best thing of all was as the carriage was being drawn
up to the door there was a rather fat big man running some way
behind and Ada, on her pony was galloping close to the man's
heels (which was very dangerous) when all of a sudden the fat man
stumbled and fell and Ada leapt completely over him. A great
many people saw it and laughed. Her pony stopped for a moment
and then gave a very high leap just as though she was leaping a
fence. I wonder the fat man was not hurt, but he got up and I
don't think he minded it.'

There were other forms of welcome that brides, new to the

family, did not always at first appreciate. Mildred, the new wife of another of Hannah's grandsons, Sydney Buxton, who later became Postmaster-General, first Earl Buxton, and Governor General of South Africa, was somewhat dismayed by the way the many Buxton, Gurney and Barclay relations wandered in and out of each other's Cromer houses—including hers—so that privacy was impossible.

'Today,' she wrote, 'I have been introduced to my fortieth Buxton relation. Today has been the crack shooting in the Cottage Woods at Northrepps which the Barclays have. We had an enormous luncheon in a barn, a regular feast, and out of thirty people present only six were not relations. I was much interested in comparing Sydney,' the bridegroom, 'to his relations, much to their disadvantage.'

A few days later Hannah was able to write on her eighty-first birthday, for all her previous sorrows: 'Surely goodness and mercy have followed me since I was born at Bramerton in 1783! Today I go a picnic with the children, but far more grandchildren; with these I am encompassed, but do not mind the numbers for myself; I rather feel the immense work for the servants, often more than sixty to feed in the day.'

Ellen writes of the typical reception at Northrepps of news of even more to come:

'Oh such a wonderful, joyful and intensely exciting piece of news arrived today. Edward and Emily have got twin babies! "A boy and girl at ten thirty last night before the nurse or doctor arrived." Intense excitement prevailed, when the telegram came. Of course the news was spread all over the house in a moment. Everyone is pleased and soon after breakfast Anna, Kitty and Laura came up in the pony chair to Northrepps Hall. In a few moments the whole house was in a sort of uproar. Everybody ran to tell everyone and everybody made such a noise that some of the maids came to see what was the matter. They thought something dreadful had happened. Longing for letters to come about the twins, which was born first? How big are they? And

all about them. Yesterday we heard the sorrowful news that
Henry Edmund had shot Gerald Upcher badly in the eye, but it
is rather comforting to hear that it was entirely Gerald's fault,
that he got shot and not in the least Edmund's.'

Presently Ellen is writing: 'The delightful days of Northrepps
are fast drawing to a close. I think that everything at Northrepps
is so *vastly* supperior—because everything in it is so old and old-
fashioned. One of the beds in the night nursery belonged to
grandmama's grandmother.'

CHAPTER TWENTY-THREE

The Storm Breaks

To John Henry's amazement, when he went to call one afternoon at a cousin's house, Abbey Lodge in Regent's Park, which was a great family centre, he learnt that Mary Jary was waiting for him, apparently ready for a reconciliation. He was so overcome he could not even bring himself to see her and slipped out of a side door into the park to compose himself, thus inadvertently saving himself from further ignominy. For Mary Jary was expecting another child by William Taylor which would be born before the divorce went through. If this child could be 'proved' to be John Henry's, by the simple expedient of a temporary return to him, it would be legitimate and, on coming of age, could inherit a share in the Gurney estates.

But John Henry did not return to Abbey Lodge. His generous offer to take on the first of Mary Jary's illegitimate children had merely produced the suggestion among gossips that perhaps none of her children were his. The offer no longer held good. He petitioned for the marriage to be dissolved.

Neither the divorce nor Mary Jary's subsequent marriage to William Taylor is recorded at Somerset House.

However, a marriage appears in the parish register of the then small hamlet of Perivale, Middlesex, dated twenty-four days before the birth of their second child, Alice Maude Mary.

'11.3.1862. Wm Taylor, bach, of full age, gent, of Perivale. Father John Taylor, gent. and Mary Jary Gurney, spinster, of full age, of East Harptree, Somerset. Father Richard Hanbury Gurney, gent. by licence.'

East Harptree was another romantic name from Dan's book, which he describes as the feudal residence of one of his crusader

ancestors. As a wedding present, Mary Jary gave William the
lordships of two manors, from which offices he became a County
Councillor and Colonel of the 2nd Cinqports Volunteers.

Hudson died in 1864 at the age of ninety, having cut Mary
Jary out of his will, and left his fortune to John Henry for his
lifetime with the estates entailed to their two sons and any other
legitimate children of Mary Jary's. Ironically enough, for all
Mary Jary's concern over 'blood kinship', of which she had none
with William, all her children by him were weaklings. Only one
of the several born after their marriage lived long enough to claim
a share in Hudson's fortune. In spite of consumption, Alice
Maude Mary lived to be thirty-one. As her sole heir, William
gratefully raised a splendid tablet to her in West Ham church.
Meanwhile John Henry had barely a year to enjoy his £1,200,000
inheritance. In 1865, the hitherto private firm of Overend,
Gurney and Co. Ltd., of which he was the youngest partner and
his Uncle Dan the eldest, started a public issue of £50 shares, only
part of which had to be paid at once, with the rest available to be
called in later. The partners, knowing that some of the assets
might thus be shaky, guaranteed their personal fortunes to make
up any bad debts. Little did they guess that these would amount
to £3,000,000.

John Henry resigned from parliament and gave up his house in
Mayfair. He sold Hudson's house in St. James's Square, withdrew his book with the expensive bird plates from the printers
and, most painful of all, for he knew how much his little son
Richard loved it, sold beautiful Catton Hall.

He wrote to him from Catton on September 7th, 1865:

'My dear Dick, I quite know what you feel about Catton, I feel
very much the same myself, but it is a great blessing to know that
after all, our happiness does not depend on *where* we live but how
we live. Your loving father. J.H.G.'

A Liquidation Trust was formed so that all possible assets
could be gathered, and various members of the family
readily bought shares in it. Samuel Gurney Buxton, second

son of Catherine of Colne House, bought Catton Hall, in which his descendants continued to live till a few years ago. At Gurney's bank in Norwich a new partnership was formed omitting the names of John Henry, Dan and one of Dan's sons. Presently, as the wealthier Barclay cousins came in, having already invested money in the sinking firm of Overend, Gurney and Co. Ltd., they poured more in, and among other changes Gurney's Bank became known as Barclay's Bank which it has remained ever since.

On 'Black Friday', May 11th 1866, it clearly looked as though the original partners had dumped dud assets on the public. John Henry was appalled to find himself among those accused of robbing the poor, with the shadow of prison bars looming over them all.

Before the case, John Henry made over all his estates to his eldest son, Jack, so that whatever disaster befell him, Keswick and Northrepps would remain in his immediate family. When the case against Overend, Gurney and Co. Ltd. came to court in 1869, John Henry was to hear the Prosecution say:

'No such case of gigantic fraud has ever come before the public since the South Sea scheme. That the defendants, with cold-blooded determination, guzzled three million pounds out of the pockets of the public, who, though they might have some sympathy for gamblers, have nothing but scorn for the defendants . . .' and so it went on, till the Solicitor-General replied:

'Of unauthentic, uninformed, ignorant and cruel opinion and abuse they had had enough and to spare. For some years they had lived in an atmosphere of calumny and misrepresentation and so strong and untiring had been the efforts of those opposed to them that there was scarcely a fact connected with the case but what was seen through clouds of mist and prejudice—enough to disturb the sight and judgment of the calmest man on earth.'

The Solicitor-General went on to say that their conduct throughout had been that of honourable men. As an old and reputable firm, they had done all that was possible to avoid going bankrupt. They had given up their own salaries. They had poured their own personal money in, sold their homes in a last bid to pour more, and many of their rich and successful Barclay relations had so much trust in the firm that they too had poured money into it.

Letters were produced in court from John Henry which made it all too clear that his intention had all the time been of the best, and the general feeling was that if his Uncle Samuel, who had founded the firm, had been alive, he could have steered it out of trouble, but no ordinary businessmen could.

Next day, in the summing up that took three and a half hours, the Lord Chief Justice observed that Overend, Gurney and Co., was hopelessly insolvent.

The jury left to consider their verdict. After being absent for only a few minutes they returned with the verdict 'Not guilty'.

The announcement was received with an extraordinary outburst of applause which lasted several minutes. After it was all over John Henry went quietly off to live in the south of England till he had readjusted himself to his 'new and very much lowered state'.

Hannah's generosity to Dan, after the crash, made it possible for him to go on living at Runcton so that 'the bankruptcy troubles hardly aged him at all'. He had lost almost all his money, and she allowed him £2,000 a year for the rest of his life so that he could continue to bring up at Runcton, as Hannah herself was doing at Northrepps, the orphaned family of one of his own children. Life with the Troubridges is deliciously described in the diaries of one of them, Laura, in which their octogenarian grandfather, Dan, was so confused by then by his life-long search into his ancestry that he came down to breakfast convinced that he had been created an earl. The children passed it off as just a dream.

Hannah and Dan, as the only survivors of the eleven brothers and sisters, like their cousins Hudson and Anna, grew increasingly close together in their old age and wrote frequently to each other, visiting each other whenever possible with their large parties of 'children-grandchildren'.

Laughingly, she used to say to Dan in their great age—'The fact is, Dan, you're so young, you're no companion at all to me.'

Hannah's birthdays had always meant a great deal to her, as a time for summing up and looking back. Falling as they did when the family all gathered together for shooting, they were important days, usually with giant picnics. It was not till she had had her eighty-seventh birthday that Dan, in his documental roaming, discovered that they had always been a month out. Hannah thanks him:

'Dearest brother, your enclosed certificate of my birth is very amusing to me as it shows I have never known my true birthday. I always thought it was September 15th and not October 15th. No doubt on our dear mother's death, no one knew accurately, and September 15th was adopted. So I am a month younger than I thought. But . . . why am I kept so long? is the solemn question.'

'I have handsome new carpets in my drawing-room and dining-room. How unreasonable in my eighty-eighth year!' she writes later.

The carriage still came every morning at eleven to drive her out to call at Colne House and on a few old lady residents in Cromer.

Catherine had now given up her house near London. When her five exceedingly good-looking daughters were aged between ten and eighteen, she made Colne House their only home. She once wrote:

'Home is very quiet and my sweet girls a lovely group. We have the exceeding pleasure of our new conservatory—the present to me of my six darling sons. It is a most sweet pleasure and the indulgence I can best bear. The cheer of the flowers and the gift and the charming object with the girls make it a venerable enjoyment.'

A friend writing of a Sunday at Colne House when Hannah was there said:

'Only those who know the beautiful room, the fine conservatory, the views from the window, the declining sun throwing shadows across the bright green lawn, can fancy the scene, nor can I adequately describe the individuals forming the groups at the window. On the ottoman seat, the Dowager, so diminished in size, delicate, refined, in a rich black silk dress, the shawl of a thin material bordered with white, very feeble but animated, summoned all to come close by her, her hand clasped in that of her dear son Fowell, and he so gentle, loving and cordial to her. Then on chairs and stools of various heights, the grandchildren grouped around her and beginning at the youngest each in turn repeated a portion of a Hymn.'

The beautiful room, the views and the green lawn are still there at Colne House Hotel. And so is the great conservatory, a period piece supported by cast iron curves, backed by tree bark and ferns, with a graciously domed aviary forming one wall.

'The precious grandmother looked so small and white, but so lovely in her calm acquiescence,' wrote one of the grandchildren.

Hannah herself describes her life in her last year, 1872, in which her youngest son Charles died in Scotland leaving her with one survivor, Fowell, of her original eleven. She writes to her brother Dan:

'This delightful morning is most pleasant and I have been basking in the sunshine. You are out and able to walk and enjoy it. I really hardly can walk, and it is some weeks since I have been in the garden,'—it was February—'but I drive out in the closed carriage and find it a great refreshment, even when the weather is dull. I call at Colne House door and on a few old lady residents in Cromer who come into the carriage to speak to me. Catherine often joins me in the drive or comes up with the girls to dinner and at home I am quite rich now with Effie and Sarah Maria, besides my constant companion Priscilla.' These were Priscilla's and Andrew's daughters. 'So, though without much excitement we have pleasant little variations and most truly I desire to give thanks for the great mercies I enjoy—such merciful indulgences—and I know you feel the same for yourself, dearest

brother, but I feel your weak hand is a great cross and incon-
venience to you. I have some rather troublesome infirmities.'

Her daughter-in-law Catherine was worried one morning to see
a crowd of girls in the bow window making bunches of violets and
leaving a mess of leaves and stalks but Hannah, being wheeled in
Anna's chair, merely smiled sweetly at them and said, 'How sweet
the girls looked and their flowers. Do turn me to see them better.'

She had no final illness. On the day she died she was carried
down as usual and when she heard that Catherine was coming to
dinner she said, 'How pleasant. I must go up now to be getting
ready.' But upstairs she dropped into a nap from which she
never woke.

There was of course a large luncheon party at Northrepps after
the funeral, with the same routine as for the wedding, christening
and big shooting lunches.

Six months later John Henry heard the news that Mary Jary
was dead. Their son Richard seems to have supposed that she had
been already dead for thirteen years.

In a description of his childhood, the 'loss of his mother when
he was four years old' is followed without a break by his admiring
her grave from a train. Surely Richard and his brother must have
eventually learnt the truth, yet, in their meticulously kept family
records, not a mention is made of their mother's indiscretions,
divorce and second marriage. Even Somerset House, *Burke* and
Fox-Davies appear to have been denied the information, though all
three record William Taylor's second marriage, two years after
Mary Jary's death, to Miss Schill of Stuttgart.

Over sixty years after the Mary Jary scandal, a responsible
professional genealogist working on Dan's lost link, asked to see
all the family papers at Keswick. However, only selected documents were brought out of the locked muniment room. Another,
promised access to the Secretissimum, called only to hear that
the key could not be found. Thus Mary Jary's skeleton has rattled
for many years considerably louder than the results of her
imaginative and passionate nature warranted.

CHAPTER TWENTY-FOUR

. . . *Unto the Seventh and Eighth Generation*

THE following year, in 1873, John Henry and his two sons, Jack, twenty-four, now the owner of Northrepps, and Richard, nineteen, came to live there, adding more bird cages but still no bathroom. In fact no alterations were made to the house except to add the verandah outside the drawing-room window to merge with the little summerhouse, which they used as an aviary, beside it. Much of Hannah's furniture remained with the red leather chairs and other pieces that had been originally bought for Northrepps, dating back, like the fire engine, to the eighteenth century. To these were now added relics from Earlham, Catton, St. James's Square and Thickthorn.

Presently Jack announced that one of his great-uncle Samuel's granddaughters 'had accepted him' and at Hill House a whole wing with a huge bedroom, dressing-room overlooking the sea and even bigger drawing-room with thirteen windows was built on for their honeymoon. 'We mean to furnish Hill House right sumptuously,' he told his brother.

'Then,' said his father, 'I must pay you rent for Northrepps Hall as you will cease to live there and I shall continue to do so.'

Jack and Maggy Gurney were married in London and returned home by train, arriving at North Walsham which had recently become the nearest railway station. At the lodge gate at Northrepps Hall, crowds of villagers and young relations were waiting to manhandle the bride and bridegroom up the drive. Among them was 'bright Eva' of Colne House, who wrote: 'the gate being open by mistake the horses dashed through and we all had to run behind, feeling rather small.'

The honeymoon lasted for over a year while Keswick was being modernised, during which time John Henry's first grandchild, Gerard, was born in the bridal suite at Hill House.

When Jack and Maggy moved to Keswick, Hill House became their holiday home. John Henry had a path made from Northrepps Hall through the woods and across the fields so that while they were there he could pay a daily visit on foot with the dogs.

It was a great event when the railway reached Cromer in 1877, thus ending the coaching days. It had been brought gradually nearer, and as a preliminary, the navvies mapped the line out by digging away the soil and then leaving it for some months. When the summer came, millions of field poppies appeared and the scarlet ribbon stretching for miles was a most remarkable and lovely sight. At last came the time when the line was finished and the first train of three heavy engines and their tenders tried the rails and bridges bit by bit, to the astonishment of villagers and cattle.

The part of the line that passed through the park at Northrepps Hall, far from being considered an eyesore or a noisy nuisance, was regarded by Richard and his father as a great improvement to the scene, as good if not better than leaping deer or kangaroos, which they later reintroduced, for adding unexpected movement to the scenery.

Though Richard was allowed a pony as a child he was not considered fit enough to ride a horse and so drove everywhere in a light dog cart, bumping over fields and rough ground, claiming that in the gig he could do everything, including shooting, that was to be achieved on horseback except jump fences. When he was unable to go out he painted and modelled in clay, decorating his works with stylised vegetation. He and his father went abroad a great deal and brought back souvenirs ranging in size from the pair of terracotta lions on the gatepost to the fifteen feet high lunar 'sundial', which still stands in a flowerbed.

Although Richard was so small that he could not sit on a chair without a footstool and so delicate that he had to rest frequently on a sofa, the young ladies of the neighbourhood found him exceedingly attractive and there were many sighs when he and Eva of Colne House, also a granddaughter of Samuel Gurney, 'fixed' their marriage one Saturday evening and took the congregation by surprise on Sunday morning when their banns were read.

Eva reports that after the wedding in Cromer, 'We drove through Northrepps where crowds stood in the rain and threw flowers that were like wet sponges and rice that was like nursery pudding, both of which left traces on my peacock blue dress.' For their honeymoon they went to America to visit Richard's step-grandmother, Eliza.

Eva wrote from Fifth Avenue Hotel, New York, in September 1881:

'Darling Mother, Here we are most comfortably established in this gorgeous erection but terribly hot. The houses are very bright coloured scarlet with staring green shutters and a great many with creepers on them and tiny gardens in front. The elevator passes usually in the middle of the street but when it turns a street corner it goes within a foot or two of houses and windows.'

They went by train to Atlantic City where Eliza was living, and were met at the station by her carriage.

'We got into grandmother's carriage and there waited while one of the horses danced on its hind legs and nearly upset us. We then proceeded, as we thought, to the hotel but found it was grandmother's. It was too dark at that hour and in her shady drawing-room to see her well but she seems a most sweet and charming person sitting in her high green velvet chair. She was, to my surprise, as young looking and lovely as her photo of twenty years ago. She is not at all strong and the excitement was so great she cannot see us today as she wished. I had no idea she was in her eighty-first year.

'Grandmother was one of the first settlers about nineteen years ago and has a very charming villa. We are about two blocks off her. Everything is of wood with great verandahs and lattice false doors and window shutters to keep out the heat.'

Eliza's relations made them wonderfully welcome and spoke of everyone in Norfolk as though they knew them all.

'Grandmother certainly is a most wonderful old lady and by no means shows her age and loves to talk and is quite clear in every respect, sees very well and is very cheerful. Her hair has much colour and her face is quite plump. She is most wonderfully sweet and full of love. She sends you much love.'

If this was Mary Jary's confidante, how interested she would be to see Mary's 'white baby' again, now well and happily married! Clearly Eliza had a tremendous fascination for the young, for Eva repeatedly referred to her delightedly and to how much they looked forward to the hour's call each day at five o'clock—which she was surprised to find was the fashionable new time to call in America.

They toured the States staying with friends of friends, and one hostess gave Eva a foretaste of the telephone at Northrepps Hall, though it was twenty-five years before it reached it, and then only in a very early form on the wall, with a handle to be turned vigorously before making a call.

'Her own bedroom,' Eva wrote, 'was very perfect, and next to it, the telephone! through which she talks to her parents or her married sister at any moment and by which she can also call the police, fireman or doctor. She merely rings her bell to the central office and orders her wire to be connected to anyone she likes! We talked to her sister and I was *introduced* by telephone!'

They had intended to return to see The Grandmother on their way home but now heard from her daughter that from the moment they had left, her mind had begun to wander and she was sinking fast. A few days later came a telegram to say that she had died. The honeymoon couple returned to Atlantic City for the funeral.

While they were away Jack wrote that the worst storm of the century had blown down the whole of the Long Wood, including the ilex trees at the end of the kitchen garden, which he had already started replanting. He had also started to rebuild barns, cottages and other ancient buildings on the estate that had collapsed and later built almshouses and a reading room in the village where Richard and Eva could read aloud to the inhabitants.

Richard and Eva divided their married life between '25, The Drive', in Hove, Sussex, and Northrepps Hall where John Henry, now a gentle benevolent grandfather, continued to live. He wrote to Richard at Hove when the children were at Northrepps.

'I have just been up to the nursery to bid them goodnight and found them all, as usual, very happy, which is most pleasant to see and to enjoy thankfully. I took your two little dogs for a walk in the garden and there to my great pleasure I found some of the tiger lilies which I have so long wished for, splendidly out, so I cut one and left it at Hill House. It reminded me of the Earlham garden when I was a child.'

When our mother was born at Hove, her grandmother, Catherine, wrote to her daughter Eva from Colne House: 'My darling child, How sweet it is to write to you in such delicious circumstances. I fancy you so happy and thankful that the charming baby on your arm or perhaps near, in the pretty pink-ribboned bassinet, and Richard so happy with you, and about you. I join too, at a distance. And to have "Rachel" is so sweet it gives a sort of sanctifying feeling to her little self. She shall hold such a special place. I must get her a silver box directly, and the nicest washing Summer cloak I can find. How I love her! Your tenderly loving Mother.'

Quintin, aged five, wrote his first letter to Northrepps.

'Dearest Granfather, The bird flies about the nursery and it did eat crumbs of Tiffy. Baby is quite well? Is the white calf well? From Quintin.'

The calf was given to Eva by an old woman in Northrepps. She came one day and said, 'I do love Mrs. Gurney and I do love my little white calf so I want to give my little calf to Mrs. Gurney.'

And so began the herd of ancient British white cattle in the park at Northrepps.

When the fifth child (Gladys) was born, our uncles Quintin and Christopher, my mother Rachel and Aunt Chen were taken by their father into his dressing-room to see the new baby, and were asked to think of a name for her. 'Let's call her after someone we love,' suggested Quintin.

'Yes,' my mother agreed. 'Let's call it Grandmother.'

Eva wrote to John Henry at Christmas. 'Dearest Father, the children's delight in the rocking horses *was* and *is* most, most amusing. They all walked to church with us, Chen in her perambulator and all came in for the hymn at the beginning looking such a pretty little row in the free seat by the door. Chenda enjoyed the big turkey downstairs as much as anybody.'

A Christmas dinner was held every year in the coachhouse for the old people and in Jubilee Year, 1887, the whole population of the parish assembled at the Northrepps gate, and formed a long procession headed by the oldest inhabitant, who was over a hundred, in a donkey cart. The other infirm and the children of the village followed in Bath-chairs and perambulators with schoolchildren with flags, singing as they marched with the rest of the guests to the long tables laid out in the coachhouse and stable yard. Here they ate a roasted ox that had been cooked in many portions on the fires of the principal inhabitants.

In the spring of 1890 John Henry died not long after a pleasant stroll in the woods, viewing his son's tame owls.

The following year Richard and Eva made the first bathroom at Northrepps with the grand Water Closet Corridor beyond it, leading to the schoolroom which was built over the new dining-room looking towards the wood. At the same time the Georgian pillared porch was moved up to the stables to shelter the coachman's cottage. It was replaced by an ornate red brick and loftily glazed vestibule, the perfect foil for the Victorian potted plants and shell and bamboo shooting sticks. A new sunken terrace with intermittent spheroids rising from the retaining wall like the decapitated heads of the enemy was made to combat the damp creeping up from the trench built to keep Anna in her wheelchair out.

'My darling,' Richard wrote to Eva, 'The house is defended by enormous ditches and a great mess it all is but I'm glad to be here. The hall looks charming with its lovely paper, particularly by lamplight. I see floods of daffodils and the air is full of the song of blackbirds and thrushes.'

Now that Richard had settled permanently in Norfolk again he became a magistrate, and Deputy Lieutenant, while his brother was High Sheriff, and in 1896 he was High Sheriff of Norfolk himself. But diabetes and asthma were sending him more and more often to rest on his sofa.

'My boys are gone back to school,' he wrote on the last Sunday of his life. 'Quintin is taller than his mother. Rachel is running up fast.'

The elder children had already outstripped their father in height and eventually grew to be well above average height. None inherited their father's delicacy, and all five are still alive and energetic today, in, or coming up into, their eighties.

Quintin was sixteen and the youngest only seven when their father died, aged forty-four. Eva lived on at Northrepps Hall as a widow for twenty-seven years with her children and grandchildren about her, just as Hannah had done for twenty-seven years before her.

Eva's five children grew up to love Northrepps in a boisterous and energetic way, riding and hunting and experimenting with their new motor cars and meeting their many cousins for shooting and dances even more than the earlier generations had done, for the railway speeded even their local movements.

My mother was the first to marry, but not to a relation. My father had broken his leg hunting in Norfolk and my grandmother took him to Northrepps to nurse him. My mother weaned him off his crutches by taking them away and placing her charming self out of reach. However, he took no chances at the wedding, and clung to them throughout it.

The inevitable 'take off' that survives in almost every family wedding story was, at Gladys' wedding, the dogs pulling the wedding cake off the dining-room table on to the floor and eating half of it while everyone was in church. My grandmother quickly had the rest cut up and handed round in small pieces and nobody noticed.

Merlin and Rhalou were born while our great-grandmother, Catherine, Lady Buxton of Colne House, was still alive. When she found she was going blind, she learnt off by heart as much of the Bible as she could, repeating it, as she dressed, to her lady's maid, who was expected to correct her. When she went deaf also, she was still able to tell the time from the vibrations of her watch, which chimed—and still does—every quarter of an hour. Her birthday parties continued annually till there were so many candles round her cake that they were too hot to go near. She was ninety-seven when she died, and so her life had over-lapped not only with our generation but also with those of nearly all the children of the Devoted Four, who first came to Northrepps at the end of the eighteenth century.

Now a high percentage of their descendants not already living there, took houses or stayed with each other in and around Cromer.

'More relations come to Cromer than ever,' wrote Mildred Lady Buxton who had been so dismayed by them when she was first married.

> 'Buxtons to the right of us
> Barclays to the left of us
> Gurneys, Hoares, Pelhams
> Bellowed and thundered.

'This is literally true and so much is my temper improved with age, that I like it. Many of them are rather plain, I regret to say—some of the Buxtons are frightful.'

But normal visitors were not put off and Cromer continued to grow in universal popularity, particularly after the Great Eastern

Railway had commissioned Clement Scott to write articles in the *Daily Telegraph* extolling the beauties of the scarlet field poppies that sprang up on the newly turned earth where the cliffs continued to fall into the sea. He called them Poppyland and yet another railway line—the Poppy Line—was opened that passed by them and on through the Northrepps woods on the coast side of the house. Now, whichever way the family went, there was a bridge to cross or pass under. It was all part of a network that had been spread over north Norfolk. With their small flint-built booking offices and paraffin-lit waiting-rooms with fires burning in their cottage-type grates, their stations were sleepy places except in the summer season when the trippers passed through them, and on market days, when sheep and cattle and farm produce left their goods yards. When the First World War came, The Poppy Line brought materials for defending the vulnerable coastline—barbed wire for the cliff tops, stone for the pillboxes, concrete and guns.

Our uncles Quintin and Christopher fought and our Aunt Chen nursed in the First World War, and this was where we came in.

Twenty-five years later, when the Second World War began, the eight Northrepps grandsons and some of us girls were in the services from the beginning. All but one of us survived. Hugh, of Northrepps Hall, one of the Little Ones of our time—always exuberantly cheerful, inventive and musical, was killed after parachuting into enemy occupied country with the Special Air Service.

Once or twice some of us met at Northrepps when we were on leave, but the gaps between visits grew longer and longer, when Northrepps for most of us was just something that went with us. But the time came when we went back—Merlin, Rhalou, Erroll, Lorema and I—and Dick and Eve and all the others who had been in the nursery after us. Joe and Anthony and Pam were already there. And now we brought our own babies and watched them playing where we had played. And soon it was our generations' children who were climbing to the tops of the trees and defying the red flag at Overstrand. It was our children who stayed out in the woods till the moon rose to watch the badgers come out, our sons who shot pigeons in the Green Drive.

And now it is our baby grandchildren—the eighth generation of Northrepps grandchildren—whom we set down on the rug in front of the drawing-room fire after Sunday tea, to creep round the chairs to look in the toy cupboard and climb on to great-great-Aunt Chen's knee. Uncle Christopher, the grand-father and great-great-uncle of the current batch of babies, is still there, but wishing to see his successor installed is now moving into one of the houses on the estate, while his son Joseph and his family move into Northrepps Hall to carry on the tradi-tions of nearly two centuries.

The nursery at Northrepps is being white-washed and the night nursery windows polished so that another generation can look down into the backyard, where the peacocks fly down to feed with the bantam hens, and Billy Silver's successor ambles across the cobbles with a piece of plank from the kangaroo cage that would nicely fill the gap in the bottom of the rocking boat. In the sunny corner under the pear tree, presently the pram will sway again with a Labrador stretched out beside it, a direct descendant of one of those buried up in the woods.

Index

Gurney, Joe (Joseph John)—*cont.*
Berridge), 23, 32, 59, 60, 61–2,
249; master of Northrepps, 250
Kitty, Catherine, of Earlham
(*1776–1850*), 73–6, 79, 85, 90,
96–8, 137–9, 140, 201, 210,
211
Louisa of Earlham (*1784–1836,
m. Sam Hoare*), 96–7, 100,
102–3, 104, 132–6, 175, 176;
early romps, 73–5, 80–1, 83–
5, 87; Hampstead, 106; Norfolk,
107–8
Mary Jary (*1829–72, m. 1st John
Henry Gurney, 2nd William
Taylor*), 161–2, 198, 205–6,
224–8, 244; elopement, 229–30;
m., 234–5
Maggy (Margaret) (*m. Jack Gurney*),
48, 241, 242
Priscilla of Earlham (*1788–1821*),
35, 74–6, 95, 98, 105, 116,
136
Pamela of Northrepps, 49, 58–63,
249–50, ill. of, facing pp.*1*61,
145 and endpapers by
Quintin (*b. 1883, m. Pleasance
Ruggles-Brise*), 37–8, 245, 246,
247, 249
Rachel of Keswick (*1755–94, m.
Robert Barclay, later of Bury Hill*),
68–9, 70–2, 73–4, 82
Rachel of Earlham (*1788–1827*),
63–4, 85, 87, 89–90, 98, 102,
116, 137, 140–1, 143
Rachel of The Grove (*1795–1817*),
108, 123, 124–7, 128
Rachel Jane (*1828–1905, m. T.
Fowell Buxton II*), 139, 202,
219–23, 230–1
Rachel of Northrepps (*b. 1886, m.
Rev. Rosslyn Bruce, D.D.*), 52,
245, 246, 247, 248, 250; in
my happiest Northrepps memories, 15, 19, 26–7, 32–5;
enjoys Zeppelin raid, 26–7
Regicide, The (*Sir Thomas de*),
murdered Edward II, 1327, 65;

(*ignominiously chased across Europe,
d. of exhaustion at Bayonne, 1333*)
Richard (*1742–1811, m. 1st, Agatha
Barclay, 2nd Rachel Hanbury*), 68,
82, 83–8, 94, 100, 109, 110,
111, 112
Richard Hanbury Joseph, of Northrepps (*1855–99, m. Eva [Sarah
Evelyn] Buxton*), 42, 227, 230,
235, 240, 241; 243–4; 245;
247
Richenda of Earlham (*1782–1855,
m. Rev. Francis Cunningham*), 74, 75,
85, 127, 178, 184, 196, 200,
210–11, 214, 215; artist, 87–
8, 99
Richenda, Aunt Chen, of Northrepps (*b. 1888*), 26, 27, 30–
2, 50, 54–6, 57–8, 246, 247–8,
249, 250
Ruth (*m. Joseph Lubbock*), 54, 55,
149–50; ill. facing p. 161
Samuel of Earlham (*1786–1856, m.
Elizabeth Sheppard*), 73, 74, 99,
117, 139, 141, 174, 175, 202,
212, 216, 217; signs of financial
genius, 103; buys Colne House,
143
Gurneyite Orthodox Friends Sect, 195
Gurney Light, 172

Hadduck, Elizabeth (*b. 1691, m.
John Gurney*), 68, 76, 91
Hanbury, Rachel (*d. 1825, m. Richard
Gurney*), 83, 143; of Northrepps,
83–4, 91, 109–11, 122, 127–8
Hanbury, Sampson (*m. Gatty Gurney,
1795*), 84, 92, 102
Hamond, Charlie, 218, 221
Hamond, Philip (*m. Chenda
(Richenda) Buxton, 1856*), 216
Hampstead, 103; Hill, The, 102–4,
132–6, 189; New End, 129–34
Happisburgh, Has'bro', sands, 172
Harriet (*Pooley*), 29, 49, 53
Hay, Lady Harriet (*m. Dan Gurney*),
66, 146 (*d. 1837*)

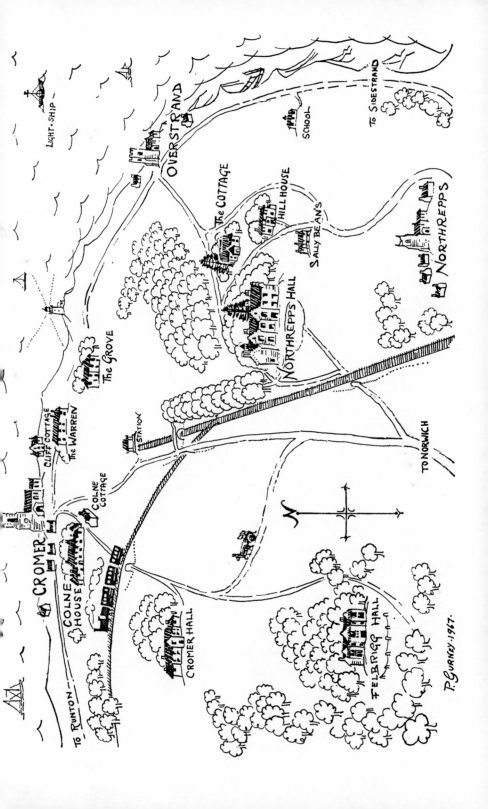

LIGHT-SHIP –

OVERSTRAND

To SIDESTRAND

SCHOOL

The COTTAGE

HILL HOUSE

SALLY BEANS

NORTHREPPS HALL

To NORTHREPPS

The GROVE

CLIFF COTTAGE

The WARREN

STATION

COLNE COTTAGE

To NORWICH

CROMER

To RUNTON

COLNE HOUSE

CROMER HALL

FELBRIGG HALL

P. GURNEY. 1967.

Printed in the United Kingdom
by Lightning Source UK Ltd.
2325